The ceremonial dancing began.

She braided her hair and wore her authentic Indian costume, a beautifully beaded white buckskin dress.

Hawk saw her, and a smoky-sultry look lit his face.

Wynne had been just as stirred by Hawk when he stripped off his jeans and shirt. She'd struggled to control her own trembling desire at the sight of him, his limbs lightly oiled, his leanly muscled body displayed to perfection by his breechclout.

She wanted him, and tonight could be the last time she'd ever see him.

As the fire crackled and its hot tongues shot up in abandon, right and wrong disappeared. There was no "should" or "ought" in the drumbeats or the dark eyes that caught hers. There was only man and woman and the deep cloak of night wrapping around them.

Dear Reader,

When was the last time your heart ached over an epic story, thrilled to a romance that spanned generations? This month in Special Editions, the ever popular Nora Roberts will satisfy that craving. The saga of the irrepressible MacGregor clan, introduced to you with *Playing the Odds* (#225) in March 1985, finally reaches its poignant conclusion in *For Now, Forever* (#361).

With the publication of *For Now, Forever*, we are also reissuing the entire award-winning series, *Playing the Odds* (#225), *Tempting Fate* (#235), *All the Possibilities* (#247) and *One Man's Art* (#259), in a special Collectors Edition. Look for them, with their tartan covers, at your local booksellers, along with this month's Special Editions.

Don't we all dream of finding that one great love? Nora Roberts's fifth book in the MacGregor Series goes back in time to tell how Daniel MacGregor, founder of the MacGregor dynasty, first wooed and won unflappable Anna Whitfield. You've seen Daniel as an inveterate matchmaker when it comes to marrying off his three children—but in *For Now, Forever*, Daniel is the one who's met his match! Whether standing alone or read with the other four, Daniel and Anna's story will capture your heart, for theirs is undeniably the love of a lifetime.

One reader wrote, "When you bring Daniel into any story, the pages truly come alive!" Come share in the MacGregors' joy and drama, and let them make your romantic dreams come true.

Warm wishes,
The editors

ANNE LACEY
Golden Firestorm

Silhouette Special Edition

Published by Silhouette Books New York

America's Publisher of Contemporary Romance

To Carol once again,
for favors too numerous to count.

SILHOUETTE BOOKS
300 East 42nd St., New York, N.Y. 10017

Copyright © 1987 by Martha Corson

ISBN: 0-373-09365-9

First Silhouette Books printing February 1987

America's Publisher of Contemporary Romance

Printed in the U.S.A.

Books by Anne Lacey

Silhouette Special Edition

Love Feud #93
Softly at Sunset #155
A Song in the Night #317
Golden Firestorm #365

ANNE LACEY

lives in Baton Rouge, Louisiana, where she enjoys exploring antebellum homes up and down the Mississippi River as well as frequently revisiting two favorite river cities, New Orleans, and Natchez, Mississippi. She is admittedly an adventurous lady, having lived in Arkansas, Oklahoma, Arizona, Mississippi and several places in Texas. She has traveled extensively in the United States, Europe and Canada and keeps a bag packed at all times for unexpected trips.

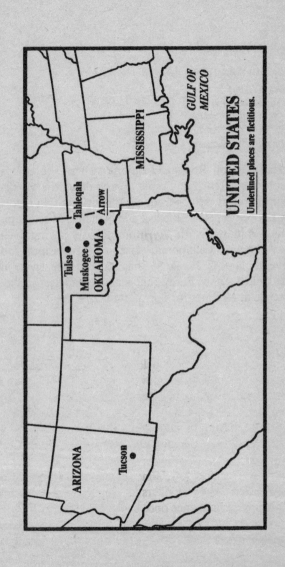

UNITED STATES

Underlined places are fictitious.

GULF OF
MEXICO

MISSISSIPPI

Tulsa
Muskogee • Tahlequah
OKLAHOMA • Arrow

ARIZONA

Tucson

Chapter One

The fire leaped higher, sending orange tongues of flame writhing up into a tar-black sky. Incandescent sparks crackled and snapped in rhythm with the drum beat as light from the flames silhouetted the figure of a dancing man.

Scantily clad in breechclout, belt and moccasins, the dancer's bronze skin glowed, and a sheen of sweat highlighted rippling muscles beneath sinewy flesh. With his black head cast up to the night and his agile feet in motion, he might have been a reincarnation of his ancestors, the proud and peace-loving nation of Choctaws.

"Ah!" came a low, almost guttural murmur of approval from the onlookers as Hawk Saddler captured and held his audience once again.

"Ah!" Wynne Norwood heard the sound that tore from her own throat even as her heart swelled with love and pride. Oh, what a magnificent man Hawk Saddler was! How fascinating! How intelligent, gifted and charming!

And how was it possible that she had existed for twenty-nine years without ever knowing him?

Just as fantastic was how she could have possibly fallen in love with him so quickly, so effortlessly. For years Wynne had said that she didn't believe in love at first sight. That it was nothing but silly infatuation from which the dreamers were certain to awaken, rudely and sadly.

But then, just two mornings ago, she'd gone to meet Hawk Saddler, the noted Indian activist. As part of Indian Pride Week at Wainwright College, Mr. Saddler had been asked to address the United Indian Students' Association and attend the ceremonial powwow. He was flying his private plane into Arrow, Oklahoma's tiny airport, and he wanted to visit a couple of the Indian enclaves nearby. Wynne was to act as his guide and chauffeur once he touched ground.

Wynne certainly hadn't been flustered or overly impressed by the assignment. She met visitors all the time in her job with the college's information office. Already this year she'd greeted the governor of Oklahoma, and the vice president of the United States, not to mention several movie stars and rock performers.

But from the moment Hawk Saddler stepped out of his Cessna, whipped off his aviator glasses and trained those snapping black eyes on her, Wynne was lost to all reason.

Lost—yet perversely, she found a part of herself too. She'd always had a haunting sense of a piece being missed, an essential and integral section of her life misplaced. She'd groped around, sometimes almost blindly, trying to find a part of herself that would sufficiently cover the wound.

"You simply feel inferior because you're a woman," the leader of one feminist group had assured Wynne. "But once you get in touch with your feelings, you'll get over it."

"You simply feel inferior because you're an Indian woman," the leader of a tribal consciousness-raising group had said. "But once you develop a true pride in your heritage, you'll get over it."

Wynne had never been able to convince either group that she didn't feel inferior. Dutifully, she'd "gotten in touch with her feelings." But, still, she hadn't "gotten over it." She kept on feeling like there was something vitally urgent and important to her happiness. But what? Where?

"You're tired, darling. You've been trying to do too much and no wonder!" Tom had said. "You look after me and the kids and you have a hard job."

No, not even Tom, Wynne's late and dearly loved husband, had understood what she meant when she cried that "Something's always missing!" But Tom, who could be understanding even when he didn't understand, had simply held Wynne close and comforted her while she sobbed.

Then, just a month after the night Wynne had confided her feelings to Tom, she'd begun crying for him. Dear, kind and tender Tom, dead far too soon—before he was even thirty.

After the bizarre accident that had killed Tom four years ago, Wynne felt even more fragmented than before. Nevertheless, she made strides of the sort that both feminists and tribal improvement groups could applaud.

"Mrs. Norwood, you're a credit to your profession!"

"Wynne, we're so pleased with your work that we're making you an associate rather than an assistant. You'll also be receiving a sizable raise along with your promotion."

"Wynne dear, our Tom would be so *proud* of you for the way you've carried on without him!"

Even with kudos and praise in abundance, Wynne still felt the obscure yawning ache. She'd never dreamed the thing that could complete her might be another person—especially since she'd loved Tom so much.

But, suddenly, there he was, standing right in front of her. Hawk Saddler—"professional Indian" some of his detractors had said, although they would never have dared say it to his face. Not with his whipcord muscles and all that lean, taut, barely reined-in strength. Hawk Saddler—writer, lecturer, businessman and militant activist. Adviser to the federal government on Indian affairs—Hawk Saddler, the most beautiful, sexy and desirable man in the whole wide world!

Wynne had never felt like this about Tom. She'd never felt like this about *anyone*.

Hawk was tall for a Choctaw, but he had his tribe's characteristically handsome and fine-featured face with a high forehead and deepset eyes. No large hooked nose or fierce mien jarred an onlooker's sensibilities. But Hawk Saddler was all Indian and proudly Indian. He proclaimed it with the headband he usually wore and his turquoise and silver ornaments. He sent the message again with his straight, midnight-colored hair that almost, but not quite, brushed his shoulders.

Because Hawk had specifically requested that there be no demonstrations or large gatherings at the airport, the college had kept secret the date and time of his arrival. Wynne had been a reception committee of one and Hawk Saddler was obviously pleased when he stepped out of his plane. Those jet eyes in the tawny face had met Wynne's and then his legs had rapidly eaten up the distance between them. All the while, neither of them had been able to tear their gaze from the other.

And with each of those strides that Hawk took toward Wynne that fissure inside of her began healing and closing although she was not actually aware of it at the time. No, at the time she'd simply been numbed with surprise and joy.

Now, with her eyes riveted on the dancing Hawk, Wynne did more than remember just how it had begun between them. She began to actually relive it.

The small plane appeared to circle the airport once, then it banked to the right, straightened out and came down for a perfect landing. It glided up to the gate where Wynne stood waiting.

A lithe figure leaped down. He spoke briefly with a man who came out of a hangar wiping his hands on a greasy rag. Wynne could not hear what the men said, but she did hear them laugh in a burst of male camaraderie. Then the lithe figure turned, and she recognized it to be Hawk Saddler.

He wore neither his headband nor his silver and turquoise. Instead he was dressed in a light blue flight suit, and somehow the omission of his usual symbols immediately made him a man to Wynne, not just a public figure of legends and quotes.

"Hello," he said softly, managing to infuse even that one word with a wealth of meaning.

"Hello," Wynne replied.

Hawk carried a bedroll and nothing else off the plane. He gestured toward the white station wagon with Wainwright College emblazoned on its door. "Yours?"

"Ours for the next few days," Wynne heard herself reply, and he smiled. Like everything about Hawk, it was an absolutely devastating smile—debonaire, full of dash.

Their eyes still held, as though unwilling to part, and now their hands seemed to move together instinctively. He must have dropped the bedroll, but Wynne didn't notice. His warm hard hands closed over both of hers.

Belatedly she remembered her manners. "Uh—I'm Wynne Norwood."

"Of course, you know who I am," he replied. "Call me Hawk."

"Uh—yes." Even more belatedly, Wynne tried to turn their clasped hands into a proper, professional handshake. Hawk simply laughed, and the sound was young, happy and free.

Slowly he released her hands and reached down for his bedroll. "Please tell me you're *Miss* Norwood."

"No, I'm not." Wynne stopped, amazed by the dark shadow that immediately crossed Hawk's face. "I'm a widow."

That brief shadow disappeared, and he flashed her a sunny look of relief. "I'm naturally sorry for whatever befell your husband, Wynne. Still and all, I'm glad you're an eligible lady."

She shot back an impish look of her own. "Right now, so am I!"

Why, she was actually flirting with Hawk and not thinking a thing about it. She'd never been a flirt! Wynne Norwood had always been wary of men she'd just met, Indian or non-Indian alike. In addition to everything else, Hawk Saddler had a formidable reputation as a lady killer. But absolutely none of that mattered to her now.

Hawk tossed his bedroll into the back seat of the station wagon, then opened the door on the driver's side for Wynne. "Your names aren't Indian," he complained as he got into the car. His tone was light enough to tell her that he didn't consider this a major disaster.

"No, and my clothes aren't, either," she replied as she watched Hawk carefully take in her appearance. He gave a nod, seemingly approving her navy business suit, white silk blouse and sensible pumps.

"In my job I find that it helps to adopt the usual uniform." Wynne spoke a little nervously as his piercing gaze swept over her again.

"And I find, in mine, that I'd better look just as tribal as I can," Hawk shot back. Then they laughed together, easily and naturally.

He made her pulse leap even while her blood slowed to languid, heavy yearning. He seemed too close, definitely encroaching on her territorial space, and yet he sat quite properly on the passenger's side. The depths of his large black eyes seemed inscrutable, but she felt as if she could decipher their every expression and fathom all of his emotions.

He was actually interested in her. He cared about getting to know her. She read that much at a single glance into his jet eyes, and the knowledge set her trembling.

She started the engine of the big, unwieldy station wagon. "Where would you like to go first?" she asked Hawk brightly. "Do you want to see the town and the college? Or the factory that the Creeks operate outside of town? Or would you prefer to go to your motel and unpack?''

"Unpacking takes me about five seconds," Hawk said. "Actually, what I'd really like to see is something to eat. I didn't have time for breakfast this morning, and I'm starving!"

"Oh, sure." Wynne put the station wagon into drive, and it lurched off like an awkward elephant. She chose one of the nicer restaurants in town, and as they took their seats there she realized that it was one of the more intimate ones as well. Booths gave added privacy, and the lighting was pleasantly dim.

Hawk perused the menu swiftly then ordered a steak, baked potato and salad. He insisted that Wynne eat something, too, so she selected a chef's salad. It was barely past 11:00 a.m., and she wasn't very hungry yet.

A pleasant-faced waitress took their orders and disappeared. Then Hawk's piercing eyes swung back to Wynne. "Tell me, Mrs. Norwood..." His voice was deep-timbred yet soft with a caressing undertone. "Why don't you have even one Native American name?"

"Just downtrodden, I guess," Wynne flashed back and Hawk roared with surprised laughter.

More seriously she added, "Grove was my maiden name. That's considered Indian in Oklahoma. As for Wynne, I think my parents believed that life would be easier for me if I had a nice familiar Anglo name. My Cherokee grandparents were aghast. They wanted me to be named Raven."

"A raven and a hawk," he mused. "Birds of a feather?"

He was fast with a quip, too, Wynne was happy to see. She had always liked a man with a good sense of humor.

"So you're Cherokee?" he probed.

"Actually, I'm Native American melting pot—Cherokee, Creek and a little Choctaw, too." As Wynne smiled she saw his gaze move lower, zeroing in on her mouth. Suddenly her lips tingled, as though awaiting a kiss. No man's stare had ever done *that* to her before! But then no one else had ever set her hands to shaking in her lap or her heart to pounding. No, not even her sweet late husband, Tom.

Hawk reached for his water glass. Over the rim his eyes continued to study Wynne while he drank. He radiated health, life, vitality. His dark hair was glossy, his eyes alert and clear, his skin smoothest bronze. Momentarily Wynne's own gaze rested on Hawk's hands. They were a trifle small for a man's hands, she knew, although they looked large compared to her own. His fingers were long and shapely. She had felt their touch once and now she yearned to feel it again.

"Are you full-blood?" Hawk queried, his eyes still seemingly fascinated with Wynne's mouth.

So he was going to continue asking her questions. Well, it was one way to get acquainted, she supposed, although Wynne couldn't quite shake the feeling that she was being grilled.

"No, I'm not full-blood. I had an auburn-haired Scottish grandfather," she replied.

Hawk sighed. "So few of us have pure blood anymore. Well, I'm sorry about the Scottish grandfather, but I expect I'll forgive you for it."

Again he spoke lightly. Clearly he was teasing her and yet, without knowing it, he had sent a barb stinging straight into Wynne's heart.

She had been crazy about her Scottish grandfather. He'd had a bushy beard and a hearty laugh. He used to settle her atop his wide shoulders so she could see parades, fairs and tribal festivities. He'd called her "my wee papoose" when she was tiny and "little blood-thirsty squaw" when she grew older and used to beat up kids twice her size. Oh yes, her grandfather had uttered all sorts of remarks that would thoroughly outrage a militant, consciousness-raised Native American like Hawk Saddler. And yet Wynne had never minded because she knew that her grandfather loved her every bit as much as she loved him. Their relationship had been very close and special.

"You're full-blood?" she asked Hawk.

He nodded with a smile, his teeth flashing strong and white in his tawny face. "I'm three-quarters Choctaw. A Chickasaw crept into somebody's teepee a few generations back." Deftly he swung the conversation around to Wynne again, posing another question. "Do you have any children?"

"Two," she said proudly. "A boy and a girl."

She saw that shadow again. Briefly it flitted over Hawk's square-jawed face and then it disappeared.

"Stephen is ten and Winona is almost six," she volunteered.

"Winona!" Hawk seized eagerly on the child's name.

"So *I* happen to like Indian names," Wynne said with a little shrug. "We call her Nona."

She could almost guess Hawk's next question or two, but she didn't want to get into all of that just yet. No, not now, Wynne thought. Not when things are positively *blooming* between us—and not when my answer might end it all!

"How about you, Hawk Saddler?" she asked with a bright gaiety. "Shouldn't you state your marital status, too, and tell me whether or not you have kids?"

Oh yes, she was flirting outrageously—she who was never a flirt! Why, Wynne knew perfectly well that Hawk was unmarried. That pertinent little fact had been mentioned in numerous articles about him that she'd read over the past few years. So his reply, unanticipated and wholly unexpected, came as a complete shock to her. .

"Like you, Wynne, I've been widowed—although it happened so long ago it might have been another young man in a totally different lifetime. I was just eighteen and my wife was a year younger. She died in childbirth and the baby with her."

"But—" Wynne stopped, thinking of her own two relatively easy deliveries.

"Go ahead and say it. You're right, women aren't supposed to die in childbirth anymore. Not even when this happened, twenty years ago, were they supposed to die. But we were reservation Indians. Neither of us had ever been more than twenty miles from our homes. We lived with the other Choctaws near our tribe's sacred mound, Nanih Waiya, outside of Philadelphia, Mississippi."

Hawk paused and drew a breath. "At that time we were still very much isolated from the rest of the world. Often, people living in the next county didn't even know there was an Indian reservation in Mississippi. Anyway, my wife went to the local Indian clinic to give birth. Do you know who staffs those clinics? Third-rate doctors, most of them, some even with alcohol and drug problems. Or, at least, that's the way it used to be. Anyway, for my wife, things went wrong...." His voice trailed off and his slim shoulders hunched involuntarily.

Wynne sat silent for a moment, thinking of Hawk Saddler's several college degrees, his frequent appearances on national TV and his travels around the world, most of which he made as pilot of his own airplane. "How far you've come," she marveled.

"Yes." Without a trace of false modesty, Hawk agreed. "It's been a long, long trip from Philadelphia, Mississippi. That's why I said it seemed like it had happened in another lifetime."

"You live in Arizona now, don't you?" Wynne asked, trying to remember what Hawk's press release had said.

"Yes, I have a ranch outside of Tucson. I left Mississippi the week after my wife died, though I go back once or twice a year to visit my family."

Hawk looked back up into Wynne's eyes. "Forgive me for interjecting a somber note," he said and deliberately extended his hand, waiting for hers. When Wynne's arose spontaneously from her lap, Hawk's hand covered it closely and warmly, making her heart bound for joy. "I wanted you to know it all. What happened to my child-bride almost twenty years ago has been the driving motivation behind everything I am and do. She was killed by indifference—the kind of indifference that wouldn't have happened if she'd been a nice WASP lady."

You can't know that for sure. Wynne practically spoke the words aloud, then she bit her tongue in time to stop them. She didn't want to contradict Hawk because she respected what he had become and what he had done, and she didn't want anything to end this magic between them. Hawk gave her hand an electrifying squeeze, then released it.

"Back to you, Wynne." He smiled with genuine feeling and his tone lightened appreciably. "Have you always lived in Oklahoma?"

"Yes, right here in Arrow," she replied.

"Was there much Indian prejudice?"

Wynne shook her head. She was about to add that she'd had friends who were white, black, brown and even yellow, thanks to the one local Chinese family, when Hawk spoke again.

"Prejudice varies in Oklahoma," he said thoughtfully. "In some areas, Indians have been treated worse than dogs. In others—" Again he shrugged. "I've seen towns where *everybody* had Indian relatives or friends."

"That was mine," Wynne said softly.

"You were lucky. Very lucky," Hawk emphasized.

"Yes," she agreed.

Oh, why was she so hesitant to fully speak her mind? Wynne wondered. Why was she afraid to let Hawk know the whole truth about her life, opinions and friends? Wynne had never been reluctant to speak up, but now she just knew that she couldn't, not quite yet. A dedicated Indian activist might not understand that her husband had been white.

Their food arrived to interrupt her thoughts. Hawk began eating hungrily yet neatly while Wynne retossed her salad and forked through it.

Professional Indian. She didn't like having the thought cross her mind, and yet, where Hawk was concerned, it was obviously a fact of life. Wynne knew that had she been asked just who she was, she would have responded, "Woman, widow, mother, daughter-in-law, public relations associate." Then, and only then, might she have mentioned "Indian." Her racial inheritance was not dominant and uppermost. It wasn't constantly on her mind. In fact, she actually forgot about it completely for days at a time. Then an invitation would arrive, asking her to attend something as frivolous as a stomp dance or as serious as a tri-state tribal meeting, and she'd think, "Oh yes, I really should go to that. After all, I'm Indian."

But Hawk Saddler, she was sure, would have answered the very same questions of his identity with, "I'm an Indian man...." So Wynne had to be careful.

At the same time she felt as though she understood him. Since he'd grown up on a reservation that was bound to make a difference. Reservations as such no longer existed in Oklahoma so Wynne knew little about them except that they tended to foster a strong feeling of isolation from other communities as well as interdependence within the group.

Hawk glanced up from his food and smiled at her, interrupting Wynne's train of thought. It was such a sweet and beguiling smile that she felt her heart lurch and her breath catch in her throat. Somehow Hawk had simply arrived in her life already being someone *dear*, just as her children had. But she'd had nine long months to learn to love each baby before it was born while Hawk Saddler should have been an absolute stranger.

"I'm glad I'll be here for three days," Hawk said in his soft, deep-timbred voice. "Already the time seems too short. Will you be able to show me around, Wynne? Or do you have to spend most of your time at the office?"

"Hawk, you're a prominent VIP and the college's guest of honor. Why, I'd be slaughtered if I didn't take you to each and every place you wanted to go! Unless, of course, you prefer to drive yourself," Wynne replied swiftly.

"I detest driving." His deep-set black eyes sparkled mischievously. "I've never been very good at it."

"Oh, of course not. You merely cross oceans and continents in your plane," Wynne gibed.

"That's different. I would so hate to wreck the college's station wagon," he added piously.

"I'll explain this quirk of yours to the office. I'm sure they'll understand," Wynne said solemnly, although inwardly she was absolutely dancing with happiness and glee. Oh, he really does want to be with me!

Their lunch finished, Hawk refused to let Wynne pay the bill. She insisted he obtain a receipt and submit it to the college with the rest of his expenses. "Oh, okay," he said, negligently shoving the receipt inside his flight suit, and they went outside and got back into the station wagon. The small incident was nonetheless telling. He did not take money very seriously. Either he had enough of it not to be concerned, or it simply wasn't one of his higher priorities.

Clumsily Wynne put the station wagon in gear, and almost tore out the transmission. Hawk shot her such an alarmed look that she laughed, the happy sound lilting out into the perfect Oklahoma day. It was early May, balmy and cloudless, the temperature in the late seventies, and the sun shone down benignly.

"What's so funny?" Hawk asked as Wynne began to back jerkily out of the parking space.

"That horrific expression on your face. That—and a thought I just had. I wondered when you'd *finally* take the car keys away from me. I guess that by two o'clock you'll have had enough of my driving."

"Guess again," he said and extended his left arm until his hand lay on the seat directly behind Wynne. He could let his arm drop at any time and it would encircle her shoulders, she realized with a thrill. "I plan to hold out at least until three!"

First, Wynne drove Hawk to see the town of Arrow. He dutifully admired the courthouse square, the new civic center building and the large modern motel where he was to stay. "Now, I'll take you to see the college," Wynne offered.

"Before you do that, show me where you live," Hawk directed. His arm slid down to gently encircle Wynne's shoulders for a moment, then returned to its previous perch. But the brief touch made her skin burn and her breath grow ragged.

"You want to see *my* house?" Wynne exclaimed breathlessly.

"Sure! Then after I've gone I can imagine you in your usual setting. That always makes me feel closer to people—until I can see them again."

Gracious! He wasn't even trying to pretend to be casual about their obviously mutual attraction. Wynne admired Hawk's honesty and frankness, but the thought of showing him where she lived made her heart skid into overdrive and caused little prickles of alarm to tighten the nerves beneath her skin. She knew she mustn't act hesitant to show him her house or he would be sure to grow suspicious.

Would her in-laws, Barry and Peg, be outside? Wynne wondered, panic-stricken. If either of them were, she could scarcely toss off a nonchalant wave and drive on by. No, she would have to stop and introduce Hawk to them. Then what would he think?

I'm just not ready to have this magic end quite yet, Wynne argued with herself. It's been so long since I was interested in a man! And I've never been so interested in anyone as I am in *this* man.

Reluctantly she turned off into a residential area and crossed three intersecting streets. Then she turned right and the awkward, bulky station wagon suddenly shot ahead, consuming more than its rightful share of the street.

"Watch out!" Hawk warned her as another car approached, coming from the opposite direction. The two vehicles passed uneventfully but Hawk said, "Whew!" and pretended to wipe drops of perspiration off his forehead.

"It wasn't that close," Wynne protested.

"What do you mean it wasn't close?" Hawk argued back. "You made that poor scared sucker eat the curb!"

"I did not!"

"Did too!"

They sounded like squabbling children except that they kept smiling at each other, their eyes holding and lingering. Then Hawk tore his gaze away from Wynne and looked at the various houses in the suburb. "Nice," he said and gave a low whistle under his breath. "Very nice!"

Wynne felt his expression grow speculative and, once again, she could read his unspoken words. "No, I am not wealthy," she said with a short laugh. "My in-laws own the house and the children and I live with them."

"Then they must be wealthy," Hawk surmised. "Oil money?"

"Just indirectly," Wynne said. "My father-in-law works for an oil company and has for thirty years. He bought a lot of their stock through an employee purchasing program. The company has done quite well."

"Obviously," said Hawk.

Wynne turned onto her own street. "We're the buff-colored house, third from the end. Oh! I see Nona forgot and left her bike on the lawn again. That little rascal! Steve never forgets his. He's such a responsible child," she explained to Hawk.

"That sounds typical of the kids' birth order," he remarked. "The first child is usually a compulsive, responsible, over-achieving perfectionist while the second kid is a blithe spirit."

"Which child were you?" Wynne asked as they neared the large buff house.

"Can't you guess?" Hawk teased.

"First?" she said tentatively.

"Bingo! And you?"

"Fourth—but I was the first girl," she explained.

Hawk grinned at her, then looked away, his eyes narrowing as they passed the house where Wynne lived. Mercifully, no one was on the lawn or in the carport.

"Hmm . . . Buick in the driveway—"

"My father-in-law's," she supplied.

"Nice flower garden."

"My mother-in-law's."

"You get along with the folks okay?" he inquired.

He was the darnedest man for asking questions. "Oh, yes. I've known them all my life. They're lovely people."

"What?" he said in mock surprise, his glossy black eyebrows arching. "No in-law flak at all?"

"Well, they tend to spoil the children," she hedged. "I guess that's natural. Tom was their only child."

"Where is your bedroom?" Hawk said abruptly and Wynne almost drove the station wagon off the street. She felt color spring to her cheeks.

"See the upstairs front window, the one on the right?" she managed to say matter-of-factly. "That's mine."

"Okay, I've got a fix on you now, Wynne Norwood. So lead on."

"Where?" Wynne said, anxious both to please him and to get out of the neighborhood as quickly as possible.

"Wherever! College. Local Indian sweatshops or watering holes. Nearby picturesque lake—I'm sure you have one."

"No, as a matter of fact, we don't. It's dry as a bone all around Arrow," she informed him.

Hawk slapped his forehead. "Why, of course it is! I should have realized. Any place those redskins got to live was usually too dry to grow tumbleweeds. Very well. Substitute the nearest Lovers' Lane and let's park."

"Hawk!" Wynne exclaimed, feeling her face flame anew, but he simply laughed at her.

Wynne wouldn't let herself even speculate on Hawk's last outlandish suggestion. She drove straight to the college and, since this was a very familiar area for her, she rattled off names of the various red brick buildings they passed. "See that circular building, Hawk? That's the Zachary Thayer auditorium where you'll be speaking tonight," she informed him. "Usually it serves as a theater in the round."

"I never would have guessed," he commented dryly. "Who was old Zack?"

"A famous Indian fighter," Wynne admitted.

"Ouch!" Hawk winced.

Wynne was less familiar with the large Creek enclave located almost fifteen miles out of town. She had to admit she'd rarely visited there, and she could tell that her reply was not necessarily the one Hawk would have preferred to hear.

The Creeks' factory was located at the end of a wide boulevard. A large gray-painted building, it looked rather drab and run-down, rather like a prison camp squatting on the edge of a wide flat field. But instead of guards and electrified fences there were signs welcoming visitors. Off to one side of the gray building was a parking lot for employees which was well-filled with cars and pickup trucks.

"What do they make here?" Hawk asked as Wynne stopped before the entrance. This led into a gift and souvenir shop while the factory lay behind.

"Toy tomahawks, kid drums, Indian dolls—" Wynne began.

"Trinkets and feathers," Hawk said scornfully. "Each year fewer and fewer of those are sold. We have to train our people to do more than that!"

"The Creeks also make fish lures and hooks plus printing the cards they're stapled to. They operate a nice little printing business as well as cast metal." Wynne was glad to display a little more knowledge of present Indian activities although she had her father-in-law, an avid fisherman, to thank for the information.

Hawk's brooding look lightened. "Well, that's some better!" he said in relief.

His scorn for certain of the items being produced did not extend to the workers themselves. Hawk charged right into the large shop where most of the people were occupied and introduced himself, shaking hands all around.

His sudden and welcome appearance shattered the Indians' characteristic passivity. Eagerly they clustered around him, laughing and talking. Everyone in that large shop had heard of Hawk Saddler. To them, he was a figure of influence and success, this slim man with the light bronze skin who was still dressed in his blue flight suit. Why, Hawk Saddler had eaten dinner at the White House and been photographed conversing with the first lady. His reputation was such that the world stopped to listen whenever he made a speech, wrote a book or uttered a thundering condemnation. He was proof that an Indian really could realize the great American dream, and they held him up as an example and inspiration for their children.

Hawk had insisted that Wynne accompany him inside, and as the flow of excited words washed over her, she thought that Hawk actually sounded more like a politician than an Indian activist as he shook hands and cracked jokes.

"Think they'll vote for you?" she teased when they were back in the station wagon again.

"No. They're going to send me to Hollywood. Watch out!" he yelled. A yellow school bus had stopped in front of them and Wynne, intent on watching the play of expressions across Hawk's face, had not braked in time to suit him.

"Uncle!" Hawk said and held up both his hands. "I surrender."

"What?" said Wynne, perplexed by her plight of trying to watch Hawk and the road all at the same time.

"Give me the car keys, please!" he pleaded.

Secretly Wynne was relieved. This big, balky white elephant wasn't nearly as responsive as her small Nissan. "It's a lot easier for me to drive my own car," she admitted.

"I should hope so!" said Hawk fervently.

"That bad?" she asked in dismay.

"Yeah." But then he removed any sting of reproach by reaching boldly across the seat and kissing her.

Chapter Two

Momentarily the world stopped. It tilted up on its axis, reversed poles and then started to move once again, with absolutely nothing the way it had ever been before. Or so it seemed to Wynne as her lips and Hawk's clung together, then parted gently.

She'd known there was good chemistry between them. She'd felt the sparks fly when they'd touched and the warmth rush over her when their eyes had met but nothing—*nothing* had prepared her for the impact of his kiss.

It took the breath out of her body, and when Wynne breathed next, she took in the warm air he'd exhaled. She tingled all over. And this was just a straight, simple, lips-only kiss. What would have happened if he'd *really* kissed her, allowing his lips and tongue their full range of expression?

His kiss had been soft, gentle, tentative, as if to give her time to object or withdraw had she wished. His firm lips had parted little, if at all. And yet when those same lips pressed on hers, Wynne felt as though the world had been upended.

When his face moved slowly back and away from hers, she searched Hawk's eyes and found them smoky looking. *Desire,* she deciphered, and her heart gave another joyous leap and bound. She wanted him, too, so much she was actually aching in yearning as her body, which had been deprived of love for so long, relearned physical response to a virile handsome male.

Hawk gave a low whistle under his breath. "Wow, I feel like I've been sandbagged!" His gaze washed caresses over Wynne's forehead and lips, then down to her breasts and thighs. Finally, he looked back into her eyes. "You, too?"

"Oh, yes," she breathed.

His black eyes sparkled with that glint of mischief. "Yes, this is definitely going to be an eventful three days!"

Did he think—? Oh, he must mean...! The heavy hammer of duty and responsibility slammed down on Wynne, crushing and ending her spontaneity. She thought of her position at the college, which commanded admiration and respect. She thought of her two small children who looked up to her as their way-shower. She remembered her in-laws with their generosity and her own family with their high expectations.

Everything came with a price tag attached, and Wynne realized that although she wanted to be close to Hawk, the necessary price now seemed steep. She could not allow herself to be branded as cheap.

Haltingly, she groped for words. "Hawk, you mustn't think that I'm—er, I . . ."

"Yes?" he said attentively and helpfully.

"I mean, I'm not a—a loose woman," she blurted.

He gave a shout of laughter. "'A loose woman,'" he repeated incredulously. "From what old, dried-up crone did you ever hear that antiquated phrase?"

"Please don't laugh at me," Wynne said and discovered, frighteningly, that she was actually near tears.

Hawk sobered immediately. "I was laughing at the words, not at you, Wynne." His large thumb, rough and warm, brushed her trembling lower lip. "My God, you're about to cry!"

"I know it's silly . . ."

She longed to add, "And it's thoroughly uncharacteristic and totally unlike the stoic Indian maidens you undoubtedly admire!" But every word she uttered only seemed to make things worse.

"If a person feels strongly about something then it isn't silly," Hawk said, his wonderful rough thumb gently tracing the contours of Wynne's lips.

But I don't feel like taking a strong moral stance! Wynne thought almost desperately. I just feel like a hypocrite—because what I really want to do is sink into your arms and melt! I want to turn off my head that echoes those dull words of duty and responsibility and be nothing but a woman, alive and responsive again! Oh, I want so much what I just can't allow myself to have!

For the space of a minute Wynne wished she were someone else. One of those confident and independent career women she was always reading about, responsible only for herself, to herself. Then she could have a fling with a man, if she wished. She could toss caution to the wind and let down her hair, both literally and figuratively. Right now the long straight strands were pinned up so properly and primly. She wanted to laugh seductively, open her arms wide and watch Hawk's eyes turn smoky again.

His quiet words interrupted her train of thought. "Wynne I want you to know that I did—and do—respect you completely. I made a careless remark which I think you've misinterpreted. I certainly don't want you to think I've embarked on some campaign to seduce you."

Hawk's words, meant to reassure Wynne, had the reverse effect. Although today was too soon to allow herself to be seduced, she wanted him to ultimately succeed. She'd spent enough hours in Hawk's company to know that he sparked a wanton and hungry longing all through her. But now he'll begin treating me like ninety-year-old Aunt Fanny, Wynne thought despairingly. Oh, why didn't I just keep my stupid mouth *shut*?

And in that wretched frame of mind where duty and desire collided head-on, what happened next was the last thing in the world that Wynne expected.

Hawk swept her back into his arms. Masterfully, he stroked her face and hair, great bold sweeping strokes that seemed to drench her in flames. Then his mouth dropped down to fit perfectly over Wynne's and, when her lips opened instinctively, his tongue darted through them.

He possessed her completely with that kiss, his hot lips a singeing pressure on hers, his tongue a bold delicious marauder, which sought to touch and awaken each tiny nerve within the cavity of her mouth.

That kiss told Wynne that Hawk still found her wholly desirable. She sagged with relief in his arms until the magic they created together seemed to be an essence that danced gaily between them.

She felt ecstatic. She melted, yielded, pressed and clung to the firm body wedged so tightly against hers. Why, she could feel her breasts flattened to their tips on the solid wall of his chest.

At that moment Wynne wasn't sure she could deny Hawk Saddler anything. He had only to claim whatever he wanted.

Instead he drew back from her as swiftly as he'd advanced. His breath came in ragged gasps and his face looked flushed. His eyes, alight with that smoky desire, studied her, and Wynne thought he had never been so handsome.

"I'll drive now," Hawk said and took the station wagon keys from her limp hand.

That was when Wynne's last doubt died. She barely knew him—but she loved him.

They shared a second perfect day together. Hawk visited several far-flung and mostly Indian schools where he exhorted the fascinated children to study hard and stay in school. Avoid tobacco, firewater and stronger substances, he counseled further, and hold tight to your dream for the future, whatever it might be.

"That was a splendid talk, Hawk," Wynne said, almost misty-eyed when he walked off the third stage.

"Good." He gave her a weary, crooked smile. "Now, let's grab a handy six-pack somewhere. Man, am I parched!"

"Hawk!" she cried in shock, remembering what he'd just told the children about alcohol. Then she began to laugh.

They bought the beer and hid out in a grove of trees like naughty children. There they sipped beer and exchanged confidences and kisses. Hawk talked about his ranch and Wynne told him about her adventurous parents who'd retired from their jobs, bought a camper and set out to see the U.S., Canada and Mexico.

Both of Hawk's evenings had been wholly consumed by speeches and meetings. Now it was morning once again, the third and final day of his stay. Also, as Wynne was about to discover, not everyone was absolutely thrilled that Hawk Saddler was in town.

"Why do you have to leave so early, Mama?" Nona complained at breakfast.

"Yeah," Steve chimed in. "You got home so late last night that Nona and I were already in bed asleep."

Guilt struck Wynne again, hard and fast. Then she rallied quickly. "Look, kids, it's just for one more day. Then I'll be back on my usual schedule again," she promised.

Her mother-in-law shot her a look that was much like relief. In Wynne's absence, Peg had to feed the kids their supper, supervise homework and cajole them into baths and beds.

Hey, folks, just let me have these three days, Wynne thought—all you big folks and little folks too. Then I'll go back to being dutiful, responsible, reliable, predictable Mama. Oh God, how I'm going to miss him when he's gone!

Would Hawk really miss her too? Would he think about her? Call her and write, as he'd said he would? Or was she a fool to believe she could stay in touch with someone as busy and important as Hawk?

"Who you showin' 'round this time?" little Nona asked.

"Hawk Saddler," Wynne replied and simply pronouncing his name sent up a glow from deep inside of her. "He's a noted Indian activist."

"Oh!" said Steve admiringly. At ten, he was obsessed by all topics and things Indian. My own little budding activist, Wynne thought. "Can I meet him, Mama?"

Before Wynne could reply, her father-in-law rattled his morning paper and looked over the rim of his spectacles at her. "Say, isn't Saddler a real firebrand type? The kind of extremist who stops just short of taking scalps?"

Wynne's heart sank but she managed a calm, "No, I really don't think so. His speech at the college was quite—quite conciliatory."

"Humph!" said Barry Norwood. "I guess he'd almost have to talk that way at the college. Half the students aren't Indian. But I remember him on TV, rompin' and stompin'. Why, he was a whole war party all by himself!"

Wynne's politically astute mother-in-law leaned over to refill her husband's coffee cup. "Hawk Saddler *used* to be a firebrand, dear, but that was fifteen years ago at Berkeley. I think he may also have been one of those Indians who seized Alcatraz. But like so many radicals and extremists of the sixties, he finally realized that verbal attacks just drove away the very people and dollars his cause needed. Now he's toned down his rhetoric and polished up his image."

"Oh," said Barry, who'd always had less interest in political matters than his wife. Wynne, as usual, was amazed by her mother-in-law's recall.

"Of course, one always wonders," Peg Norwood said thoughtfully as she took her seat across from Wynne.

"What? What does one always wonder, Granny? Steve piped up.

"What does Hawk Saddler really believe? Is it his old line of Indians' superiority and Indians' rights? Or is it his new line?"

Nona chose that moment to upset her glass of milk. Wynne dodged the splatters and pools, then mopped fast and furiously with her paper napkin. So she scarcely heard her father-in-law's remark that had to do with the inability of leopards to change their spots.

Finally their very last hours had arrived. Hawk had finished making speeches and participating in rap sessions where he continuously urged young Native Americans to make the most of the educational opportunities offered to them.

The last scheduled event of Hawk Saddler's visit to Arrow, Oklahoma, was the evening of ceremonial dancing—the lovely ancient dances so inadequately described, Wynne often thought, by the cliché word "powwow."

She braided her hair and wore her own authentic Indian costume, a white buckskin dress, which was elaborately and beautifully beaded. Matching moccasins were on her feet, and when Hawk saw her, that smoky-sultry look lighted up his eyes and suffused his whole face.

Wynne had been just as stirred by Hawk when he stripped off his jeans and shirt. She had struggled to control her own almost trembling desire at the sight of him, his limbs lightly oiled, his lean and muscled body displayed to perfection by his breechclout.

The firelight, dancing, chanting and the rhythmic, ritualistic beat of the drums fired her blood and filled her senses. The leaping, twirling male figures, now wearing war paint, were all so beautiful. But there was that special and particular one from whom she could scarcely tear her gaze, who left her body smoldering.

She wanted Hawk! She needed him and—cruel thought that it was—tonight really might be the last time she ever saw him, Wynne knew. She wanted that agile body beside her in bed, wanted the fantastic rake of his lips over hers and the sensuous glide of skin on skin. She wanted to cover his strong broad hairless chest with a hundred kisses, wanted to let her hands wander over that body that drew her like a magnet and explore its source of strength.

As the fire crackled, and its hot tongues shot up in abandon, right and wrong disappeared for Wynne. There was no "should" or "ought" in the drumbeats or the dark eyes that caught and held hers. There was only man and woman and the deep cloak of night wrapping around them.

The tempo of the pounding drums grew faster. Wynne could feel Hawk watching her and she wondered if he could read her desire in the sway of her body, in the golden, fire-lighted glow of her eyes, in her parted lips and desire-heavy limbs.

If she never saw him again— Wynne bit her lip to halt that thought and the rush of tears it engendered. Then, when her tears were blinked away and she looked back again to the dancing men, Hawk was gone!

She found him standing a short distance away. He used a motel towel he'd brought to scrub sweat, oil and paint from his face. He dropped the towel across his bare shoulders and looked directly at her.

Wynne looked back, not moving, not even hearing the chant or the drums that rose all around her. She didn't see the numerous bronze bodies in motion. She saw only Hawk.

He walked over and took her arm. "Shall we go?" he whispered, and what Wynne read in his eyes was so deep, so important and all encompassing that she saw no need to reply at all. Her arm, slipping around his flat hard waist, said it all.

They couldn't keep from touching each other as they walked. His bare thigh brushed her buckskin-covered one, making her skin prickle with hungry sensations while their shoulders rubbed and meshed together.

Back inside the familiar station wagon, they moved toward each other instinctively. Hawk's kiss on Wynne's open and responsive mouth was fierce, indeed almost burning. But she didn't care—she returned his kiss just as rapturously. Surely once, a young Choctaw brave must have claimed his mate just like this, Wynne thought. Hawk's fierce possession of her lips made her head swim, her heart pound and her senses clamor for all of him. She loved him! Loved him as though she always had, as though they were longtime lovers instead of brand-new ones.

Then Wynne felt one of Hawk's hands curling avidly over her breast while the other moved boldly beneath the hem of her dress, making her knees tremble. Next that loving yet aggressive hand cupped and lightly squeezed her knee, its touch hard and its strength so exciting.

With a new boldness that Wynne hardly knew as her own, she took Hawk's face between her hands and drew his lips down to cover her eager mouth again. Her hunger for him was a live and flaming thing, and she felt him respond delightedly to her caresses. He leaned closer to her, inviting more of them, his breath gone ragged.

His bold hands on her grew even more audacious, stroking up and down, awakening her breasts until their nipples bloomed and flowered for him beneath the beads and buckskin. At the same time, Hawk's other hand glided between Wynne's soft thighs, setting them afire. Gradually they drifted apart, seeking pleasure in response to his gifted fingers.

If his hand goes any higher up my skirt I'll probably scream, Wynne thought distractedly, feeling herself grow molten hot at her very core.

Then, before she quite knew what was happening, Hawk had fallen forward across her lap. Slowly and gently his hands raised Wynne's skirt. His mouth, hot and wet, glided up along her inner thighs, making everything that had gone before mere child's play. Desire struck Wynne as fiercely as lightning splitting a tree; she cried out, her fingers tangling in the coarse, thick blackness of his hair. Rhythmic waves threatened to overtake her, to drench and drown her in pleasure.

Abruptly Hawk's exciting, tantalizing mouth was gone. He straightened up in the car and looked across at Wynne. In the light from the bonfire, she could see dimly that he looked just as shaken as she felt. When he spoke, his voice wasn't quite steady. "Let's go back to my place."

His place. His motel room, he meant. Wordlessly Wynne nodded her assent. She simply couldn't have done otherwise.

The motel with its quiet and spacious room lay only a short distance away, and as they rode, their hands clung together. Wynne had no illusions about what was going to happen. She and Hawk would make love and, for them, it was right and good because they both desperately wanted and needed each other.

Hawk swung the station wagon into the closest available parking space to his room, then leaped out and hurried around to open the door for Wynne. He'd been doing that for days now, always gallantly opening doors for her. But never had she appreciated the small courtesy quite as much as she did now.

Hawk had left a single light burning dimly. The yellowish glow it cast provided just enough illumination for each of them to search the other's face. Hawk's features were taut with need and desire, but another look was present there as well. Wynne, looking up to his greater height, saw a gentle softness that usually wasn't present on the hard angular lines and planes. Hawk felt a tenderness toward her that looked even more intense than his drive for pleasure.

"Wynne . . ." He breathed her name in the barest of whispers.

"Yes, Hawk?" she replied expectantly.

His lips crushing down on hers was his answer and now Wynne clung to him wildly, feeling a primitive passion grow and swell between them. His hands gripped her to his body, one tangling in her braids, the other rock firm as it pressed against the small of her back. Insinuatingly, erotically he ground their hips together.

His kiss, his touch might have been almost painfully severe if Wynne had not been equally aroused. But, because she was, she swayed and gasped in his grip. This was exactly the way she'd wanted him to make love to her. She needed to know she could produce the same excitement in him, inciting every part of his body.

Wynne wasn't aware of Hawk's moving them until she felt the mattress of the king-size bed press against the back of her knees. Then he gathered her even more closely in his arms until they were falling backward onto the soft bed.

Taste. Smell. Touch. All ignited her, inflamed her, and caused Wynne to clutch at Hawk with trembling hands. Wordlessly, and eagerly, she urged him on.

He rained fiery kisses over her and buried her in the wide expanse of the mattress, bearing her down with his body. His hands moved like ten, they were so rapt and rapid in their movements. Everywhere they touched, they left Wynne moaning, arching up to him instinctively as she awaited the final culmination of all that he was and everything that he meant to her.

In just a minute, she thought, he'll start undressing me and then—

Instead, Hawk's hands froze. Chillingly, almost frighteningly, he jerked back from Wynne as though she were on fire, and he was being burned. Bewildered, she blinked up at him and saw his black head lowered to his chest as he held himself up off her then drew slowly away. One of his hands gripped the bedspread in a trembling, white-knuckled grasp, as though he felt pain. Indeed, as Wynne watched, a chill seemed to shake Hawk's body.

It wasn't desire, not now. This was a man resisting almost unbearable temptation—and Hawk could do it. He was strong enough, disciplined enough and mature enough to have learned restraint.

But why should he restrain himself? Wynne thought in further bewilderment. They were each consenting adults; neither was married to anyone else. Why shouldn't they have these few magic moments before all the dull days and dreary responsibilities were upon them again?

"Hawk?" Wynne said tentatively, her heart shaking her with its ominous pounding.

He moved even farther away at the sound of her voice. "Forgive me, Wynne," he said lightly, although his face did not reflect his voice. Rather, it looked tense and troubled.

"Wh-why should I forgive you?" Wynne stammered, raising herself up on one elbow.

"Because I almost got carried away," he replied still in that easy, smooth voice that the harsh lines of his face belied. "You're such a beautiful woman, I'm sure you know from past experience how easily men can be aroused."

No, she really didn't know, Wynne thought, her throat contracting with hurt. She wasn't experienced with "men" at all! Tom had been her first boyfriend, her high school and college sweetheart. Since his death, she'd spent a few dignified and sedate evenings with an older businessman in Arrow and she'd kept expecting that Rick Thompson, a younger man in her office, would ask her out. Neither man would try to hustle her into bed—in fact, she didn't feel irresistibly drawn to either.

Her experience with men consisted solely of Tom and Hawk. But Wynne didn't say this as she propped herself up on one elbow. Instead, the hurt of rejection and condescension was so pronounced and severe that it ran like chill embalming fluid in her veins. Because if Hawk assumed her experienced with men, then—undoubtedly—she was just one more in a long string of women to him.

Although just why he had decided to hold off, when he could have had this woman so easily, Wynne couldn't imagine.

She saw her breasts still rising and falling unevenly, evidence of their thwarted desire. Her whole body felt cold and rigid now. She might have described herself as a statue except that she was aching so. From the lump in her throat all the way down to her toes, curling in shame in her white beaded moccasins, she ached.

Meanwhile, Hawk stirred around the room, picking up the towel he'd dropped at the door. Then he carried the slacks and shirt he'd worn earlier, before he'd stripped down to his breechclout, to the rack of hangers.

His face looked closed, angry, hurting. His jaw was set in a rigid line. Wynne knew she had to ask him one more question, although she dreaded hearing the answer.

"Hawk, did I—did I do anything wrong?"

"Of course not!" His emphatic denial was twice the volume of the soft inquiry. "I just realized it's getting late and tomorrow will be a busy day. Can you pick me up at seven in the morning, dear?"

That careless endearment was the last straw. Wynne couldn't think of anything Hawk could say to her that was worse! She found herself standing by the side of the bed, straightening her dress and smoothing her hair, with no memory of how she'd gotten there. Nor did she know what force had propelled her into sudden motion. All Wynne knew was that she had to get out of there as fast as possible. Otherwise, she was likely to burst into tears and disgrace herself completely or—or else she would grab up one of the heavy bedside lamps, break it over Hawk Saddler's head and then have to stand trial for murder!

"Keys?" she said in a single clipped word.

"Ashtray by the door," Hawk said automatically.

"I'll pick you up tomorrow morning at seven," she gasped, almost breathless in her humiliation.

"Thank you—Wynne." At last Hawk stopped moving around hanging up clothes. He stopped and looked at her, *really* looked at her.

"Are you all right?" he said as if something he saw in Wynne's stricken face had touched a responsive chord.

"Oh, yes," she replied, stammering and flushed with embarrassment. Sure. Fine and dandy. Peachy keen. Desperately Wynne's hand searched the ashtray and plucked out the car keys while her other hand turned the knob of the door.

"Sleep well," Hawk called.

Wynne jerked her head in assent, already knowing with certainty that she wouldn't be able to close her eyes all the horrible night long. Oh, why had she ever thought that she was anyone special to him? Or that their passionate kisses and caresses felt as magical to Hawk as they did to her? What a silly, love-starved fool she'd been!

He was still watching her, but Wynne couldn't return Hawk's easygoing farewell. By then she couldn't have spoken at all. A thick cord seemed to be around her throat, stifling her larynx.

Then, mercifully, she was through the door, outside and alone. In the protective black darkness only the stars, twinkling down maddeningly and tauntingly, could see her.

Wynne stumbled to the station wagon and crawled in wearily behind the steering wheel. She gripped it with both hands and then she fell forward, her arms cushioned by its circular ring while her face, streaming tears, pressed down against her arms.

Something awful had gone wrong and not knowing what on earth it could have been didn't help her at all.

Alone in his motel room, Hawk dropped the shirt he'd tried three times to hang up. Savagely, he kicked at it and swore under his breath.

Wynne's face, stunned, white and pinched, as it had looked during that brief interchange at the door seemed to rise up to haunt him. Had he made a mistake? Hawk wondered suddenly. Had she really wanted him to go further?

No. Surely not. Wynne had taken pains to tell him, immediately after they had exchanged their first kiss, that she wasn't the sort of woman to play around.

Hawk had respected that. In fact, his already high opinion of Wynne had shot up another several notches. Over the years he'd had his fill of the easy women, the promiscuous ones, the casual-about-sex ones who considered taking a man to bed with the same seriousness with which they'd order a cup of coffee.

Hawk had survived several years of hell raising when he was in his twenties, but now that he had matured, he had been looking for a woman from whom a commitment would really be important. He was ready to marry the right woman, settle down and raise kids.

And Wynne was that woman; his exact and perfect woman! The woman he had almost despaired of ever finding until three short days ago, when he had stepped out of his plane and seen her eager, happy, beautiful face as she stood by the gate waiting for him.

His heart had soared off at that moment, and he wasn't earthbound yet. *There she is,* a little voice had whispered inside of him, and Hawk, well-grounded in Indian mysticism, would never discount an inner voice.

He'd been disturbed to learn of Wynne's previous marriage because he was a possessive kind of guy. He'd always hated to share what was his! And, since Wynne was his and he knew it beyond all doubt, that former husband had briefly hung before his eyes like a wraith. But what the hell? Hawk had reasoned to himself. He, too, had been married before.

Wynne's kids were two smaller wraiths. Damn! Hawk had thought. He was interested in having kids of his *own*, not raising some other man's! But when he thought of the rough row that so many Indian kids had to hoe, he knew Wynne's would need a strong father figure. Why, they might even need someone to support them as well. Hawk wondered if Wynne was dependent financially on her in-laws and whether that was the reason she and the kids lived with them.

Anyway, he could deal with two kids, he'd decided, especially if they both looked a lot like Wynne. And she certainly seemed healthy enough to bear another one or two. Magnanimously, Hawk had vowed that he would treat his stepchildren just as well as he did his blood children.

Events with Wynne had been clicking along at a nice, steady pace—until tonight. Until she had looked so gorgeous in her white buckskin dress, until her eyes had followed him, warming him, while he danced.

Everything had come together then. The hot flames leaping ever higher, the lithe physical movements that aroused the sense of his own body with its needs and pleasures, and Wynne—especially Wynne, looking at him so eagerly, so almost—hungrily.

In the station wagon, she'd simply dropped into his arms as though she belonged there. They'd come together with a passion and desire that transcended sheer bodily hunger and glowed like a golden firestorm.

Had he misread the signals? Hawk wondered now, remembering how her body had curved passionately and pliantly around his. Was it possible that she just happened to find him irresistible too?

Abruptly, Hawk stopped pacing. He listened, frowned, then listened again. He realized what was worrying him; he hadn't heard Wynne drive off.

He knew the heavy, grinding sound of that station wagon's engine by now. It always sounded like a threshing machine going full blast.

Hawk quickly darted for the door and wrenched it open. Yes, there was the station wagon still parked exactly where he'd left it. In the moonlight, its white paint gleamed. God, had something happened to Wynne? Sheer terror seized him—the terror of a man who had already lost one woman he loved.

Then he saw Wynne crumpled over the steering wheel, crying bitterly.

Hawk suddenly forgot how to breathe. In the scant minute or two since she'd left his room, could she have been mugged or stabbed?

Feet bare, clad only in his breechclout, Hawk darted out, his heart hammering in a terrified new rhythm. He wrenched the door open on the driver's side, screaming, "Wynne!"

Startled, she raised her wet face to his—and it was certainly wet. Streaming, in fact. But as Hawk drew deep restorative breaths at seeing her stir and move naturally, he didn't even pause to wonder about the cause of her tears. He simply forced his way into the car and caught her to him.

Chapter Three

Wynne blinked in astonishment as Hawk flung the car door open. The interior light flashed on, illuminating his suddenly gaunt-looking features, then she felt herself hauled up to rest against his rock-hard chest. His hands stroked and gentled her with more softness, more consummate tenderness than she would ever have expected him or any man capable of.

"What—?" she stammered.

"I kept waiting to hear you drive off but you didn't leave," he explained rapidly, one hand rising to unconsciously muss her hair. After he had tangled it a bit further, the hand moved down to stroke her tensed shoulders. "What is it, Wynne? Why are you crying?"

"I—I . . ." Faced with Hawk's obvious concern, Wynne felt her eyes filling again and a knot gathering in her throat. Why had she ever thought that loving someone was wonderful? Love could hurt you like nothing else in the world when the love went awry—or when it died, as it had with Tom.

"Tell me, darling!" Hawk implored.

Were her ears deceiving her? Wynne thought in wonder. Had Hawk really called her "darling"? Yes, he had—and this time he'd sounded like he meant it, too. Not like that earlier, casual "dear" that had cut her to the quick.

"Tell me!" Hawk urged once again.

"I was just feeling—" Wynne stopped, knowing that she simply couldn't tell him the *truth*! But what on earth could she say?

"Wynne, talk to me!" Hawk implored.

He was cuddling her now, almost rocking her, and she felt his lips that earlier had been fired with passion now moving over her forehead and cheeks with an absence of desire. These kisses sought only to comfort and console. They did not demand any response from her.

But he waited for a verbal response.

"I, uh, was just feeling blue because—because you're leaving tomorrow—" Wynne stammered.

"That was the worst case of 'blue' I've ever seen. Why, you were sobbing!" Hawk's voice was quite gentle, but his even and measured tone of voice told Wynne that he didn't buy her explanation.

"Well, uh—I knew I was going to miss you a lot. We've grown close. And your leaving means, I—I have to go back to the office and things there aren't..." Wynne's voice trailed off again under Hawk's skeptical stare.

She was the world's worst liar, and always had been. So much for the myth about inscrutable Indians.

"Wynne!" Hawk gave her a gentle little shake but his lips continued to glide down her temples. "Tell me the truth," he urged, his breath so appealingly warm as he spoke against her skin.

So nothing but the truth would do.

She drew herself a little bit aloof from him, the better to protect herself if Hawk should find her answer appalling. "Why did you stop making love to me?" Wynne blurted. "You seemed to find me attractive at first, but—but then you pulled away like I was poison! You turned so cold—"

She was unable to finish her sentence because Hawk gave a great whoop that was part ruefulness, part laughter and part pure, happy war cry.

"Well, you *did*!" Wynne said, both accusing and defensive. "You know you did." But she couldn't say more because his hands were gliding up her bare arms and now their touch was distinctly sensual again. She swallowed hard.

"My precious, beautiful, darling woman—" Hawk spoke in a slow, very measured tone of voice. "Did you actually think I didn't *want* you?"

Miserably, Wynne nodded and then found herself caught again in his arms. Hawk laughed once more, a spontaneous sound of relief. "Wynne, you've sent me mixed signals. I haven't known which one to believe. I've been terrified that I might offend you or frighten you away."

"You have?" she said in surprise, automatically swiping at the tears on her cheeks.

"Oh, Wynne—" All at once his arms were a vise about her, and she could do nothing but relax in their wonderful clutch and cling to him. She felt Hawk draw a deep breath and then came his amazing, incredible words: "Oh, Wynne, don't you know I'm going to *marry* you?"

She couldn't move in the huge vastness of her surprise. In fact, had someone yelled "Fire!" at that moment, Wynne was sure that not a single muscle of hers would have twitched. She was just that shocked.

"What did you say?" she managed at last, her voice no more than a breathy whisper.

"You heard me. I'm going to marry you! Unless, of course—" Hawk paused and Wynne detected the first note of his own uncertainty "—unless you don't want that," he finished.

"Oh, no," she sighed.

"Does 'oh, no' mean yes, you will?" he teased.

"Oh, yes, Hawk!" At last she could move and talk again, because his great black eyes were glowing down at her and she could see his sincerity in their depths. He meant it! Why, he really meant every single word!

Joy flooded Wynne then, a new sort of relieved and unencumbered joy. It was joy of a sort she'd never felt before. But then with Hawk, the whole world and certainly every emotion was brand new.

"Oh, Hawk, I love you!" she said in a happy gasp.

"And I love you dearly," he replied. "I hadn't intended to make my declaration of honorable intentions quite so soon, but I certainly can't let you think—" Mercifully he stopped, letting the misunderstandings and profound misery fade away into the nothingness they were now.

Then Hawk tipped Wynne's face up and kissed her, his lips hot and demanding once again. They swayed together, clung together, pressed and moved, trying to get ever closer together.

Their hungry kiss went on and on. Finally Hawk broke it to utter a husky whisper. "You have two choices. You can push me out of this car, drive home

and protect your honor. Or you can go back inside with
me and share what I know will be a deep and meaning-
ful experience. And an even further commitment between us. But make up your mind quickly! I want you
so much I'm about to turn purely savage."

"Oh, you are, are you?" Wynne teased, her lips no
more than a fraction of an inch from his.

"Um-hum," he assured her. "You're about to be
dragged by your hair, locked in my room and kissed by
a love-crazed man from your head to your feet. And
that's just for starters!"

"Sounds like I'd better go willingly then," Wynne
smiled.

Then Hawk's kiss wiped out every other thought
from her mind.

Back in his room they moved together spontaneously. Wynne let her eyes close, allowing awareness
to enter through other senses.

Warm. Smooth. Soft. Her hands glided up and
around Hawk's neck and face, tracing his features as if
she'd been blind. Long and slender, flared at the tip—
his nose, she deciphered. Twin cavities, slightly sunken,
and she knew she approached his eyes. Hairy and thick,
she found his bristling black eyebrows. All the while, his
own hands were gently yet relentlessly stripping away
her clothes.

She felt the buckskin dress fall away, then her bra and
half-slip followed. "You're so gorgeous!" Hawk whispered almost reverently, and Wynne opened her eyes
lazily to see his dark head bending down to her breasts.
Then his hands cupped her two gently swelling mounds,
and his tongue lapped caresses over them. Ecstatically
Wynne sighed.

After a moment, she felt his hands moving down to strip away her panties. Then Hawk knelt on one knee, urging Wynne to lift first one leg and then the other until the moccasins had been discarded as well, and she was totally nude.

Slowly, Hawk ran his hands up and over the calves of her legs, then his mouth followed, arousing, awakening and preparing her. Wynne felt herself trembling inwardly and then outwardly until her frame shook unsteadily.

"No fair," she said and heard her voice shake, too.

"What?" Hawk asked, his own voice considerably less than steady.

"*You're* still wearing clothes." She sighed, her voice too languid to be accusing.

"This?" In one motion, fluid and deft, he stood up and his breechclout disappeared. "Better?" he asked.

"Much better," Wynne approved and they flowed together again as though impelled until all the hard, angular planes of his body were softened and pillowed by her cushioned curves.

"Let's take a shower," Hawk whispered against Wynne's hair. "I'm all greasy from this oil."

"Umm, you are a bit slippery," she agreed, letting her hands glide over him again. She heard the sharp intake of Hawk's breath when her hands dipped below his navel.

"Yes—shower," he said unevenly.

Wynne followed him into the bathroom, her eyes riveted on the smooth flow of his athletic body as he moved around, turning on the shower and adjusting its water temperature and flow. He might have been a Greek god, though one cast in bronze, and now Wynne understood why those statues had featured men vir-

tually free of body hair. Without that partial conceal-
ment, all their muscles could be seen and appreciated
more fully while the interplay of sinewy muscles—the
bulges of biceps, the jutting forth of a ropelike calf under the pressure of performance—had been all the more
evident.

"Oh, Hawk, you're beautiful, too!" she breathed.

"Saying things like that will get you dunked in an ice
cold shower," he growled and lunged for her.

"Oh, no—not an icy—" Wynne stopped protesting
as a cascade of warm water, the absolute perfect temperature, slashed down over them. The water, landing
needle sharp, then trickling lazily down her body was
another contrast in sensation.

"Here, scrub me," Hawk urged, thrusting soap and
a rough washcloth into Wynne's hand. He swung
around, presenting his broad back and slender buttocks. Wynne scrubbed away until Hawk turned back
to face her.

He slicked his black hair back from his drenched
face, took the bar of soap from Wynne and swiftly
rubbed it over his arms, chest and legs. She saw that
smoky desire flare in his eyes; eyes which scarcely left
hers, even as he soaped himself. Wynne glanced down
to follow his darting hands and fluid movements and
saw that he was fully aroused.

Hawk rinsed himself, revolving slowly beneath the
spray, then turned swiftly and seized Wynne from behind. "Next," he said huskily, pressing his hardened
flesh against her.

She gasped as his hands worked the bar of soap over
her breasts. Slowly, ever so slowly and sensuously, he
moved. His face he nuzzled against the softness of
Wynne's neck until his lips moved languidly to the nape.

"Oh, yes," she breathed as she felt herself being returned to her previous peak of arousal.

Hawk's hands slid lower, soap foaming between them, as he stroked Wynne's stomach, sought the indentation of her navel, and leisurely dipped lower to lave the tops of her thighs.

Wynne flamed beneath the stroking of Hawk's hands for he sought out the soft slopes and curves of her body, as well as finding her acutely sensitive depths. Again and again those marvelous hands of his stroked, caressed, rubbed and touched.

She wanted him! Indeed Wynne wanted Hawk so much that she heard herself make a little whimpering sound of longing. His tongue plunged swiftly into her small shell-like ear and he rubbed himself insinuatingly against the backs of her thighs. He was ready and so was she.

Wynne turned in Hawk's grasp and their lips crushed together. He caught her long wet hair and pulled her head back, to let his lips taste the sweetness of the newly soaped skin on her neck. Wynne whimpered again, her body aching and burning for him; Hawk answered, plunging his tongue deep into her mouth.

She writhed against him, her legs shaking, and he broke their kiss to stop to turn off the shower. Rapidly he handed Wynne out, then enveloped them both in long white towels, snatching up a smaller one at the same time. "C'mon," he urged tenderly.

"Where?" she said automatically, her mind misted and fogged with desire. "What are you going to do with me?"

"You have to *ask*?" he growled and led her over to the bed where he whipped back the bedspread.

As Wynne dropped down to the mattress on one knee, she felt Hawk whisk away the towel that had blotted most of the water off her body. Her wet hair he turbaned quickly with his smaller towel, then he pressed her down against the yielding softness of the bed.

His damp body swiftly topped hers until they were touching in a hundred separate places, all of them erotic. "I love you, Wynne," Hawk whispered and then re-emphasized his words with his lips and hands.

"We're actually going to get *married*?" she whispered incredulously into the wet blackness of his hair.

"Oh, yes," he breathed and now an aggressive knee moved, parting her legs. "From the first day, I knew you were mine!"

"How soon?" she asked breathlessly, her excitement and exhilaration increasing with every one of Hawk's gentle yet demanding movements.

"Ten seconds after I saw you. Oh, Wynne, I want you!"

Wynne answered with a wordless lift of her body, flowing up to meet Hawk at the exact moment when he descended fully onto her. In a single, thrilling and ecstatic second, Hawk fused their bodies.

Ancient primitive rhythms, soft murmured words of love—they might have been linked just like this through a timeless eternity that stretched all the way back to the dawn of time. This was more than just a joining of bodies. This was a complete communion of hearts, minds and kindred blood.

Wynne had never imagined that lovemaking could really be so important. She had never felt before that she had missed anything significant in the man-woman relationship, yet now she knew better. With Hawk, she had found the other side of her soul. Like twin flames, they spiraled higher and higher until reaching extinction together in the sky.

A sunburst, then a firestorm! The great combustion threatened to devour them both in its epic explosion, until a shower of sparks rained down around them.

Slowly, slowly, Wynne came back to full consciousness again. Hawk lay gasping, his head buried on her breast, and her own breath came almost in ragged pants.

"I have never—ever—experienced anything like that! Oh, God, Wynne!" Hawk's voice was that of a man deeply and profoundly moved.

"That's because there's never been anything like *that* before," Wynne assured him, and then buried her suddenly wet face into the inviting crook formed by his neck and head.

"You're not crying?" he said incredulously.

"Just a little, from absolute happiness!" she replied.

They lay quiet and still in the near darkness, their bodies relaxed and limbs lying indolent, their heartbeats slowed to normal. Their bodies were fully dried now from heat and passion. Even Wynne's long hair was practically dry, and Hawk rubbed a strand lazily between his fingers.

He lay on his back, Wynne's head pillowed on his chest. Beneath her cheek she could hear the strong regular beat of his heart. "Your hair is downright *silky*," Hawk said in a low whisper.

"You sound surprised," Wynne commented, and turned to press a kiss over one of his hard male nipples.

His free hand found the small of her back and stroked there lazily. "I am. Indian hair is heavy and coarse, haven't you heard?"

"Must be the conditioner I use when I shampoo," Wynne murmured.

"More likely it's that Scottish grandfather of yours having the last laugh," Hawk grumbled. But he continued to rub her hair between his fingers as though fascinated by its texture.

"Hawk—" Wynne stopped herself. She had to speak out now, quickly, before she lost her nerve again. Hawk needed and deserved to know the whole truth about her.

"Humm?" he breathed, his fingers falling from Wynne's long midnight strand of hair.

She drew a deep breath. "I really loved my grandfather," she said, easing into the subject gradually.

"Yeah...sure." Hawk's voice sounded profoundly sleepy. "He's gone, then?"

"Yes. He died when I was pregnant with Nona." Even now their last visit remained both a shining memory as well as a wrenching one to Wynne. She could still see her grandfather lying against the alien starkness of white hospital sheets and attended by a busy white-clad nurse. "Why, here's my girl!" her grandfather had exclaimed, his voice surprisingly strong when he saw Wynne.

The nurse had turned from adjusting the bottle hung high on a pole. She smiled at Wynne, too. "You must be Mr. Jeffries's granddaughter. He's told me so much about you."

Later, just a few hours after their happy visit, Wynne's grandfather had died quietly in his sleep.

It had been her first experience with grief and loss. Dismally, Wynne had felt that life would never be entirely whole and complete for her again.

That feeling had lasted until Nona was born and Wynne had seen her new child's coppery hair. Then she'd understood that a part of love never entirely dies.

She leaned over Hawk urgently now, ready to explain to him what she'd learned at that time. That love was never really lost but may come full circle again in ways wholly unanticipated.

"Hawk—darling, there's so much I have to tell you," Wynne began. "It's important—"

She stopped abruptly, aware of the regular rise and fall of Hawk's chest, his closed eyelids and barely parted lips. He was asleep.

Disappointment stung Wynne momentarily. She had been all set to tell Hawk right now about Tom. But the past three busy, exciting days had taken their toll on Hawk, and he slept now from understandable exhaustion. Unless Wynne wanted to awaken him, which didn't really seem like a very good idea, her revelation would have to wait. She sighed softly, wondering if she'd ever have quite as good an opportunity again. She had frankly wanted the militant Hawk caught with his defenses down, so what better time could there have been than when they were both warm and replete from their blissful lovemaking?

On the other hand, maybe it wouldn't matter to Hawk now—now that they were so much in love, and he'd asked her to marry him. Wynne swallowed hard, trying to force down her doubts and opt hopefully for the happiest, brightest solution.

Wynne yawned, suddenly aware of her own exhaustion. *Yes, it was all going to be all right,* she assured herself as she cuddled up beside Hawk's strong relaxed body. She intended just to watch him sleep, but his rhythmic breathing and the warmth of his body lulled her into another yawn. Suddenly, like a diver soaring off a high cliff and jackknifing into the deep sea far, far below, she slipped into another state of consciousness. Deeply and completely she slept.

"Wynne . . . Wynne. Wake up, honey." Hawk was shaking her shoulders gently, but she was so deep in sleep, so deeply down in her own dreamless sea that at first she couldn't even stir.

"Wynne . . . sweetheart, it's three in the morning. We've got to get you back home. I don't want your father-in-law coming after me with a gun!"

Wynne couldn't help smiling at the image of Barry with a gun of any kind. She stretched sleepily, still not quite able to force open her heavy, heavy eyelids. "The best Barry could do is land a hook in your mouth and reel you in," she murmured.

"Honey, you're mumbling so I can't understand you. C'mon—wake up," Hawk coaxed, half laughing.

"Can't yet," Wynne informed him.

"Okay, just don't fight me and I'll try to dress you. Although I must admit, I've had a lot more practice in doing the opposite."

"You're bragging," she accused, but the buckskin dress dropping over her neck muffled her words so she had to repeat them.

"Bragging? Not really. 'Cause none of it ever really meant anything. Not until now, with you.'

Next, Wynne felt him cupping one of her feet in his hand. He dropped a kiss on it before sliding on one of her moccasins. "Tha's nice," she sighed.

"Just for that, I'll do the same to the other foot," Hawk replied and did. "Now, up we go!"

Wynne blinked and found herself standing beside the bed. "Underwear?" she asked.

"Don't take that dress off just to add a bra," Hawk instructed. "You can carry your bra home in your purse. Your panties too."

"No!" Wynne objected, trying to shake off her sleepy state. She smiled at Hawk, but he was still a little out of focus for her. "What if I'm in a car wreck?"

"My God, that's a dreadful thing to think about!" he protested. "Especially since I'm such a good driver."

"Oh, are you going to drive me home?" Wynne asked, muffling another yawn against the back of her hand.

"I sure am, lady. Now that I've got you, I'm not taking any chances on losing you! I sure don't want you out alone at this hour of the night, especially when you're sleepwalking."

"Am not." Wynne's eyes opened another crack and she was able to see Hawk standing in the middle of the room, wearing jeans and a pullover shirt, dangling the station wagon car keys rather impatiently from his right hand. "How can you be so wide awake?" she marveled.

"Trained myself to be. It's an asset anybody in the public eye should learn. How to fall asleep in ten seconds and how to wake up just as fast. I'll teach it to you. But, now, let's go."

"Underwear," Wynne insisted.

"Oh, no!"

Eventually they compromised on panties, which Wynne pulled up her long and shapely legs. When they reached her knees, she glanced over to see Hawk watching her with a grin. "Look away," she instructed.

"Not on your life!" he retorted.

She made a face at him, turned her body slightly away and drew the panties up over her buttocks. "Maybe I was too hasty—" Hawk said, reaching out for her and drawing her into his arms.

Wynne allowed him one deep lingering kiss, then pulled away when she felt a wayward hand starting to glide over her body. "Three in the morning," she reminded him. "I do have to get home."

Hawk sighed and opened the motel room door for her. Wynne resisted the urge to look back and memorize its utilitarian features and ordinary furniture. She couldn't help but feel as though she were leaving a honeymoon bower.

The cool night air cleared Wynne's head and woke her completely. She needed to concentrate to give Hawk instructions on how to reach her house, although she was also amazed at how many landmarks he'd noted when she'd driven him there before.

"Front door?" Hawk asked as they glided up toward the buff brick house.

"No. We hardly ever use the front door. We go in and out through the door leading into the carport," she told him.

"Okay," he said agreeably.

"There's no need for you to get out," Wynne urged as Hawk stopped behind Barry's Buick. "See, the door is just a couple of steps away, over there to the right."

"I don't care. I'm still walking you to the door," Hawk said, jerking up on the parking brake. "It's the way a man treats a lady."

"Thank you, kind sir," Wynne said. At the patio door, Hawk leaned over and their lips met in another lengthy kiss.

"I love you, Wynne Norwood!"

"I love you, Hawk Saddler!"

"See you in about—" he glanced at his watch where green numerals glowed in the darkness "—three and a half hours."

"I'll be ready," Wynne promised and then slipped inside the house.

She bolted the door and listened, smiling, to the familiar roar of the station wagon as Hawk drove away. Suddenly the truth struck her.

Oh, horrors, I *still* haven't told Hawk about Tom! she thought with a renewed sense of panic.

For the next five minutes Wynne paced the kitchen floor and again went through her maybe-Hawk-won't-mind routine.

This time she couldn't convince herself. Because, in her heart, Wynne knew that a militant like Hawk was going to mind quite a bit that she had been married to a white man.

Wynne paced the floor some more. Maybe I can keep stalling was her next cowardly thought.

Of course, Hawk would be back here at her door by seven. But if I were all ready to go, Wynne thought, and outside waiting for him, I could surely make up some story about why I wasn't inviting him in to meet the family.

What? Everybody has measles. Mumps. Chicken-pox. . . .

Great thinking, Wynne Norwood. Besides, you're such a really adept liar he'll be sure to believe any tall tale you spin. Why, just look how readily Hawk believed you tonight!

Wynne stopped pacing and found herself staring at the coffee maker. Each night, before Peg went to bed, she fixed the coffee and water so that Wynne, who was usually the first one up, had only to plug in the pot. Peg was always doing thoughtful things like that—Barry, too.

Her in-laws had not loved her like a daughter-in-law but, rather, as though she'd been the daughter they'd never had. They had provided much of Wynne's strength and support when Tom died, and they were the influence to which she willingly exposed her children every day.

Was she ashamed of them? Ashamed of her children? Ashamed of having been married to a marvelous man like Tom Norwood?

No, of course not! Wynne answered her own questions even as her heart began to throb. It's just that I love Hawk so much! I couldn't bear to lose him, too!

But, deep inside of her, a strong, tough-minded voice whispered to Wynne that any man who could not accept the past that had so nurtured her—the husband, children and in-laws—was not a man worth having.

She drew a deep breath and wiped away a single tear that fell. *I do love Hawk so!* she thought one last time. Then, resolutely, Wynne switched on the coffee maker, poured in the water and went off to bathe and dress.

No thoughts of going back to bed even crossed her mind. Wynne knew she was through sleeping for the night.

Hawk did not sleep much after he returned to his motel room. He felt too exhilarated and fulfilled, too happy and content with what his life had suddenly become, to waste time lolling around in bed.

On the other hand, his mind prompted, a tired pilot is a careless pilot. You're flying back to Arizona, remember?

He had meant to tell Wynne more about his place in Arizona, Hawk recalled as he crawled back into bed. She'll love it, he thought hopefully and punched his pillow into shape.

They still had so much to discuss. So much to learn about each other. But the love and the desire to spend the rest of their lives together would surely carry them through the difficult patches. Meeting Wynne's kids and in-laws, as he undoubtedly would do today, was one. Another was introducing her to his own family, essentially rural people who still lived on the reservation in Mississippi. Would a modern, up-to-date Indian like Wynne be able to understand his mother's various superstitions, his father's clinging to the old tribal traditions? And would she be able to understand about Heleema?

Sleep, Hawk reminded himself.

He slept for an hour, then he rose and began grooming himself carefully. He showered, scrubbing his straight shoulder-length hair. Then Hawk used his razor as he had every day since he'd met Wynne although hair growth on his face was practically negligible. Still, it made him feel better to know he presented her with smooth-shaven cheeks each and every time they happened to kiss.

Like most Indian males, Hawk didn't grow many facial hairs. He also compensated in typical fashion with a thick growth of hair on his scalp and would probably never be bald. Just one of life's little trade-offs, he reflected.

He dressed carefully, too, in the one pair of neat, dark slacks he'd brought and topped them with a pima cotton shirt. A headband next. Hawk debated between the three he'd slung into his bedroll. Then he put on his silver and turquoise belt and added his matching necklace and bracelet last. On the little finger of his left hand he wore a wide silver ring given him by his mother when he was still a child. It had fit his middle finger then.

Hawk glanced at his watch and saw that he still had time left. He snatched up the notebook and pen that always accompanied him on his travels and sat down to write. But even as he worked away diligently, his eyes strayed frequently to check the time.

Hawk certainly wasn't going to risk being late for a meeting as important as this one!

Chapter Four

While she waited for Hawk to arrive Wynne became a bundle of nerves having an all-out anxiety attack. At the breakfast table with her family she was even clumsier than little Nona, dropping first her fork and then her spoon. Finally she simply sat in frozen silence, her nervous fingers reducing the toast she couldn't eat to an anthill of crumbs.

Wynne had also sipped too much coffee since she'd gotten home hours before, and now she was jumpier than ever due to an overdose of caffeine.

Even before Hawk pulled into the carport, Wynne's family had been watching her in astonishment. The children telegraphed a look of mutual inquiry, then both shrugged their shoulders in bewilderment. Although the gestures made by Wynne's in-laws were less noticeable, Wynne saw them as well. The eloquent eyebrow Barry lofted and Peg's barely perceptible shake of her head.

Nobody knew what was wrong with Mama.

Then Hawk drove up and everyone knew in a flash. Wynne leaped up from the table so fast that she flung her paper napkin straight into her coffee. With horror she saw the saturated paper dissolve into a ghastly brown goo, but she was in too much of a hurry to stop now to clean up the mess.

"That's-Hawk-Saddler-outside-I'll-just-greet-him-first," she said in one single gust of breath as she flew past her mother-in-law's chair.

"Oh? My goodness, dear, be careful!" Peg cautioned for Wynne, having thrown open the main door, had walked straight into the screen door beyond.

She recovered her balance in an instant, let the screen door slam behind her and scurried down the concrete carport just as Hawk stepped out of the station wagon.

At sight of him, Wynne stopped short. He looked gorgeous, absolutely gorgeous, and she was touched that he'd obviously dressed in his best to meet her children and in-laws.

While Wynne admired Hawk's appearance, at the very same time her heart sank a trifle because of it. Peg and Barry, who would indignantly deny any trace of Indian prejudice or, indeed, prejudice of *any* kind, still liked their minorities dressed like mainstream Americans. A "melting pot" was fine just as long as everyone looked properly melted and melded.

Hawk Saddler, wearing his trademark headband and his turquoise and silver, looked quite Indian indeed. Of course, Wynne knew he'd assumed that he would be meeting an upwardly mobile Indian family.

She had to tell him the truth now, this very instant, before his smile could reach its widest at sight of her or before he could catch her close for the kiss that was already written in his eyes.

"Hawk, there's something you must know," Wynne blurted in a panic to have the secret told and Hawk's reaction over and done with. "My husband, Tom, wasn't Indian. He was white. Both of my kids look more like Tom and his family than me, except that—that Nona also looks like my Scottish grandfather."

Hawk blinked. He stared at Wynne, opened his mouth to speak and then clamped it closed again. She waited for him to assimilate what had to be a shock. Waited to see that shadow slide over his face, the shadow she'd seen twice before.

Then, in dismay, Wynne saw the growing darkness of a thundercloud instead. Hawk's black eyebrows rushed toward the bridge of his nose in the start of a ferocious scowl. His lips thinned and his nostrils flared.

"I—I'm sorry I didn't tell you before," Wynne whispered miserably and inadequately. She could read the irate question blazing in his hard ebony eyes.

Before Hawk could make a reply or Wynne add anything further, the carport door opened and Peg's clear voice rang out. "Do bring Mr. Saddler in, dear. We're all so eager to meet him—Steve in particular."

Thank God for Peg! It wasn't the first time that Wynne had blessed her mother-in-law's existence. Peg always seemed to know the exact right moment to step in and defuse an argument. Today, of course, she could scarcely have known an argument was even brewing, but her timing was perfect as usual.

"I'm sorry you're upset, Hawk," Wynne said tremulously. Then she squared her shoulders and tilted her head toward Peg, still framed in the doorway. "Will you come inside for a minute or two and meet my family?"

For a perilous few seconds Wynne didn't know whether Hawk would agree or not. She saw his thinly veiled shock and fury, saw Peg's waiting stance at the screen door, and suddenly the outcome of *everything* that Wynne Norwood wanted for the rest of her life seemed to hang in the balance.

Then Wynne felt Hawk's hand brush her back. His touch didn't feel like it usually did, for now this hard hand seemed somehow aloof. But she understood that he would follow her inside.

As they neared Peg, Wynne saw her mother-in-law swing the door wider in welcome to them, and finally the angry man behind Wynne spoke.

"Good morning. It's nice to meet you, Mrs. Norwood. Thanks for inviting me in," Hawk said in a perfectly level and even tone of voice.

Hawk heard himself talking automatically, with the least awareness of what he was saying. This had only happened to him once before in his life, when he'd asked questions of the brash young doctor who had just informed him of Tishti's death in childbirth. Later, Hawk had heard from both his mother and sisters that his questions had made perfect sense. So maybe he was making sense this time, too. At least neither Mrs. Norwood—a slim, gray-haired, pink-cheeked lady—nor Wynne had gasped or regarded him with alarm.

Hawk felt like he'd been coldcocked. That was the only way he could describe how Wynne's bombshell affected him. If her kiss had sandbagged him, this unpleasant revelation had hit like a sack of cement. Hawk was so stunned he still felt numb, but even as he cursed the incapacitating numbness he felt it start to ebb. In its stead came horror and fury—he knew he was mad enough to strangle Wynne—and absolute outrage that she hadn't leveled with him about this from the beginning. Why, she'd had *days* in which to tell him!

But worse than either his numb shock or his rising anger were the ugly pictures alive and burning in his brain. He saw Wynne's beautiful golden body, so lithe and sinuous, just as she'd been last night with *him*. Only in Hawk's vision of horror she was clutched in the hairy arms of a burly white brute and moving on a bed with him.

And this wasn't just a momentary nightmare, either. That scene of Wynne and a man of another, different race had actually occurred many times. Inside this proud buff brick house lived the proof of it, Wynne's children sired by that man.

How could she? That question, above all, was something Hawk simply could not understand. Why had she chosen to marry a paleface? Had Wynne thought she was getting a superior bread-winner—or lover? Or had she somehow become the unfortunate victim of the man she'd married? Sometimes white men married Indian or Oriental women to have an obedient slave who would wash the "master's" back or feet, put up with his brutality or drunkenness and accept his having other women.

Given the two choices, Hawk would rather have cast Wynne in the role of unhappy victim. Yes, maybe that was what had happened. If she had been very young and very dumb.... Young, maybe. Dumb—never! Nor had Hawk found her spineless or filled with feelings of inferiority. So he was back to square one—and absolutely furious with Wynne all over again.

Everything flashed through Hawk's mind in rapid-fire sequence. Meanwhile he followed Wynne inside the house where she lived and his rage was tempered suddenly by his almost morbid curiosity. Although Hawk had often been in the homes of the rich and famous or the hovels of the poor and underprivileged, he'd not often been invited into upper-middle-class white homes like this. Nor would he have accepted most such invitations even if they had been forthcoming. But since he was actually here, however reluctantly, he determined to learn all he could. Maybe, in the learning, he could find something to help him either excuse or better understand Wynne.

Hawk passed through the kitchen still half-dazed by all his tumultuous thoughts. Automatically his mind registered the numerous kitchen appliances that white families seemed to find so essential. Not just a fancy stove and refrigerator, either, although both were here. There were also a dishwasher, microwave, food processor and coffee maker. Lesser appliances—toaster, mixer, yogurt maker—dotted another counter. Hawk was through the room too quickly to really note all of them. He spotted a portable color TV set and guessed that there would be several more TVs scattered throughout the rest of this large house.

Not that Hawk himself couldn't have afforded everything he saw displayed. He could have easily—he just preferred a simpler lifestyle. But his books had always done well, and he commanded considerable sums of money from his numerous speaking engagements. He had a savvy financial planner, an Apache friend who looked like Geronimo and had acquired his MBA from Harvard. Burt had guided Hawk's excess income into mutual funds, blue-chip stocks, bonds and gold where it had all either multiplied or split, been reinvested and then gone on to multiply and split some more.

"—Seen you often on TV, Mr. Saddler. Goodness but you must have an interesting life!"

Wynne's mother-in-law had found her tongue, and was now talking away briskly. Hawk forced himself to listen to the older woman as Wynne led them into the living room.

"I've told Wynne and my husband that I was *sure* you were one of the Indian activists who seized Alcatraz Island back in the sixties."

Hawk blinked in surprise. It had never occurred to him that a woman like Wynne's mother-in-law could be interested in such things.

"Yes, I was," he admitted.

"I thought so!" Mrs. Norwood exclaimed in triumph. "That event represented a great coming together of different tribes, didn't it? The understanding that all of you would have to stand together, whatever the previous tribal differences, to achieve the goals you all sought?"

Now Hawk had a handle on Mrs. Norwood. A "knee-jerk liberal," he and his brothers or sisters-in-the-cause would call her. But such women represented money as well as considerable political clout and smart activists had learned not to offend them. "Yes, that's true," he said automatically.

"My grandson, Steve, was asking— Oh, do come meet my husband and the children. Wynne dear, will you make introductions? I'll go brew a pot of fresh coffee."

Hawk's overly sensitized ears heard the second "dear" as Mrs. Norwood addressed Wynne and, although Wynne didn't appear to mind, he thought it *stank* of condescension.

Wynne wore that white, pinched look again, Hawk observed. But this time it didn't go straight to his heart. He was warier now and far more skeptical.

"Dad, this is Hawk Saddler," Wynne said in a small low voice. "Hawk, my father-in-law, Barry Norwood."

Hawk glanced at the man to whom he was being introduced, and then his gaze sharpened in a kind of glum despair. Barry Norwood was big and burly. Wearing a knit shirt, as he was today, the thick white hair that covered his arms was exposed. Tufts of it also poked through the man's shirt, open at the throat. Hawk had no doubt that Barry's son could easily have been the demon lover he'd visualized so clearly with Wynne.

Meanwhile, both she and Barry stood waiting. Reluctantly Hawk stuck out his hand and felt it taken with a similar reluctance.

Just as his own gaze had swept over Barry, now Hawk felt the older man taking his measure. Barry's washed-out blue eyes lingered on Hawk's headband and hair, their expression something less than appreciative. Yeah, and I know your type, too, fella! Hawk thought. You're the sort who'd like to bleach the red heart white.

Suddenly the children materialized, the little girl peeking around her grandfather's leg, the boy stepping up to stand by Wynne's side.

Hawk took one look at them and felt his heart sink all the way to his moccasins. To him, Wynne's mixed-breed children were the worst thing of all. Why, they looked like Hanzel and Gretel! Hawk could easily imagine these two strolling through the Black Forest and happening onto a witch's gingerbread house.

What he could *not* imagine was these children actually belonging to Wynne, even though she was now drawing them forth with an arm around each kid's shoulder.

Oh, Wynne, Wynne, Hawk thought in despair. I'm just not ready for this!

"Hawk, this is my son, Steve," she said, her voice filled with pride, "and my daughter, Nona."

"Hello," Hawk said and then could think of absolutely nothing else to say. He knew more was expected of him. The children stared at him wide-eyed, and the tension of the adults was an almost palpable presence hovering in the room.

Little Nona saved the day. "Gosh," she said, craning her neck up to look at Hawk. "You're the most Injun-lookin' Injun I've ever seen!"

Wynne and her father-in-law burst out laughing and Hawk felt himself smile, too, despite the overall heaviness of his heart. "That's what I am," he said.

"You've got to 'scuse Nona," the boy piped up and turned to pin his sister with a scathing look. "Don't you remember anything, dummy? I've told you how we were Indians too."

"Yeah, but I don't look like *him*!" Nona said with a child's refreshing honesty.

No, she certainly didn't, Hawk thought. With those auburn curls and grass-green eyes, Nona looked like she'd come straight from the British Isles.

"Well, you don't look like Mama, either," the boy retorted, "or like Grandpa or Grandma Grove. Neither of us does. But we're still part Indian just the same.

Don't tell anybody, kid, and no one will ever guess, Hawk thought cynically.

"Let's all sit down," Wynne urged, obviously anxious to change the subject.

"Wynne, you and I need to leave for the airport," Hawk said pointedly. He couldn't wait to get out of here.

"Yes, I know." She didn't quite meet his eyes. "But let's stay for just a minute longer. Peg's bringing coffee for us."

Politely Hawk sat down when the others did. There seemed nothing else to do without creating a scene. Out of the corner of his eye Hawk could see that Wynne's boy, Steve, had taken the chair nearest him. Barry Norwood sat in the other and Wynne and Nona were on the sofa.

"Here's fresh coffee... " Peg bustled in, a welcome distraction, and Hawk soon found himself holding a cup of black coffee and declining either sugar or cream. Apparently, Wynne took her coffee black too, Hawk noticed, although she seemed to stare down at it with a faintly nauseous expression. Just an hour or two ago such a look of sick dismay on her lovely face would have caused Hawk alarm. He would have anxiously asked her what was wrong or if she felt all right. Now he had no such questions. He knew she was all right. Any Indian woman who could stand to marry white, to live with white people and have kids like these, had—in Hawk's opinion—a very strong stomach indeed.

"Mr. Saddler, sir?"

Hawk almost gave a leap of surprise. Wynne's son had eased out of his chair and now stood by Hawk's elbow. A sneaky little brat! "Yes?" he said and immediately regretted the curtness of his voice. *Oh, dammit,* he thought, *this mess is not the poor kid's fault!*

"Yes, Steve?" he tried again and this time his voice was better modulated.

"What tribe are you, Mr. Saddler?"

"Choctaw," Hawk answered automatically, studying the kid at closer range. Oh, sure, the boy had dark brown hair but no real Indian's hair had ever possessed those soft waves. Also, the kid had a very fair skin, the kind that would fry after an hour in the hot sun, Hawk thought disparagingly, and he had certainly inherited old Granddad Norwood's washed-out blue eyes.

"Choctaws are neat!" the boy exclaimed. "Why, 'Oklahoma' is even a Choctaw word. See, Nona—" He turned to look at his sister. "Oklahoma means 'red people.' That's why Oklahoma was known as 'the home of the red man.' That's right, isn't it, Mr. Saddler?"

"Right," Hawk agreed tightly.

He didn't like the boy's proprietary manner, acting like *he* had a right to call himself Indian when he looked the way he did.

"Choctaws built burial mounds," Steve went on excitedly. "You can still see some of their mounds in Mississippi and Arkansas. And Choctaws probably started the custom of calling a real dumb person 'a turkey.'"

"How's that?" Barry Norwood asked his grandson.

"Well, Choctaws would gobble like a turkey when they wanted to poke fun at someone who was acting silly or showing off."

Yeah, that's what I think you are, kid, a real little show-off, Hawk thought. The extent of his own hostility toward a ten-year-old almost frightened him.

"Is that true, Mr. Saddler?" Mrs. Norwood asked brightly.

"Yes," he replied, reaffirming Steve's assertion. "Even today, a turkey gobble is a characteristic Choctaw call of defiance. But whether or not Choctaws are responsible for the phrase that calls someone 'a turkey,' I couldn't say." Hawk turned to his coffee. It was so hot it practically burned his tongue but he downed most of it in one long swallow.

"My goodness, Steve, where do you learn about all these things?" Mrs. Norwood asked her grandson with obvious admiration.

While Steve explained that he read all the books about Indians that he could find in his school library, Hawk saw young Nona peering at him shyly. When she realized she'd caught his eye she smiled, and that smile, identical to Wynne's, was like a hand squeezing his heart.

Nona's skin was not quite so pasty white, either, Hawk noticed now that she was sitting near an open window. It was lightly burnished with gold tones. Unlike her brother, this kid would tan readily.

Hawk realized, only when Nona ducked her head onto Wynne's shoulder, that he'd been returning her smile with a relentless stare. *Oh great, Saddler, now you're scaring the little kid to death!*

Automatically he drained the last of his coffee and, summoning up his best company manners at the same time, he rose from his chair. He thanked Mrs. Norwood for the "delicious coffee," assured Barry and the kids that it had been "a pleasure" and then looked at Wynne in an expression that brooked no arguments. "We must go now."

To his relief she rose readily and set down the cup of coffee she'd scarcely touched.

Mrs. Norwood followed them out to the car, still chattering a mile a minute. Barry had obviously corralled the kids since they didn't come out, too. Hawk was grateful for that much.

They rode three blocks in silence. Hawk's face was unreadable in the early-morning sunlight, and its very immobility and unreadability unnerved Wynne even further.

"Say something, Hawk!" she burst out at last.

"About what?" he replied carefully.

"About what you're obviously thinking. Me. My in-laws. My children," Wynne said, then caught her trembling lower lip between her teeth.

"I'm pretty upset," he admitted. "I can't understand how you could marry a white man."

"But *why*?" Wynne cried, feeling her heart wrench.

Hawk threw her an incredulous look, then turned his attention back to the road. "My God, Wynne, the white man slaughtered the Indians, enslaved the blacks and stole much of the West from Mexico! Now that's history, and you know it."

"I didn't marry history," she said steadily. "I married one very good and kind man because it just so happened that we loved each other."

Hawk winced and threw her a black look of betrayal. "I guess that was one giant step up the social ladder."

"Oh, Hawk, it wasn't anything of the sort! Tom and I were kids. The last thing we cared about was any so-called 'social standing,'" Wynne sighed. Then she drew herself up sharply. Why in the world was *she* sounding defensive, even apologetic. *Hawk* was the one with the problem! As that realization came to Wynne she began to get good and healthily mad.

"Maybe we'd better start at the beginning. How did you meet your husband in the first place?" Hawk asked.

"How does any couple happen to meet?" Wynne heard the raw, sharp edge to her voice, but she felt helpless to alter it. "I knew Tom all my life. Our mothers were close friends—"

"Is your mother the one who's a half-breed?" Hawk asked tensely.

"She's half white, yes," Wynne said. She knew Hawk wouldn't be able to miss the chill in her voice, but suddenly she didn't care. What the hell sort of word was *half-breed*? And what had such an ugly, racist word to do with her mother? "My dad, you'll be relieved to know, is one hundred percent, genuine American Indian!"

"You can skip the commentary, Wynne."

"I just wanted to be sure you have all the players straight as well as the color of their epidermis," she said sarcastically.

Hawk heaved a great slow sigh but Wynne saw his knuckles whiten on the steering wheel as he struggled to hang on to his temper.

"Okay, so you met Tom while you were a kid. When did it get serious?"

"High school," Wynne answered and gazed wearily out of a window. "Tom was a year older than I was. We never really dated anyone else. After I graduated from high school and Tom had finished his first year of college, we got married. Obviously, we were both quite young, but it worked out just fine."

"I'm sure all your parents were absolutely thrilled."

At that crack, Wynne's head whipped back and she stared at Hawk. "As a matter of fact they were," she said in a tightly controlled voice. "I believe I told you that Arrow is a very enlightened town. There's little discrimination."

"So what happened next in this bi-racial love story?"

Wynne chose to ignore that jibe. "Tom continued college and I had a baby. But the following year, after Steve had been born, Tom stayed out of school and worked so I could start college."

Hawk threw her a frankly startled look. "He actually did that?"

"That and much more," Wynne said fervently. "Tom learned to change diapers and cook edible food and do lots of things most men never even bother to learn. But he certainly wasn't a wimp!" she said, seeing the contemptuous look that had started across Hawk's face. "We just happened to have had a fair and equal partnership."

Hawk clenched the wheel again, his knuckles whitening anew. "That's a hard row for even a liberated male to hack. Are you telling me that your white husband managed it?"

"He managed it with grace and very few moments of rebellion," Wynne said through gritted teeth.

"What would you have done if he'd beaten you up when he was drunk?"

Hawk's quiet yet tense question took Wynne completely aback. *"Beaten me?"* she repeated in amazement. Then her voice turned fierce. "Hawk, I would probably cut out the heart of any man who ever beat me—or my kids! So you can certainly forget that one. Beat me...sheesh!" She ended with a long drawn out hiss.

"That's what often happens to Indian women who marry whites. In my business you get to hear all the dirty stories."

"I'm sure you do, and I'm sorry for that. It's obviously left you very suspicious of people. But please forget the usual clichés when you discuss my marriage. Tom was a good, steady, loving husband who never drank more than a couple of beers, and I loved him and was very happily married to him!"

She saw Hawk's face pale with her words, and his jaw tightened. "What is it?" Wynne asked. "Why does that bother you more than anything? That Tom was decent and kind and that I loved him?"

"No, that's not what bothers me most," Hawk said, low-voiced.

"Then *what*?" When she saw Hawk's jaw tighten again, Wynne thought he wasn't going to answer, but finally he did.

"Why didn't you tell me about all of this sooner? No, don't bother to look surprised that I'm upset. If you had learned anything about me at all, Wynne, you should have known I would mind this greatly. But no. Instead of honestly telling me the truth right off the bat, you wait until four days after we've met. You wait until I'm half in love with you—"

Wynne realized, even before Hawk, that he'd made a slip of the tongue, but she pounced on the revealing error nonetheless.

"Oh, are you just *half* in love now, Hawk? Last night you vowed you were in love forever. Moonlight changes things, I guess."

"That wasn't what I meant!" he roared. "I meant to say you deliberately waited until you knew I was half out of my mind in love with you!"

"That wasn't what you said," she pointed out contrarily. "But don't worry, Hawk. I won't hold you to anything we discussed last night, certainly not love or marriage! Don't you think I saw the way you looked at Steve and Nona? Well, my kids just happen to be wonderful people, even if you don't like their skin color. And, God knows, I wouldn't want them to have a stepfather unless he thought that they were great!"

Hawk shot her a look that managed to combine anger as well as a certain level-headed coolness. "Wynne, I think we'd both better shut up right now or we'll be saying a lot of things we'll regret later." He looked back at the highway and gave his head a confused shake. "I've lost my bearings. Have we passed the airport turnoff or what?"

"No," Wynne said lifelessly. "It's around the next corner."

She knew Hawk was right. They wouldn't get anywhere if they kept arguing. Besides, none of their heated words would change any facts. Hawk would still be Hawk, and she'd still be Tom's widow and the mother of his children. So she and Hawk would simply have to say goodbye.

This was a calamity too great for easy tears. Ever since their time together last night, Wynne had felt bonded to Hawk. In a single session of lovemaking, they had possessed each other so utterly that Wynne now felt like he was as dear to her as anyone else in the world. He was her perfect and ideal mate, the man she must have unconsciously been looking for all of her life.

She couldn't compare her feelings for Hawk to the way she loved her children. Although both emotions were love, the specifics couldn't be more different.

The airport sign loomed up. In just a moment they would arrive, and Hawk would fly out of her life as suddenly as he'd flown into it. Wynne felt her breath catch in her throat as pain seized her without warning. I'll never see him again, she tried to tell herself and felt only disbelief at the words. Because not to ever see him again would be so monstrous!

Suddenly Wynne felt Hawk's gaze on her. She looked up just in time to see him wrench his eyes from her rigid face and look back at the road. But something in his sad gaze had been as troubled as her own feelings.

Hawk stopped in a designated parking lot, then came around to help Wynne out. She knew she ought to bid him farewell here and now, and drive away. But she was loath to lose these last few minutes with him. She would think back on them for the entire rest of her life, she knew.

They walked inside the small terminal, Hawk carrying his bedroll, and at some point their shoulders brushed together. The very last touch of him, Wynne thought.

Hawk excused himself to go change into his flight suit and see to his plane. "I won't be long," he said to Wynne.

But he was gone a long time. Ten minutes passed, then fifteen crept slowly by. Oh, this is impossible! Wynne thought and turned back toward the entrance. Why was she torturing herself by hanging around? Why should she stay to wave as Hawk flew out of her life forever? I'll go home and get busy and—and—

And just simply die! she concluded dismally.

Still, Wynne had marched resolutely through the entrance and was halfway down the walk when a single realization was borne in on her. She couldn't drive home because Hawk still had the car keys!

"Oh, damn!" Wynne hissed under her breath and, just at that moment, Hawk came racing down the walk after her. He caught her arm and swung her around.

"Were you going to leave without even telling me goodbye?" he demanded.

Wynne looked up into his strong handsome face that, already, she knew almost as well as she knew her own. Oh, Hawk was so nice looking in his blue flight suit! Memories of her first glimpse of him came back to haunt her. Of course, he'd also been so handsome when he'd appeared at her house earlier this morning, dressed to meet the Indian in-laws she was unable to produce.

"Were you?" Hawk demanded again and gave her shoulder a gentle little squeeze of warning.

"I can't," Wynne said lifelessly. "You've got the car keys."

"Oh, so you noticed that. I didn't mean to go off with them." A faint semblance of a smile touched Hawk's lips. "But now, since you want to run out on me, I'm glad I did."

Wynne bit her lip to stem the threatening tears. Only one person is running out on anybody in this particular love affair! she thought bleakly. Then, incredulously, she felt Hawk's arms go around her tightly.

"Dammit, I love you!" he said, his lips pressed against her hair.

At the touch of his body on hers, Wynne went weak with remembrance and longing. Last night, in each other's arms, they had been like one person. Although physically they were less close now, she still felt like they were the two halves of a solitary soul.

"I love you, too!" Wynne heard herself saying, her voice husky with unshed tears, her fingers tracing the hard muscles of his shoulders and back. "Oh, Hawk, I—"

"What?" he whispered gently, but she heard a new vibrant note singing in his voice.

"You were right, Hawk. I should have told you sooner about—about Tom and the children. But I fell so deeply in love with you! Can you possibly understand how I fell so much in love with you?" she blurted, rubbing her nose and forehead against his smooth chin. Oh, he felt so good and he smelled so fresh, clean and wholesome!

"I might," he admitted. "That might be the one thing I understand best of all, Wynne." He sighed and folded her even closer and Wynne swayed in his grasp, seeking to be closer still.

"Now, can *you* understand about me?" he asked her. "I didn't grow up in a nice town with white friends and white relatives. I grew up outside Philadelphia, Mississippi which is still notorious, even today, because five workers for black civil rights were once killed there. We feared and dreaded white people—and not without reason! Any time they came on the reservation it was usually a carload or two of drunk young punks, spoiling for a fight."

"Yes, I can understand that," Wynne whispered. "But, Hawk, you speak now of brotherhood, of equality. Do you mean that or is it all just a PR ploy?"

He hesitated for a long moment, as though giving Wynne's question thoughtful and serious consideration. "Oh, it's partially PR," he confessed. "Peace. One world. Brother joining hand with brother—that sort of thing is very popular these days. I'm smart enough to know what's politic to say."

"Then you really don't mean it?" Wynne asked, her heart sinking rapidly, because this was a concept that was of vital concern to her.

"I *want* to believe it," Hawk said after a moment. "It's an ideal to which I'm striving, too. I know I fall short a lot of times. I know I must seem awfully narrow-minded and prejudiced to you, but we Indians really did catch it in the neck for generations."

Wordlessly, Wynne nodded and then Hawk tilted up her chin so that their eyes met. In his she saw a reflection of her own. They were each sobered and frightened yet not entirely unhappy, either. As long as they could hold each other close, they could not be wholly unhappy. Then that fierce current of mutual desire came swirling up anew, hot and demanding, and Hawk pressed his lips over Wynne's.

Their kiss became a crushing, almost bruising one as they gripped each other so tightly, each aware of the perilous forces that threatened to rend the whole fabric of their love.

At last Hawk tore his lips from Wynne's and took a step back from her. "We'll work it out, honey," he said hopefully. "I don't pretend to know *how*, but I really believe we will."

"If two people honestly love each other, it ought to be possible," Wynne agreed, feeling alive once again from the force of their passionate feelings.

Gently Hawk's rough thumb traced the outline of her lips. "We won't say goodbye—because it's a long way from being over between us. I'll write you, Wynne. Don't expect long letters because I'll be traveling cross-country, but I'll stay in touch."

"Okay," Wynne managed to say, choking back her unasked question of when she would see him again.

Then Hawk kissed her goodbye, dropped the car keys in her hand and walked rapidly away.

Chapter Five

The first week that Hawk was gone he sent Wynne two postcards. One came from the University of Nebraska at Lincoln while the second was postmarked from a tiny town in North Dakota that she had never even heard of. Both messages were similar. "Missing you... thinking of you... hope to see you soon."

The second week Wynne received one postcard, mailed from Albuquerque, New Mexico. Since it featured the Potomac River, she wondered if Hawk had actually been there in Washington, D.C., or if he'd just had the card conveniently handy. He still missed her and thought of her, he wrote.

The third week she heard nothing at all.

Wynne tried not to feel hurt, unhappy, rejected. Good Lord, woman, she argued with herself, you spent less than four days with the man! But once the chips were down and all the cards on the table he decided that a relationship between the two of you would never fly. It's just that simple.

There's nothing simple about it at all! Wynne's sore and throbbing heart cried back. What about those hours when we were alone in his motel room?

He didn't do anything that you weren't just dying for him to do! The voice of logic shouted back to her. So stop sniveling and feeling so sorry for yourself!

But she continued to cry herself to sleep at night. Life had never felt so bleak, except perhaps right after Tom had died. Wynne didn't understand why this loss of Hawk seemed a similar calamity or why, perversely, in the very midst of all her grief and desolation she no longer felt that horrible aching emptiness at the center of her being.

Even without Hawk's physical presence or much hope for the future, Wynne still felt whole at long last. Hawk remained that other part of herself, a perfect masculine complement to her femininity. It didn't even matter that Wynne had failed to *like* everything about the man. Obviously, the sheer knowledge and fact of his existence were what she'd sought for so long.

It was all very strange. And very heart wrenching too.

Every day Wynne went dutifully to work and sat in her small office handling the various matters that arrived. She was supposed to prepare a report on Hawk's successful speeches and his meetings with Indian students. It would be reviewed by the regents at their next regularly scheduled luncheon.

But that routine task suddenly appeared beyond Wynne's ability to achieve. She'd written a scant four paragraphs about Hawk Saddler and every day she reviewed and polished them, but further words just wouldn't come. "Wynne, is that Saddler report ready yet?'' Rick Thompson had begun to ask her. Finally, one day the clincher came.

"Dr. Roxie has asked about the Saddler report," Rick informed Wynne, and he wore a worried frown.

The "Saddler report." That's what it was to everyone except Wynne. Finally, she realized that the reason she couldn't finish it was her instinctive reluctance to have everything that concerned Hawk over and done with. She still wasn't quite ready to say goodbye.

Wynne gritted her teeth, forced herself to resume writing and, eventually, the chore was done. Rick read her report and pronounced himself pleased by it, but Wynne herself had utterly no idea whether it was good or dreadful. She'd totally lost all sense of objectivity where Hawk was concerned.

The phone on her desk rarely rang, but Wynne still couldn't stop herself from pouncing each time it did.

"Mama—" a tearful Nona might wail. "Steve and his friends are goin' to the Hamptons' pool, but they won't take me 'cause they say I'm just a baby and I'll drown."

"Nona, tell Steve to come talk to me this minute! Steve? Listen, young man, you and your friends are *not* to go to the Hamptons' pool! Is that clear? I don't care how well you swim, if Bob or Kiki Hampton aren't there to supervise you, you can't..."

Perhaps the next call would be from Peg or Barry. "Dear, on your way home could you stop for a half gallon of milk?" Or: "Well, Wynne, it's my water pump. If you'd pick me up at the Buick agency when you get off work—"

It was never, ever Hawk who called.

* * *

"Say, Wynne, the regents really liked your report on Hawk Saddler," Rick informed her, beaming.

Just hearing Hawk's name spoken aloud still caused Wynne's heart to jerk and twitch. Fortunately she knew her emotions didn't show on her face. Rick stood waiting for her reply so Wynne made herself look up at him and smile. "I'm glad."

Rick Thompson was another associate director in the information office. He had considerably more seniority than Wynne, however, and stood to inherit the position of director within the next year or two. He was Anglo-Saxon, tall and big, with reddish-blond hair, bright blue eyes and a button nose set in a round face that was usually beaming. A happy, friendly person, Rick's mood brightened even more when he was around Wynne. She knew that the only reason he'd never asked her for a date was his fear of having an office romance go sour. Since Wynne shared that fear, it was one reason she'd never particularly encouraged Rick.

But today her warm smile apparently gave him the necessary courage to plunge in. "Say, Wynne, if you aren't doing anything tomorrow night, how about having dinner with me?" Rick asked.

Wynne hesitated momentarily, then swallowed hard. She really didn't want to go out with anyone but Hawk, but it should be obvious by now, even to a battered but still-loving heart, that Hawk would never return. And Rick deserved a chance. The worst thing Wynne could say about him was that he looked a trifle soft in the waistline, as though he didn't get enough exercise. So she made herself flash him another smile and reply cordially. "Thanks, Rick. I know I'll enjoy having dinner with you.

* * *

Hawk sat with his chin sunk on his chest, listening to the long, wearying conversations going on around him. It seemed they'd been discussing the issue of gambling on Indian reservations for hours now. He darted a glance at his watch and stifled a sigh. God, it really had been hours!

At first Hawk had been quite interested in the subject. More and more Indian reservations were sponsoring bingo, and a few other games to bring in needed dollars. Players had flocked to the games, often arriving in chartered buses, and impoverished Indians were suddenly gainfully employed and earning substantial salaries. It was the sort of initiative and progress Hawk loved to see his people make, but adding casino gambling and horse racing, as several reservations were threatening to do, were quite different matters indeed.

"High stakes gambling attracts organized crime like a magnet," Binita Weitchpec was protesting now. "Soon you've got Mafia shakedowns, payoffs and prostitution—"

"You think our tribal police couldn't recognize Mafia?" Larry Redbear retorted sarcastically. "The last I heard they were all Italian. And as for call girls, I don't think they'll look much like you, Binita, or the rest of our women."

"Listen, our own people can be corrupted and don't think they can't!" Binita shrilled back. "Give me an unemployed Indian with debts and a drinking problem—"

Hawk mentally tuned Binita out. He didn't want to think about problems any more. His own personal one had worn a groove in his tired mind until he felt constantly weary and ineffably sad.

Wynne, Wynne, Wynne, his heart cried.

He went to bed thinking of her. He woke up each morning reaching out for her. Then, feeling considerably less than refreshed, Hawk would sit up and ponder the crumpled sheets he'd tumbled in his restless, troubled dreams.

More than once he found himself standing with his hand on the phone, wanting desperately to call her and hear the low soothing murmur of her voice. He imagined making love to her again, feeling her moving in his arms, arousing and awakening him until they came together in a fiery explosion of passion.

No woman had ever affected him as Wynne did! There had never before been one Hawk couldn't leave or forget. Even with poor little Tishti, he knew he'd been over the worst of his grief in six or seven months, busy again and wholly occupied with the new life he'd forged for himself beyond the reservation's boundaries.

But, in his heart, Hawk knew that six months from now he would still be thinking about Wynne, needing her and wanting her just as much then as he did right now. Yes, she had belonged to a white man. She had slept in her husband's bed, twined herself around in his arms, loved him and borne two children that looked just like him. The pictures were still there in Hawk's mind every time he tried to close his eyes and sleep. Had sex been better for Wynne with a white man? Had it lasted longer? Had Wynne's husband been better endowed physically? Had she gazed up at *him* with that same shiny-eyed contentment? God, he was going to go out of his mind if he didn't quit torturing himself with thoughts like that!

"Hawk, what do you think?" Larry Redbear asked abruptly.

"What?" Startled, Hawk tried to recover. His overall opinion on the gambling issue, that was what they wanted to hear now. "I favor bigger and better bingo games. Offer larger prizes. Give people a real incentive to come out to the reservations and stay in our motels and eat at our restaurants. Hell, you could run the games twenty-four hours a day, like they do in Vegas, and use relays of employees! But I have to agree with Binita that we'd be better off to avoid attracting organized crime. Surely we haven't come this far to—"

Even as he went on talking, a part of Hawk's mind stayed detached. What would Binita or Larry think of Wynne's white kids? For that matter, wouldn't he— Hawk—run the risk of being discriminated against by friends and associates like these if he had such white-looking stepkids? Surely *he* hadn't come as far as he had to throw it all away now!

But Wynne's face rose up again in the mirror of his mind, and Hawk wondered if he could live without her. All of a sudden his whole life seemed like a lot of work, worry and trouble—and nothing else at all.

I'll give it another day, he thought almost desperately.

Wynne's date with Rick Thompson and the realization that he was really interested in her inspired her to daydream of revenge. In her fantasy, Wynne imagined Hawk showing up, lonely and contrite. "I'm sorry, Wynne," he would say. "I realize now I've always loved you. Please forgive me."

"Oh, I'm so sorry, Hawk," she would reply coolly. "But I naturally concluded that you just didn't care, and I've recently married a wonderful man. Rick darling, come meet an—an old friend of mine."

Then, while Hawk gnashed his teeth in fury and dismay, Wynne would introduce him to her *second* white husband.

Wynne's fantasy overlooked a few very significant elements that, in her more realistic moments, she was quite well aware of. First, there was absolutely no way that Rick Thompson was going to sweep her off her feet. Second, even though he was really a pleasant, kindly man, the two slightly timid kisses he'd given Wynne at her front door would never make her seethe with passion or yearn to be crushed in his arms.

Rick had gotten along famously with both Wynne's in-laws and her children. In fact, Peg and Barry, unknown to Wynne, were friends of Rick's parents. "Goodness, what a nice man Rick is!" Peg had exclaimed several times during the last few days, and Wynne had gotten the message clearly. Her in-laws would be quite pleased to see her marry, if she just picked someone like Rick—and not "that firebrand Saddler," as Barry had tactlessly called him.

Both of Wynne's children, as well as her in-laws, had guessed with unerring instinct just where her heart really lay. "Mama, do you think Mr. Hawk will ever be back?" Steve asked her abruptly one morning.

"I guess he won't," Wynne replied sadly. "Why?"

"Oh, I learned some more things about Choctaws I wanted to talk to him about." Steve gave an elaborate shrug. Then on a more hopeful note he added, "Maybe I can tell Mr. Rick about them."

"Steve—" Wynne began, then she stopped, biting her lip. She had been about to tell Steve that she doubted if

"Mr. Rick" would be back, either. But Steve would be sure to ask why, and then what could she say?

"Oh, hell," Wynne muttered under her breath and got busy sorting the kids' clothes into piles of light or dark for laundering purposes. There was plenty of work to do at the office and even more to do at home. All of it seemed suddenly so meaningless for she felt so very desolate. Even worse, she knew Rick was priming himself to ask her out again, and Wynne had utterly no idea of what she should or shouldn't do about that situation.

The last thing that Wynne ever expected was that Dr. Roxie Escoban would play a role in reuniting her with Hawk.

Dr. Roxie, director of the information office, was a tall, stout woman in her early sixties. She was one-quarter Osage Indian, one-quarter Hispanic and two-quarters Anglo. *All* of her quarters were crafty and cunning.

Dr. Roxie was not one of Wynne's favorite people. Although the two women had always shared a surface cordiality, Wynne didn't approve of Dr. Roxie's "convoluted connivances"—a phrase of Rick's with which Wynne was in complete agreement.

So while she sat in her office trying to work, on a warm early June afternoon, the last thing Wynne needed—or so she thought—was to hear Dr. Roxie braying out her name. "Wynne! Oh, Wynne. There's someone come to see you!"

Dr. Roxie's voice held its coy manipulative note. Great! Wynne thought angrily, slamming down the copy she'd been halfheartedly proofreading.

"Just a minute," she called to Dr. Roxie, and it was the one and only time when she didn't immediately think of Hawk.

"May I offer you a cup of coffee?" Wynne heard Dr. Roxie say next.

"No, thank you."

Wynne's heart slammed against her breastbone, and she gasped aloud. It's someone else! she thought frantically. It's an IRS investigator because I screwed up my tax return. Or it's a policeman telling me our house just burned down. She knew it was neither for she knew just exactly to whom that low, almost musical voice belonged.

Desperately, Wynne fumbled for her purse. Lipstick, she thought and then watched the gold-tone tube drop from between her shaking fingers and roll off the top of the desk. She decided to forget about lipstick. Oh God, why did I wear my black pantsuit today? she wondered as she stood up nervously. It makes me look like I'm fifty years old and a still-grieving widow! Well, at least I washed my hair this morning. Then there was nothing for Wynne to do but walk out and face him. Her knees felt weak but she forced them to obey.

"Hello, Hawk," Wynne said as she stepped through her door. Then she fell silent, staring. He looked so wonderful—but he also looked so *changed*!

Most of him was exactly as she'd remembered. The glossy black hair and smooth bronze skin. The black inscrutable eyes. They met Wynne's, and she couldn't read their expression—or perhaps she was just too nervous and unprepared for this meeting to do so. His smile, which had alternately been debonair and devastating, was today only a faint glimmer of its usual self, no more than an upward tilt to his lips.

It took longer for Wynne to realize why Hawk looked changed because she couldn't tear her gaze from his face. He was thinner, and he was obviously tired, for dark smudges lay below his deep-set eyes. But most startling of all was Hawk's hair, which had been cut substantially shorter, and his present attire. Today he wore neither his flight suit nor his Indian garb and jewelry. Rather, he sported the junior executive's "dress for success" uniform of dark slacks, blue long-sleeved shirt and sedate maroon tie. A jacket that matched his slacks hung from his hand.

"Well, well—" Dr. Roxie harrumphed, and Wynne turned bewilderedly, to see the director gazing upon them like a benign chaperon. "Mr. Saddler and I rode up in the elevator together, Wynne. I finally realized why he looked so familiar and just who he was."

Hawk turned to the older woman. "You've been very helpful. Thank you."

"Would—would you like to come into my office?" Wynne stammered to Hawk.

"I was hoping perhaps you were available to drive me back to the Creeks' factory," he said glibly. "I know it's a lot to ask, but I'm not sure I remember the way."

Wynne's knees went even weaker still. Oh God, he was only here on business. He hadn't come to see her at all! "I'm afraid I—" she began.

"Nonsense!" thundered Dr. Roxie. She was never one to let an opportunity bypass her or her department. "Our work can wait, Wynne. We certainly want to make ourselves available to assist distinguished people like Mr. Saddler." The hard gray-brown eyes she trained on Wynne were as kindly as a cobra's. "Now, don't we?"

"Yes, of course—we'll just get our purse," Wynne said and realized she was babbling insanely.

Back behind the closed door of her office, Wynne retrieved her lipstick, drew several long, deep, restorative breaths and counted to ten. The moment she emerged, Hawk seized her elbow and guided her out, calling back his thanks to Dr. Roxie.

His hand was as warm and hard as Wynne remembered. As Hawk whisked her down the nearest staircase, Wynne tried to free her elbow but Hawk just gripped it tighter. "What are you *doing*?" she snapped, wishing she could get good and properly angry instead of feeling a perilous two seconds away from tears.

"Trying to find a dark, quiet place where I can kiss you," Hawk retorted. They reached the landing and he pulled Wynne over toward the dark side of the wall. "Here—I guess this will have to do."

He loomed over her, his hands going to either side of her face, his lips moving inexorably closer to hers. "Hawk—" Wynne's hands came up, intending to push him away. Instead they could only close over his arms, caressing him through the starched, unfamiliar-feeling blue shirt. "You left me," she accused, her lips trembling, "and you stopped writing and you *never* once phoned—"

He didn't make the apology of her fantasy. In fact, Hawk never apologized at all. He just let his lips, warm and seeking, cover her quivering ones. Then his lips left hers, and he said huskily yet matter-of-factly, "And now I'm back."

"*Why* did you come back?" Wynne asked, her arms lifting of their own volition to encircle his neck.

"Because I absolutely couldn't stay away from you even one day longer," he replied gruffly. "I can't forget you. Believe me, I tried."

How had he tried? She was afraid to ask. "Oh, Hawk!" The shift of his body now pressing against Wynne's in a dozen places, excited her and fired off a succession of memories almost too poignant to bear. "Don't say things like that unless you really, truly mean them!" she cried.

"I really, truly mean them, now and forever." Hawk leaned closer, pinning Wynne to the wall. She felt his hands tunneling through her hair, his fingers beginning to massage her scalp and the nape of her neck. She felt the overall eagerness and arousal of his body. "We're going to start all over again."

"I might have something to say about that!" Wynne threatened, but then Hawk leaned down and kissed her again. This time his tongue traced the outline of her lips and slipped between them. Wynne felt all of her senses skyrocket into ecstasy at his lavish kiss. The hot plunging dagger of his tongue revealed his desire more plainly than words. Wynne's head reeled under the welcome assault and she went weak with longing. Her eyes closed, her body shifted to allow him greater access to hers and she felt her breasts digging into the solid wall of his chest.

"I mean it, we'll start all over," Hawk repeated when their mouths parted at last. "This time we're going to make it, Wynne. Unless, of course, you have some fresh surprises to drop on my unsuspecting head."

"Wh—what do you mean?" Wynne asked, keenly aware that his hands were now gliding down to gently stroke and knead her breasts.

"Another couple of husbands. Three or four more kids I haven't met."

"No, no others, Hawk..." His hands dropped away from her breasts, leaving them aching with longing. Now they spanned her waist.

"Good! I don't think I could stand another month away from you! Now, let's get out of here," he said.

His head bent lower, his eyes like liquid flames. The firestorm of their desire threatened to whirl them away from sanity and reason, and before that happened Wynne needed to know one thing. "Hawk, do you really mean this?" she asked tremulously. "Don't—oh, please don't play with me if you don't mean it. I couldn't stand another month like the last one. I'd rather never have you back than have to go through losing you all over again."

His eyes met hers and their expression was very clear and sober. "I've never played with you, Wynne. God help me, I love you so much I've almost gone crazy from it! I want to marry you, and this time I will. I'll help you the best I can to raise your kids, and maybe you'll be willing to give me one or two more."

"A little Hawk," she said unsteadily. "Yes, I'd like that."

"Or a little Raven," he whispered.

Like people already safely enfolded in a warm and wonderful dream, they moved slowly down the staircase, their arms around each other, their eyes locked and holding.

Wynne blinked when they stepped outside to bright sunshine. Students swirled all about them as Hawk led her to the curb.

She almost choked when she saw where he'd parked his rental car. "That's a fire lane!"

"Which is entirely appropriate," he shot back. "I'm on fire for you."

"It's a wonder your car wasn't towed off," Wynne said to him reprovingly.

"Sometimes a guy has just got to take chances," Hawk shrugged, helping her inside. He leaned in the car and kissed Wynne again before closing the door. Then he went whistling around to the driver's side, the image of a handsome and happy man.

Swiftly Hawk covered the few blocks to the same motel where he'd stayed before, and Wynne blinked when he pulled up before the exact same unit. "Oh, Hawk! You asked for your old room again."

"Men remember certain sentimental things too," he said softly.

Inside, in the light of a single lamp, they slowly undressed. Hawk tugged off his tie and draped it over the back of a chair. "Sometime I'll have to get an Anglo businessman to tell me how he wears one of these chokers every day. Is his Adams' apple higher or lower than mine?"

"Probably not." Wynne smiled and looked up at Hawk from beneath her eyelashes. "Yours looks about right to me. Why are you wearing a business suit, anyway?"

"Frankly, I didn't know if you'd care or not. But I know damn well your father-in-law will like me better if I own one."

"Oh, Hawk!" Unbelievably touched, Wynne closed the distance between them. "You're right about Barry, of course. But anything you want to wear is fine with me."

"Right now I intend for that to be nothing—and that's just how I want you dressed, too." Hawk finished unbuttoning his shirt and let it fall open over his chest. Muscles rippled over the tawny skin and Wynne stared, fascinated.

"Here." Hawk drew her close and began unbuttoning Wynne's blouse. Slowly he let it drop from her shoulders and she pushed away his shirt at the same time. He skimmed off her bra next and let it fall beside the rest of their clothes. Wynne looped her arms around his waist and then gasped as she felt the exquisite contact between his bare chest and hers. She heard Hawk grind his teeth together in pleasure. Hands glided, nipples brushed, mouths moved to touch and kiss.

"Oh, Wynne, I love you so," Hawk vowed and began leading her toward the king-size bed.

"I love you, Hawk!" she whispered back fiercely.

He stretched her out on the clean, starched sheets and let his mouth play across hers—teasing, tingling, tantalizing. Then he moved, open-lipped, over her cheeks and chin, glided down her neck and trailed kisses across her shoulders.

Wynne moaned when she felt Hawk's mouth tugging gently on the tender tip of one breast. His black head oscillated, moving from one to the other, until Wynne ignited so thoroughly from passion that she felt herself aflame.

She saw Hawk's smoldering eyes as he drew back to remove her shoes and slowly strip away her slacks. When the garments were gone, he kissed a blazing path up first one of her shapely legs and then the other. Then she felt his breath burn through the filmy nylon of her bikini panties.

Swiftly Hawk tongued her small circular navel while his thumbs fondled her hipbones. Then abruptly the gentle thumbs turned aggressive, hooking beneath the nylon until that last barrier had been cast off. "God, I want you!" Hawk breathed and dropped his face, damp with desire, into the softness of her shoulder.

To Wynne's astonishment she found her own hands fumbling to open Hawk's slacks. A narrow belt slithered away and a large hook popped open. Slowly she lowered his zipper and, as his slacks gaped open, she couldn't resist sliding a small hand within. Even through his soft cotton shorts she could feel the springy hairs below and the rigid fullness of his passion. He groaned with delight at her audacity.

Wynne wanted Hawk to claim her then and there. She could see no need for further preliminaries for she felt thoroughly quickened and aroused. She whispered her desire to him as she felt her hips begin to lift and roll, following an old and instinctive rhythm.

"First, just let me do this—" His mouth, like liquid flame, moved intimately, avidly. "And this...and this!" His tongue flicked and flashed until Wynne cried out, feeling her hips rise practically off the mattress.

"Now, just this...and this..." Hawk kept talking as he built her exquisitely toward the highest point of rapture. His tongue spoke eloquently when words weren't possible, telling her of his complete devotion and adoration.

All at once Wynne heard herself gasp. She clutched his black head to her burning body until she felt sure she stood on the highest peak of all. Then with another inarticulate cry, she felt herself tumbling into a swirling vortex of purest pleasure.

Hawk drew away from her briefly to divest himself of his few remaining clothes. Then he returned to the circle of Wynne's welcoming arms.

She felt almost blinded by her overwhelming need for him. Now... quickly! she thought as Hawk guided her hands to his body. Eagerly she stroked and caressed him until, with a sudden choked sound, he moved up and over her.

Her body arched upward at the very moment when he thrust forward until, at last, they were one being again, whole and complete. Together in the heat and fire that forged their rapturous union, they moved. Clinging and kissing, their movements grew gradually faster, soaring to a final frenzy.

"Hawk!" Wynne's cry of delight was timed to the deep blissful shudder of his body. Then, drenched with satisfaction, they turned to rain kisses of awe and gratitude on one another.

"Umm..." Wynne stretched, yawned and moved while Hawk's body followed hers. He imprisoned her with one arm and one hip and she laughed softly, her eyes still closed.

"What's so funny?" His lips were only inches from her ear, she discovered.

"Not funny. Just joyful. You and me." She turned to snuggle closer to him and found him watching her tenderly.

"We're joyful all right. Wynne, do you suppose any other two people have *ever* been so perfect together?" Hawk's voice was lazy, filled with contentment.

"No." She fit her body even more closely against his and marveled at the renewed quickening of her senses. It was unbelievable how he excited and intoxicated her.

"Of course, we might just be a trifle overconfident," she teased.

"Actually, we might just be a trifle oversexed!" Hawk laughed. "Speaking of that, I'll bet if you'd just touch me—yes, right there and then kiss me in that hot wonderful way you do..." Wynne's lips interplayed with Hawk's while his hands stroked her body. Slowly he rolled over onto his back, taking her with him. A breathless time of sighs and kisses followed before he guided her astride him.

"You direct the action this time," he whispered, straining against her. "Never let it be said that I oppose a fair division of labor!"

"This isn't labor. It's too much wonderful fun," Wynne breathed. She moved slowly, erotically, until he gasped and gripped her hips.

"Wow, that feels wonderful! You're some talented lady," he exclaimed.

"That's because I have the most exciting lover in the world!" Wynne said, her voice growing ragged. Her movements increased while his surged even more powerfully than before. "Oh, Hawk, I love you!"

"I love you, honey! I always will."

And, once again, ecstasy swirled over and about them.

"I have to go to Tahlequah this weekend," Hawk said later. "Can you come with me? We need to spend more time together."

"Tahlequah?" Wynne yawned again. It was a town with a large Indian population in northeastern Oklahoma, she knew. While it wasn't especially close to Arrow, neither was it a great distance away. "What's happening in Tahlequah?"

"Dedication ceremonies for a new Native American arts and crafts center. Yours truly has been asked to bestow blessings upon it or some-such."

"You'd better go with the some-such," Wynne advised. "Frankly, I don't see you doing the Great Spirit act."

"Why not?" Hawk leaned up on one elbow and peered down at her loftily. "*I* think I'd make a great shaman," he protested, pretending to be offended.

"You're too earthy. I can't see you subduing the flesh or enduring long rigors of discomfort and celibacy to achieve enlightenment." Even as she spoke, Wynne caressed his ear with a lazy finger.

Hawk gave a light smack on one of her buttocks since his hand rested on it, anyway. "Women always try to pigeonhole a man," he complained. "As for celibacy, I just got through a whole horrible month of that. I was pining for you, I might add. Well, what about it? Can you go? We'd need to leave at noon on Friday."

"I'll have to ask Peg to keep the kids," Wynne mused. Then, as she saw that telltale shadow darken Hawk's face again, she added rapidly, "Yes, I'll go. Peg will understand."

Chapter Six

Peg didn't mind keeping Wynne's children, but she made no attempt to hide her dismay over the situation that had prompted the request. "Oh, dear," she said in her frank and forthright way. "I had really hoped we'd seen the last of Mr. Hawk Saddler."

"Why?" said Wynne, stung. "I thought you found him interesting."

"I do. But basically Barry *is* right about him. Oh, I know how prejudiced Barry must have sounded to you. But, Wynne, Hawk Saddler is trouble."

"You can't be sure of that," Wynne said almost desperately.

"Oh, no? I still remember when he was ready to run off this continent anybody who wasn't one-hundred-percent Indian. That included other minorities too. 'The hell with them. This is our country and nobody else's!'— That was exactly what Hawk said once. Yes, Hawk is just too—too Indian!" Peg finished.

"But I'm Indian," Wynne protested.

"I know, dear, but you're different—and I'm not just saying that because I've known you all your life. You're natural—human. You laugh and talk. Hawk Saddler is stiff as a ramrod."

"Peg, I had just dumped quite a surprise on him less than one minute before you met him." Again, Wynne attempted to explain.

"I know. You told me, dear." Peg gave a labored sigh, her china-blue eyes troubled. "Oh, Wynne, I do know you need a husband. You're certainly too young to spend the rest of your life alone. Tom wouldn't want you to, and Barry and I don't want you to either. But is a man like Hawk Saddler a good choice? Could he possibly get along with the children, much less love them? Oh, that nice Rick Thompson seemed like he was such a good person!"

Wynne turned to stare blindly out of a kitchen window, her hands knotting involuntarily into fists. "But I don't love Rick," she said in a low voice. "I never will. I love—" She stopped herself but she knew she'd already revealed too much.

"You love Hawk," her mother-in-law finished for her.

"I can't help it." Wynne turned back to face Peg. "We stayed apart for a month—"

"And you both suffered. At least I know you did," Peg said wearily. "Oh, I've tried to kid myself about what was happening but, in my heart, I knew."

"It's been even harder on Hawk," Wynne said shakily. "You should see him. He's lost weight and has black circles under his eyes. And—and he chopped off most of his hair.''

"Why?" asked Peg.

"To—to try and make himself more acceptable to you and Barry." Now twin tears started rolling down Wynne's cheeks. "When he showed up in my office today he was wearing a business suit and a—a maroon tie."

"Oh, my," Peg sighed. "That is a concession, isn't it?" Then she stretched her arms out to Wynne.

Wynne went straight to their comfort. "Now, don't cry, dear," Peg said briskly, patting her on the back. "If you love Hawk Saddler then—then that's just the way it is. No one has the right to stand in your way. I'll talk to Barry and explain why we must be very friendly and welcoming to Hawk. You know I can usually bring Barry around."

"You can *always* bring Barry around," Wynne said, caught between laughter and tears.

"You go pack. I'll be glad to look after the children this weekend.

By noon on Friday almost everything had dropped into place. Wynne had been able to arrange time off from her job, and she and Hawk planned to drive leisurely to Tahlequah in his rental car. The trip really wasn't long enough to justify Hawk's taking his plane, and he'd needed to have some work done on it, which a local mechanic at the hangar promised to have finished by the following Monday.

Wynne had already bidden Steve goodbye since school was out, and he was attending summer day camp. She promised to tell the eager child all about the

Cherokees and their new arts and crafts center on her return.

When Wynne snapped her suitcase closed at noon, her father-in-law was away at work, and Peg was in the kitchen packing a picnic lunch for Hawk and Wynne to eat along the way. Wynne deeply appreciated this symbolic gesture of her mother-in-law's understanding.

The only problem was five-year-old Nona. "No-oo-oo!" she howled when Wynne attempted to kiss her goodbye. "I don't want you to go 'way!"

"Nona, stop that screaming," Wynne said sharply. "I'll be back home on Sunday night."

"No-oo-oo!" Sobbing hysterically Nona wrapped her arms about her mother's legs. Wynne reached down but found herself unable to dislodge the tiny fingers that clung to her with ferocious tenacity.

"Nona, quit making such a racket and let go of my legs. You're *hurting* me!" Wynne cried.

She wasn't kidding her daughter. She felt those fierce little fingers bruising her. "No-oo-oo!" Nona wailed again.

"Nona, if you don't let go of me and stop that squalling I'll—" Wynne hesitated. Did she really want to stop to spank Nona when Hawk was due here at any minute?

Wynne had always heartily disliked spanking her children even when she knew they deserved it. That's the Indian in me coming out, she thought for Indians were usually quite indulgent of children. But now, faced with little fingers digging into her flesh and ear-splitting shrieks, Wynne popped Nona sharply on her small plump bottom.

The child's mouth dropped open in an O of astonishment, but she promptly released her clutch on

Wynne's legs. Before Nona could start screaming again, Wynne bent down and spoke to her urgently. "If you'll stay quiet and kiss me goodbye, Nona, I'll bring you back a nice present."

It was a bribe, pure and simple. Wynne knew it and so did Nona whose green eyes took on a decidedly crafty look. "You *promise* you'll bring me back a present?" she asked.

"Yes," said Wynne desperately and not a moment too soon. Peg's voice drifted up the stairs to her.

"Wynne dear, Hawk is here."

"Come kiss Mama goodbye, Nona," Wynne said to her daughter. They exchanged a warm kiss and Wynne rapidly completed her instructions. "Be a good girl and do what Granny tells you. If you ride your bike be sure and put it up. And—and don't forget to say your prayers."

"Okay, Mama," Nona said equably. "Don't forget my present."

Lord, what kind of mother am I becoming? Wynne wondered as she dashed down the stairs to meet Hawk. First, I spoil the kid rotten, then I buy her off so I can go away to spend a weekend with a man!

But any feeling on Wynne's part that she might be doing the wrong thing disappeared as soon as she reached the kitchen. Hawk's face lit up at sight of her and his eyes filled with a consummate tenderness.

He stood holding the picnic hamper that Peg had packed. When Wynne reached his side, Hawk reached out and slipped his free arm around her waist. He would not kiss her in front of Peg, Wynne knew, for he was too reserved in the presence of white people to make an open display of his affection. But Wynne saw Peg watching Hawk closely, then her mother-in-law flashed Wynne a brief conspiratorial smile.

Hawk wore clothes suitable for a trip—comfortable jeans, polo shirt and jogging shoes. Wynne's own attire was similar.

"Thanks so much for the food, Mrs. Norwood," he said, thanking Peg and guiding Wynne to the door all at the same time.

"You're welcome. Have a good trip, you two, and drive carefully," Peg urged.

Hawk didn't speak again until they were in the car. He had stowed Wynne's small suitcase and the picnic hamper in the trunk of the car. "Mrs. Norwood is a nice lady, isn't she?" he remarked as they moved off down the street.

"The very nicest," Wynne agreed, feeling grateful that Hawk had seen through to Peg's innate goodness.

"Say, what sort of trouble were you having with your kid?" he asked.

"Oh, you heard her then?" Wynne asked with something like dismay. She was hoping that Nona had quieted before Hawk had arrived.

"Yeah, I heard her, and I'm sure your neighbors all did, too," he said critically.

Wynne bit her tongue and waited until the right response formed in her mind. He doesn't really know about children, she reminded herself. But, oh, how she wished *hers* could make a better impression on him! "Nona's still awfully young so sometimes she misbehaves." She finished with a question to Hawk. "Say, why are you stopping here?"

He had pulled into a small park where he halted the compact car under a large oak tree. "C'mere," he said, making it one word as he reached toward Wynne.

"Oh, Hawk!" She went into his arms and lifted her chin for his kiss. His lips came down on hers, tasting as sweet as wine and even more intoxicating. Thirstily Wynne drank in his kisses, letting herself melt against his lithe muscled body. She felt her arms and legs start to quiver and shake as he continued to kiss her with such devouring hunger, parting her lips and letting his tongue do a delicious sword fight with hers.

A moment later Hawk drew back, panting and laughing. "See what you do to me, Wynne Norwood! he accused, making a joke of his evident arousal.

"And see what you do to *me*," Wynne shot back and stretched out her hand, which trembled visibly.

"We're going to have two fantastic nights together." Hawk caught her close once again to whisper suggestively in her ear. "I want to hold you all night long, Wynne. I want us to make love until we're too tired to move, until we fall asleep in each other's arms."

Fantastic thrills shot through Wynne. "I can hardly wait," she confessed and shivered again when Hawk's arms tightened convulsively. His tongue danced around her ear, then plunged inside to trace its sensitive contours. "Hawk, hadn't we better—?"

"Yes," he sighed and released her. "This is neither the time nor place. Here." Hawk dropped an Oklahoma road map into Wynne's still-shaky hands, then he slid back beneath the wheel. "Find us a scenic route to Tahlequah and someplace to stop for lunch in about an hour."

Wynne turned her attention to the map as their journey resumed. After a few minutes she glanced at Hawk and intercepted a look from him which immediately evolved into a slow loving smile.

"Everything is going to be fine for us now, Wynne," he said firmly. "I know we've had our problems but we've worked them out and gotten through them."

Happily Wynne nodded her agreement. It was only later, much later, that she looked back and realized that Hawk had spoken with more hope than confidence.

They left an area of dry plains and gently rolling hills as they drove northward and headed into a land of green mountains and steep valleys, dotted with rivers, lakes and ponds. The road curved through lovely hill country that was heavily populated both by Cherokees and the descendants of Appalachian mountain people.

Wynne and Hawk stopped by a clear, fast-running stream to sit on warm grass to eat the lunch Peg had prepared. "Hey, this lady really knows how to cook for a man," Hawk approved, drawing from the picnic hamper thick sandwiches of ham and cheese. There were two covered containers, one holding fresh fruit and the other potato salad. Soft drinks had been packed in ice and there was a thermos of coffee as well. Delicious brownies stuffed full of pecans and heavily frosted with dark rich chocolate were dessert. Then Hawk and Wynne dozed contentedly in the sun for almost thirty minutes.

They stopped again several hours later at a quaint roadside stand where they bought jars of honey and homemade jam. Wynne admired some black pottery set on display and homemade guilts hung on a clothes line. Attractive as they all were, she decided to resist them, but Hawk succumbed to a painting of the same wooded mountains they had just driven through showing dog-wood trees in bloom.

"Now I'll know what spring in Oklahoma looks like. I can't be sure I'll ever be back here at exactly the right time to see the dogwood," he explained to Wynne.

"Sure, sure," she said, rolling her eyes to the sky as Hawk dug into his jeans and came up with fifty dollars, the asking price. But the picture was really quite lovely, she knew, and very reasonably priced as well.

The sales clerk was a teenage girl of Indian descent. She explained to Hawk that her grandfather was the artist and he always liked to have the names and addresses of people who bought his paintings. Obligingly, Hawk scribbled his name and appeared not to notice when the girl's dark eyes widened.

"Wait here a minute, please!" she choked.

Hawk shrugged good-naturedly, and the girl dashed into a small mobile home that sat a few yards away. "I think you've been found out," Wynne warned but Hawk just shrugged again.

The girl reappeared a few minutes later. Following her was an old Indian man who wore his gray hair in long braids. "Hawk, is that really you?" the grandfather called. He had a seamed and weathered face, wrinkled yet still serene.

"Yes." Hawk stepped forward, his hand outstretched. "Have we met before?"

"Sure have," the old man grinned, meeting Hawk's hand with his own. "I'm Charlie Birdsong. Do you happen to remember where you were the week of November third 1972?"

"Late '72…lessee. Oh yeah, I sure do!" Hawk's face split in a grin. "I was in that caravan called The Trail of Broken Treaties that arrived in Washington, D.C., along with a thousand red brothers and sisters. Were you there too?"

"I sure was," Charlie Birdsong said proudly. "I heard your speech in front of the Lincoln Memorial, and I used to wonder if I'd ever see you again."

"He's talked about you a lot, Mr. Saddler," Charlie's granddaughter chimed in.

"Hey, this is great! Wynne honey, come here and meet an old friend," Hawk called to her.

"I heard the news," Wynne said with a smile as she returned to Hawk's side.

"Charlie, this is my fiancée, Wynne Norwood."

Wynne glowed as she heard herself presented to old Charlie Birdsong as Hawk's fiancée. Mr. Birdsong's shrewd black eyes narrowed on Wynne and she wondered if she looked too "modern" for his taste. On the other hand, his granddaughter wore eye shadow, which Wynne would never think of using during the daytime.

"So you're finally gonna get married, Hawk. That's good. A man shouldn't be alone." At last Mr. Birdsong smiled on Wynne. "You've got yourself a rare and wonderful man."

"I know," Wynne said with a little catch in her voice.

"Take care of him 'cause there aren't many like Hawk left. Today everybody's in too much of a hurry to make a buck. People forget the old causes, the old ways, but someone like Hawk reminds us." Charlie Birdsong looked back at Hawk. "You take care of this nice woman too. It's easy to make a woman happy, but too many Indian men just won't bother. Guess that goes for other men too."

Wynne and Hawk nodded. They were standing side by side when Charlie Birdsong suddenly raised both his hands over them. With his eyes closed, his head lifted up to the clear blue sky, he began a sing-song chant over them. Wynne felt her own eyes widen but the little ceremony had an impressive dignity. Hawk took her hand in his and gave it a squeeze.

Charlie's sing-song chant went on for perhaps a minute, possibly two. Then he stopped, opened his eyes and smiled benignly on Wynne and Hawk. "Cherish each other!" he commanded.

Then Charlie shook both their hands, told them to stop by anytime and excused himself to get back to his painting. Charlie's granddaughter beamed broadly as she busied herself about her roadside stand. She waved to Wynne and Hawk as they got back in the car and prepared to drive off with Hawk's new painting.

"What was that all about?" Wynne muttered.

"I was hoping you could tell me," Hawk said.

"Charlie wasn't speaking in Cherokee," Wynne reflected. "Not that I'm exactly fluent but I do know enough to recognize the language."

Hawk said nothing for a moment, obviously reflecting on Charlie's chant. Then, suddenly, he burst out laughing.

"What is it, Hawk?" Wynne asked.

"Honey, I don't exactly know how to tell you this." Gently Hawk leaned over and kissed her cheek. "But I think we were just married."

They spent the night in a motel in Muskogee, and when Wynne emerged from the bathroom in a long white nightgown, Hawk drew her almost reverently into his arms. "You look like a bride, my bride."

Touched, she reached out and stroked his lean cheek. "I'm glad you approve. This is a new nightgown that I bought just for you."

"Of course you know I'm just going to take it off you," he said.

"I'm counting on it," Wynne said breathily, then as he leaned closer to begin nuzzling her neck and shoulders she added a warning. "But if you think I'll settle for a Native American ceremony performed by Charlie Birdsong under the trees, you can think again, Hawk Saddler! I want a bridal bouquet and a ring, a marriage license and a *real* minister—"

"And me on display, sweating in a navy-blue suit and being choked to death by a tie," he groaned, rolling his eyes to the ceiling.

His words sent a twinge of discomfort shafting through Wynne. "Hawk, is it selfish of me to want an official wedding with all of our friends and family?"

Slowly, elaborately, he shook his head and repeated the words she had said to him just a moment earlier: "I'm counting on it."

They breakfasted leisurely next morning, then left for Tahlequah. It was another fantastic day of balmy blue skies and golden sunshine. Later in June the weather would turn scorchingly hot, Wynne knew, and begin searing the green mountains and tender vegetation. By August, only the hardiest plants would have survived, and unless there had been a lot of rain even the grass would turn yellow or brown. But right now, Oklahoma was at the peak of its beauty.

Wynne and Hawk watched for jackrabbits and cottontails as they rode along. They also pointed out birds, horses grazing in pastures and even a coyote. At least Hawk claimed it was a coyote. Wynne scoffed at the assertion, assuring him that he'd merely seen a dog.

Between the moments when they noticed and exclaimed over wildlife, they talked quite seriously, planning their future together.

"First of August?" Hawk had suggested for their wedding date."

"First of September will be better," Wynne qualified. "The kids will be back in school then. And that will give us more time, too, for everything we need to do."

"To heck with 'everything,'" Hawk objected. "Let's just get married and jump back into bed!"

Wynne couldn't resist smiling at him. Their lovemaking last night had been a radiant extension of their perfect day. They'd each thrilled to the other's touch and been propelled to new heights of glory, only to rest later in each other's arms just holding, stroking, comforting, loving.

Today Wynne's body, replete from Hawk's lovemaking, glowed with satisfaction and its secret knowledge of him. She felt tempted to seize on his offer of a quick wedding and a far longer honeymoon, but there were practical and necessary matters to be attended to.

Now she gently reminded Hawk of them. "You said you wanted me to meet your family in Mississippi. And, of course, I want you to meet my parents too."

"Yes," he agreed. "I also want you to see my ranch in Arizona to be sure you can be happy there."

"What if I don't like it?" Wynne teased.

Hawk gave an elaborate shrug. "Then I'll just have to buy someplace you like better."

"Oh, Hawk! You surely wouldn't give up a home you love—"

"Yes, I would—without a single regret or a last look back," he assured her. "That's how important you are to me, Wynne."

She felt shaken by the intensity of his declaration. "I'm going to love your ranch, Hawk. I just know I will because I'm bound to love any place that you do."

He gave her hand a pat and Wynne warmed to the subject even more. "I'll bet the kids like it, too," she enthused. "Steve, in particular, has always loved reading about the West and—"

The shadow flitting over Hawk's face stopped her happy flow. "What is it?" Wynne asked, suddenly chilled.

"Uh...nothing," said Hawk evasively.

She knew better and her heart sank. It was her mention of the children, her very own children, that had caused Hawk's face to cloud over. All at once Wynne's joy in the perfect day and their future plans dimmed considerably.

Wynne had thought, when Hawk finally came back to her with his declaration of love, that he'd made peace with her previous marriage and her children by that marriage. Since Hawk had practically said as much, maybe *he* had really thought so too. But he still hadn't. Not yet.

Yes, he had come back to Wynne—but not to Steve and Nona.

Would Hawk get over his irrational resentment of her children by the time of their September wedding? Wynne wondered.

Oh, surely he will by then, she tried to assure herself, even as fear swelled in her breast and caused her stomach to churn. They're really such dear and wonderful little kids! Everyone says so! Hawk just needs the opportunity to know them better.

But, in her heart, Wynne knew that she still had numerous and serious reservations. That's why she'd just argued gently with Hawk, holding out for the later wedding date. She and Hawk both needed more time to consider this important step as well as the chance to learn first-hand all about each other's families.

What if he never, ever learns to love my kids? Wynne thought with a sudden gut-wrenching fear. She turned suddenly to look at Hawk and found that he was watching her.

"Let me tell you what to expect when we get to Tahlequah," he said, his voice even toned and, after a moment's hesitation, Wynne gave a nod. There was no point in borrowing trouble. Not yet, anyway.

So she let Hawk get away with a not-too-adroit change of subject. And then, all at once, they were there.

Wynne would have enjoyed seeing more of Tahlequah. It had been founded by Cherokees and still served as the capital of the Cherokee Nation so its Indian roots went deep. But soon after meeting Hawk's hosts at a rendezvous point just outside the city limits, Wynne and Hawk had been whisked through town and straight to the new arts and crafts center.

By arriving early, before the formal dedication ceremonies began, Wynne had the new building almost to herself to explore. Hawk had immediately been drawn into talks with a number of other Indian leaders head by Vine Whitehead, and Vine's wife, Glenmae, led Wynne away to see the various exhibits and native artisans at work before the building grew crowded.

They found women wearing colorful Indian attire working at large looms and weaving brightly colored blankets or rugs just as their great-great-grandmothers had done. "They make me wish I'd learned more about our native crafts," Glenmae revealed to Wynne as they fingered the thick, beautiful goods.

"Me too," Wynne nodded.

"My grandmother used to do this sort of thing. I could have learned," Glenmae sighed. "But, no, I wanted a law degree. I was determined to lead Cherokee women into the brave new century and teach *them* a trick or two. Were you that way too, Wynne?"

"Oh, I got a Master's and a university job, as well as acquiring a husband and a couple of kids, but I wasn't much of an activist. I was more into Yuppie capitalism. My grandmother made moccasins and tobacco bags, water and pottery jars. Her beadwork was gorgeous! But Mom never bothered to learn any crafts and neither did I."

"Yeah, we used to be so afraid of being thought 'blanket Indians,'" Glenmae said sotto voce. "God, were we dumb! Just look at the *prices* on these things!"

"I see," Wynne muttered, and they eased out the door and into a hall that displayed artifacts museum-style.

Promptly at noon a small private luncheon was held for all the visiting dignitaries, their wives and husbands. Then the food was cleared away and the largest hall opened for the 1:00 p.m. dedication services. The whirr of the governor's helicopter, setting down on the lawn outside, was the signal to begin.

Wynne found most of the speakers interesting if somewhat repetitious. The present Cherokee chief impressed her with his thoughtful remarks on how the tribe's economic base was widening. Glenmae had a number of succinct comments on the opportunities available to present-day Indian women. But it remained for Hawk to unite all the various factions in the room, to bring them to their feet clapping, cheering and whistling. He's a symbol of something very important to all of us, Wynne realized, her heart almost bursting with love and pride as she looked up at the man on stage who was trying modestly to still the enthusiastic assembly.

What was the source of Hawk's great appeal? Wynne found herself wondering almost impersonally. Of course he had been active in Indian causes for quite a long time but so had many others. Undoubtedly Hawk was also a "credit to his people," as the old phrase went; he possessed considerable gifts of talent, intelligence and education. And, of course, there was that flair and dash—the pronounced hint of recklessness that had made him both a skilled pilot and a legendary lover of women.

But nothing that Wynne mentally itemized explained the fervor and near love with which she'd seen Hawk greeted everywhere. Indians of all tribes and even many non-Indians appeared to identify with him. Was it the simple fact that Hawk Saddler had suffered misfortunes too, but had managed to rise above his and even turn them to good use? That, undoubtedly, was part of his appeal.

The rest of it, she decided, must simply be charisma and sheer originality, because as the large room quieted and Hawk began to speak, Wynne was struck by those particular traits.

Hawk talked now of the way life must have been for long-ago Indians who lacked the material and educational advantages available today but who found peace in simple pleasures—the right ratio of sun to rain, the sight of prairies filled with buffalos and their elaborate religious rituals and attunement to an overall pervading Spirit. Hawk spoke as a mystic, almost as though he'd been there to witness it all, and he took his audience back into that long-ago world with him. Wynne could almost feel herself atop a pony, riding bareback across the rolling plains with a wide blue bowl of sky above her and a profound contentment in her inner contemplation of life. Today's lives were too busy, too filled with trivial pursuits and concerns, Hawk cautioned. Let the wise ones among this Indian audience not lose touch with their roots and their inner true sense of self.

Thunderous applause greeted his conclusion. Hawk received it with a wry look on his face as he dropped back into his seat beside Wynne. "Here you warned me not to do the Great Spirit act and I did it, anyway," he said ruefully. He looked down at brief notes he held and to which he had never once referred. "Sometimes what comes out of me isn't exactly what I'd planned."

"No, *you* were right, Hawk," Wynne said fervently. "You really would have made a great shaman. Don't ever listen to me again!"

"After we're married, I'm not even going to remind you that you ever said that," Hawk teased.

When the ceremonies concluded, a veritable mob crowded around Hawk eager to shake his hand and have a private word with him. We're never going to get out of here! Wynne thought, glancing down the long line of patiently waiting people.

They were saved by the governor. His strong politician's voice washed over them as he called, "Saddler, I need to see you!"

Hawk clutched Wynne's hand and drew her out of the crowd with him. He presented Wynne as his fiancée and she managed to tactfully remind the governor that they'd met earlier that year at Wainwright College.

"I knew you looked familiar, Mrs. Norwood," the governor said jovially. "So now you're carrying off this wild man into legal matrimony? That's certainly going to break of lot of women's hearts although, frankly, I'm not sure the son-of-a-gun deserves you."

"I don't," Hawk admitted, "but I've been hoping Wynne wouldn't find me out."

"And now I've blown your cover, huh? Well, be sure to invite me to the wedding." The governor's grin began to fade as his voice turned serious. "Now, Mrs. Norwood, if you'd just let me have a word in private with Hawk . . ."

"Certainly," Wynne said. She strolled off into another area of exhibits that she hadn't seen and was soon joined by Glenmae.

"Get used to it," her new friend advised. "Important people are always going to be grabbing your husband and pulling him into little rooms for private talks. I used to resent it a lot since I was just as active in the movement as Vine. My consolation now comes from the fact that, after fifteen years with Vine, I've demolished every chauvinistic notion he ever had. He always tells me *everything* that happens in these private tête-à-têtes and usually asks for my advice. I actually think I'm more effective now working behind the scenes of power. Hawk will probably tell you exactly what happens, too, since he's one man who's never minded women being present during serious talks. In fact, he's recommended several women I know for important tribal positions."

"Oh yes, I think he'll always talk quite openly to me," Wynne agreed.

"As far as I can tell, all that happens when women aren't present is that they all cuss a lot more. Oh, say, Wynne, look at that travois. Can you imagine moving the household goods south for the summer on *that*?"

"They say large dogs were often trained to pull a travois when the tribe moved," Wynne mused.

"Really? I always assumed they only used horses." Glenmae leaned close to share a confidence. "Don't tell Hawk, but I wouldn't live back in those days for anything! I'm just not the type to tan buffalo hides and carry my baby on my back. I want everything sanitized, up-to-date and air-conditioned in my teepee!"

Wynne laughed and nodded her own agreement. Then, for the first time, she began to wonder what she would find when she went with Hawk to Mississippi and later, Arizona.

Chapter Seven

"Stop that, Hawk!" Wynne said with mock sternness. She lay sprawled lazily across the king-size bed in their motel room in Tulsa, trying to read the Sunday funnies. Hawk supposedly was browsing through the news section but, first, a lazy elbow had grazed Wynne's breast and now he was using a big toe to tickle the sole of her foot.

He looked up from his newspaper in feigned surprise. "I'm not doing anything," he protested innocently and proceeded to tickle her sole once again.

"You—" Wynne rolled up a section of funny papers and started to hit him with it as one would discipline a naughty puppy.

Suddenly something in the paper that he'd been only half reading caught Hawk's eye. "Hold, it, honey," he said automatically and caught Wynne's arm as it started to descend.

"What is it?" Wynne asked, dropping her paper roll and snuggling up against his bare, brown shoulder.

"Uh-oh," Hawk said simply and then passed the section over to her. "I hope you were ready to tell the whole world because some reporter just did."

"What?" Wynne asked, thoroughly mystified by his comment.

"Here." A strong lean finger pointed to the brief article headlined "Indian Activist to Wed."

"Uh-oh," echoed Wynne, speed-reading down to where her own name appeared. "Good Lord, I didn't realize that landing you was such a coup."

"Neither did I," Hawk admitted. "Or I might not have made it so easy for you!"

"Be serious," Wynne pleaded, lowering the paper while anxiety clutched at her. "Do you realize what this means, Hawk? Peg and Barry may also have seen it. Or your parents or mine."

"Not mine," he said swiftly. "You couldn't pay 'em to read a newspaper. Frankly, I'm not so sure they even know how to read more than the simplest, most common English words. Anyway, I doubt if newspapers outside of Oklahoma would pick up that story."

"You're too modest," Wynne said, loving him for the trait even as the extent of his notoriety disturbed her somewhat. She jumped out of bed and dashed to her suitcase where she began rapidly pulling out clothes. "What about Steve and Nona? I don't want some kid telling them or their hearing it on TV. Oh, no! *I* want to be the one to tell my children about us."

Hawk sighed. "You're getting dressed, I assume?"

Wynne stopped in the act of skimming off her nightgown. "Oh, yes, Hawk. You've got to take me home right away. Don't you see that?"

"Yeah, I guess," he agreed reluctantly. "Let's see, where did I put my damn shirt?"

Wynne paused to glance over at him. Hawk was scowling, a formidable-looking if thoroughly informal figure with his bare feet and gaping jeans that he hadn't yet buttoned.

He'd wanted us to make love again, Wynne realized as she bent over to hook her lacy bra. He'd already announced that he wanted them to have an elaborate breakfast on the terrace and a leisurely drive back to Arrow. Now Hawk's romantic plans had just gone sailing out the window and they had to dash back instead. Wynne could tell he was not a bit pleased.

Because he was Hawk Saddler, he was used to being the center of the universe. Now he was going to have to share the top spot sometimes and Wynne wondered if he could learn to adjust to it gracefully.

She certainly hoped so because she wasn't exactly thrilled to be running back home, either. But, right now, the needs of her young children definitely came first.

Not only did Wynne have to deal with her own disappointment, but she felt the necessity to cajole Hawk out of his. Fortunately a little lighthearted teasing on her part roused him to reply. "My mother always warned me about going to motels with famous me Wynne said as the highway fell away behind them. "I mean, if I'd been there with Joe Blow I'd be having brunch on the terrace right now instead of drinking coffee from 'Fastest Foods in the West' out of a Styrofoam cup—"

"If you'd been in any motel with Joe Blow I'd be pouring coffee over your head!" Hawk said with a mock growl. "Not to mention the way I'd tear up that pretty little fanny of yours!"

"Oh, my! I guess I'd better behave myself then." Wynne glanced over and saw that Hawk had finished the breakfast sandwich he'd been eating. "How about another sausage and biscuit?"

"No. One large and very greasy one was enough. And you're darn right you'd better behave yourself. You belong to me now!"

"Not so, famous chief. We are mutually committed to each other—and that is a far cry from the human possession to which you just so erroneously referred." Wynne dropped her high and lofty tone to peer down into the paper sack from the quickie restaurant where they'd stopped.

Hawk reached over and covered one of her hands with his. "Have it your own way, Ms. Norwood. You've certainly got your hooks deep in me! However, I will still argue that I'm not truly famous, thank God! To me 'famous' is when you don't dare show your face in public, you're so easily recognized. Elvis Presley was famous. Frankly, I never want to be."

Wynne smiled over at him and noticed that Hawk's tense jaw was beginning to relax. "I don't want you to be, either. I want us to have enough privacy that we can live like other people." She dipped into the paper sack and came up with another huge biscuit. "Don't you want to split this with me? It's egg and cheese."

"Okay," Hawk said after a moment's hesitation. "Fortunately I have the digestion of a billygoat."

"Good for you." Wynne divided the biscuit and handed Hawk the larger half. "Mine gets a bit touchy at times."

"Speaking of touchy—" Hawk stopped and drew a deep breach. "Since we're on our way to tell your in-laws and kids about our plans, I guess you'd better tell me more about . . . Tom."

"Oh." Wynne was so surprised at Hawk's taking the initiative on this indeed touchy matter that she swallowed her bite whole. "What do you want to know, Hawk?"

"Just *things*. Like what he looked like. What sort of work did he do? What kind of things did the two of you do together."

Wynne considered each question carefully. "Tom looked a bit like Steve. He had the same wavy brown hair and light skin. He wasn't especially tall, and he was always a little too thin. He was nice-looking but not handsome. He worked as a chemical engineer—a very good one, too."

Wynne darted another look at Hawk and saw that he was absorbing this quite impassively. So why did she have the feeling that each of her words struck him like a blow? Because, somehow, I'm able to see inside Hawk's mind, Wynne thought, feeling her heart begin to pound ominously over the reaction she merely sensed. But Hawk was right—he did need to know certain facts about her marriage to Tom, so she determined to press on.

"What did Tom and I do together? Absolutely everything! We were friends long before we were sweethearts. I tagged along when Tom went fishing or skeet shooting, and he took me to dances and movies. We both liked the out-of-doors. After we married, we used to cook outside a lot and take the kids on picnics. And we travelled quite a lot. That was our only extravagance, but we both enjoyed it. We went to Hawaii on our honeymoon and to New York and Washington, D.C., when Steve was just a baby. When he got a little older, we took him to Disney World in Orlando. We pretended we were doing it for his sake but, actually, Tom and I enjoyed Disney World more than Steve did. Then, not long after Nona was born, we left the kids with Peg and Barry. We flew to Colorado intending to ski for a week and have a second honeymoon—"

"So how was the second honeymoon?" Hawk interrupted. "For that matter, how was the first?"

"Hawk—" Wynne warned and then, suddenly, anger erupted in her breast. For the first time she turned and glared furiously at this man she loved so much.

"I know!" Momentarily Hawk's eyes closed, and he struck his fist on the steering wheel. "I'm sorry, Wynne. I'm very sorry." His voice held the desolate note of self-reproof.

Hot words sprang to Wynne's lips, but by a miracle of self-control she kept herself from uttering them. Carefully she picked over the vocabulary and chose less inflammatory ones. "Hawk, I simply don't understand you where this subject is concerned."

"Would it surprise you to know that, on this subject, I don't understand myself, Wynne." Hawk's voice was uneven while his mouth was a crooked line of pain.

"Oh," she said and lapsed into silence. What *could* she say to him after an admission like that?

"I know that I'm the one who brought up the subject," Hawk went on, striking the steering wheel with his fist. "I know I feel absolutely *driven* to talk about Tom and your marriage to him. I want to know. I need to know. And then, when you answer, some crazy chain reaction goes off in me. I guess part of it is jealousy, pure and simple. I hate the thought that anyone else ever touched you, made love to you or that you had his kids. Most of all, I hate the fact that you actually loved the guy!''

"I'd noticed that," Wynne said tightly.

"I'm not making sense, I know, because *I* was married before, too. I would also have had a child if things had turned out differently." Hawk paused. "And I've certainly been no angel in the years since Tishti died, while I suspect that *you* actually were. Why, I doubt if you've ever been with more than two men, have you?" Hastily Hawk added, "You don't have to answer that!"

"I don't mind answering that," Wynne said, feeling a strange weariness seeping through her like a spreading stain. "You and Tom are the only two men, although I'm scarcely an angel. I—I guess I'd better tell you about my honeymoons with Tom, both of them."

"No!" Hawk fairly shouted. "It's none of my business."

"You're right, it isn't," Wynne agreed, "but I'm going to tell you anyway. Tom and I were a couple of dumb kids when we got married. Oh, he acted like he'd been around and was quite worldly wise, but on our wedding night he was actually more afraid than I was. Why, we didn't even consummate our marriage for a week. It took that long for both of us to calm down."

"Wynne, I don't need to hear this," Hawk protested.

"Yes, apparently you do," Wynne contradicted, clutching calm about her although it was fraying like a tattered garment. "And you want to know something else, Hawk? I thought making love was a very disappointing business. It was always something I thoug' could live quite easily without."

His startled black eyes swung back to her. "But you said you loved Tom!"

"Yes, I did—so I never let him know exactly how I felt. Then, after Steve was born—" Wynne shrugged her shoulders. "Things were better then. Even dumb kids finally start to learn a few things. Tom bought some books and read them, trying to improve his technique, I knew. I...appreciated that. And, soon enough, there was Nona."

"Wynne, that's enough. I—"

"I think the second honeymoon in Colorado might have been great," Wynne continued coolly. "But when we got to the resort it was late at night, and we were both quite tired. So all we did was sleep. In fact, I slept till noon the next day. Not Tom! He was off to the slopes at dawn like a big eager kid. And then...just about the time I was waking up...there was an accident on the ski lift. Three people were flung off when it broke and Tom was one of them. He was hurled so far! At least it happened fast, people say, but how fast does time pass when you're terrified? I know Tom must have been terrified." Wynne swallowed hard, feeling tears rise into her throat even at this late date. "Tom was barely twenty-six years old. And he was a good, kind, decent man. I'll always be proud that I was married to him. But you know what, Hawk?"

"What?" he said softly, his voice subdued.

Wynne blinked back her tears and saw that deep shame had tinged Hawk's high cheekbones. "You have absolutely no reason to be jealous because I didn't love Tom the way I love you. How could I? That was an inexperienced girl's love—a happy girl for whom very little had ever really gone wrong. But I'm not that girl anymore, just like you're not that same young man who grew up on a reservation in Mississippi. Things *have* gone wrong in my life, bitterly wrong. But some things, thank God, are going right and have actually gotten better."

"Wynne—"

"No, let me finish, Hawk. I'm a mature woman now. And I love you and need you in a way I never even believed possible before. I want you—I adore going to bed with you! Physically you always turn me on and making love with you is deep, rich and exciting!" Wynne drew a breath so deep that it made her breasts heave. "So go ahead. Castigate me because I grew up with the love of both an Indian man, my father, as well as a white man, my grandfather. And that's why it was easy for me to love Tom and why it's easy for me to love you, too. And keep on punishing me for having what you consider to be 'mixed-breed children.' Oh, and be sure and make life miserable for *them*, too, over something they certainly can't help! And you know what, Hawk? Even considering how much I love you, I'll soon wish I'd met anybody, *anybody*—purple, orange, green or pink—other than you!"

"Oh, Wynne!" The face he turned toward her was stricken.

"I mean it, Hawk!" she said fiercely and fumbled for a tissue on which to blow her nose.

"I know you do," he muttered and fell silent.

Several miles passed without either of them speaking. Now, while Wynne gave herself points for logic and calmness, she also began to wonder if she hadn't said too much. Could Hawk really control what he'd called "a crazy chain reaction?" If it was really involuntary and purely instinctive then he couldn't—so chewing him up, as she'd just done, was like beating a dead horse.

A roadside restaurant loomed up on the right. "I know you're probably not hungry," Hawk said, "but let's stop for a soda or something."

"All right," Wynne agreed and wished that Hawk's face didn't look quite so drawn and unhappy. His pain pierced her heart like a thorn.

Hawk veered off the highway, took the access road to the restaurant and pulled into the parking lot. Then, as Wynne started to reach for her door handle, Hawk leaned over and stopped her.

"Hawk!" She turned spontaneously at the touch of his hands, and then they were locked in each other's arms.

"Wynne, I'd rather be dead than to ever have you feel the way you just said, wishing you'd met anybody but me!" His hands crushed her against his chest and Wynne shed a few soft tears against its strong hard expanse. "I never want to do that to you!"

"I know...I know." She felt his hands tracing consoling circles on her back. "Oh, Hawk, what are we going to *do*?"

"I'll stop needling you, Wynne. I swear I'll stop it! I'll be good to your—to Steve and Nona. I swear that, too!" His voice was vehement and she felt the strong contraction of his muscles as he made the vows.

"But can you?" Wynne sobbed, beginning to cry in earnest. "Can you really do that?"

"Yes!" Hawk said fiercely. "I can. I will. Wynne honey, please don't cry. It absolutely tears me up when you cry!"

"This has turned into such a—a terrible day," Wynne said, struggling to control her tears. "And the rest of our weekend was so beautiful."

"It might have helped if we'd been able to make love," Hawk whispered softly, his lips moving against her hairline. "I was just starting to get your attention this morning when I saw the damned article that started this whole thing. Although, come to think of it, it's my own damned fault for introducing you as I did yesterday at Tahlequah. I just never thought I was important enough for my engagement to be big news."

Wynne heard the lingering surprise in Hawk's voice. He really is modest about his accomplishments, she thought with surprise of her own. And sometimes he acts . . . well, almost *insecure*.

Then she scoffed at herself. How could Hawk Saddler be insecure. The idea seemed incredible. He'd gone everywhere, done everything, knew important people in all walks of life. No, indeed! For all that she felt almost miraculously attuned to Hawk, Wynne felt sure that her intuition was really off base on this one.

"Hawk—" she began slowly, slipping back from the sheltering circle of his arms.

"Don't say it, Wynne. And don't do it. Please!" he implored.

"Say what? Do what?" she asked, not understanding his meaning.

Hawk drew a deep breath, then rushed into words he obviously feared uttering. "Don't tell me to get lost," he muttered, but his voice wasn't steady.

"Lost? *You!*" Now Wynne was the one reaching out to console Hawk. "Didn't you hear a thing I said?" she whispered, running her fingers through his thick black hair. "I love you! I want you and need you! Going to bed with you is sheer heaven! Why, I'm not about to tell you to get lost or—"

His lips sealed hers closed with a passionate kiss, and Wynne flung her arms tightly about his neck. Then, after another kiss or two, they went inside the restaurant to have cold drinks and let their troubled and turbulent emotions simmer down. Over a red-checkered tablecloth their hands brushed, met and clung.

"It *will* work out," Wynne said, trying to assure herself as well as Hawk.

"I know it will, Wynne. I think all we really have to do is remember what Charlie Birdsong told us. 'Cherish each other.'" Hawk's head bent down, his lips brushed across her four knuckles. "I do. I do cherish you."

"Same here. I cherish you, Hawk Saddler." Wynne found it hard to speak, her throat contracted by all the fervent emotions that gripped her.

"Say, I've never told you—" Hawk looked up at Wynne, his face softening, his eyes holding a faraway look. "I had an Anglo friend once."

"You!" she exclaimed in surprise. "Why, Hawk! When? Where?"

"Late sixties. His name was Mike McCormick and he was a freckle-faced redhead who came from someplace near Boston. He was active in lots of different causes, all involving civil rights. You never knew where Mike was liable to turn up—making a march with Martin Luther King or protesting wages paid to migrant workers with Caesar Chavez. He also made the trip to Washington with us. Actually—" Hawk paused "—Mike was a lot friendlier than I was. He really acted as if he liked me and pretended not to see that I was damned suspicious of him and his motives." Hawk looked back down at his and Wynne's linked hands.

"By the time I found out that Mike really had been my friend it was too late. He was dead."

Wynne's throat contracted again at the regret and deep sadness she saw on Hawk's face. "What happened to Mike?" she asked.

"Vietnam. That's what happened to him. Like all of us, he was opposed to the war. But Mike's father was a gung-ho veteran of both the Second World War and Korea, and he'd pretty well had it with Mike's liberal causes and his minority friends. So he told Mike to forget burning his draft card, or being a conscientious objector and running off to Canada. The old man said if Mike ever did any of those things, he would never be welcome at home again."

"How sad!" Wynne exclaimed. "I could never imagine telling that to a child of mine, especially if he or she had strong personal convictions."

"Mike's father could. So Mike sweated over it a lot then decided to do the so-called 'patriotic thing,' which was what his family wanted. I know I had such a bad feeling when he told me goodbye. I guess it was a premonition," Hawk added softly.

"How did you find out that Mike had really been your friend?" Wynne asked, searching Hawk's intent face.

He reached for his glass and took a sip before he replied. "Mike had a guitar I'd always admired. He even taught me to play it a little. Well, I guess Mike had a premonition of his own because, before he left for Nam, he wrote out a last will. It probably wasn't legal but nobody cared. He didn't have much in the way of worldly goods to distribute. But he left me that guitar that he'd loved better than most anything. I remember when it arrived. I took it out into the desert and sat on a hill and tried to play and sing a few songs for the rest and peace of Mike's spirit. And then I cried, Wynne. For the first and last time since I was a kid, I sat on a hilltop and cried. Because I'd never let Mike know how much I liked him—and I knew then that I never could."

"Oh, I'll bet he knew, Hawk," Wynne said, speaking over a lump in her throat. "I'll bet Mike knew!"

As she watched Hawk, his thick eyelashes swept down to veil his eyes. He drew a breath and, with one finger, swept off drops of moisture that had condensed on his tall frosty glass.

"I hadn't thought about Mike in a long, long time," Hawk said at last. He looked back up at Wynne with his eloquent black eyes. "I don't guess I've ever talked about him to anyone who didn't know him."

"I'm glad you told me," Wynne whispered, her heart going out to Hawk, even as her hand gently and lovingly caressed his. She was filled again with hope.

They reached the Norwoods' home in Arrow by late afternoon. To Wynne's relief it was not in the state of uproar she'd feared. Rather, when Peg turned from the stove to greet them with a smile her countenance was placid. Immediately, Wynne knew that the news story in the Tulsa and Oklahoma City papers had apparently not been picked up by their own small local paper.

Nona sat at the kitchen table, crayons clutched in her fist, coloring messily in one of her coloring books. As Wynne bent down to give her daughter a hug and kiss, she was grateful that Nona did not demand her present that immediate instant. And Wynne also wondered wryly if this second child of hers would *ever* learn to be neat. At present Nona's bike, her volleyball and a small pail were scattered about on the lawn. Wynne decided not to mention them yet.

"Have a seat, Hawk, if you don't mind being in the kitchen like family," Peg said hospitably. "How about a beer?"

"That would be great!" Hawk said just a trifle too fervently for one who was a light drinker. Wynne darted a nervous glance at him. She saw that he looked almost predictably uncomfortable, but she also knew that Hawk intended to try his best to be pleasant and companionable. Perhaps a beer or two would relax him and put him more at ease.

"I'll get drinks," Wynne said quickly and opened the refrigerator. In addition to Hawk's beer, she poured small glasses of wine for herself and Peg. She served Nona a glass of cranberry juice so the child wouldn't feel left out.

"Barry and Steve ran down to the hardware store," Peg explained. "They left just a minute or two before you drove up, but they shouldn't be gone long." Briskly Peg put the lid on a simmering pot and moved to a skillet where she had meat browning. "Tell me about your trip. Did you two have a good time?"

Hawk and Wynne murmured assents, and Wynne was happy to see Hawk smiling over at Nona. After a moment of skeptical observance, Nona grinned back with her wide and refreshing smile. At that moment Wynne decided that Nona had earned her present and bent down over her daughter's coppery curls to whisper that she hadn't forgotten.

"We'll look at presents after Steve gets here," Wynne added.

"Hawk, you must stay and have dinner with us," Peg urged.

"Thank you, Mrs. Norwood. I'd enjoy that," Hawk replied readily.

Wynne's heart warmed anew and she smiled at him. Hawk really was going to try his best, she realized gratefully. He was also downing his beer in record time, she noticed. She just hoped it would have the desired effect.

The four of them chatted pleasantly for ten or fifteen minutes and Hawk did relax considerably. Wynne had placed a second beer in front of him, and he sipped on it more slowly, allowing Wynne to describe the arts and crafts center, the speeches and their meeting with the governor.

"Oh, Wynne!" Peg said suddenly. "I was about to forget. Your parents called."

"Yes, I got to talk with Grammaw and Grampa Grove!" Nona added excitedly. "They're in Texas."

"Oh, I'm sorry I missed their call," Wynne said with a touch of regret. "Where in Texas were they?"

"Brownsville. But they're heading home in just a week, you'll be glad to know." Peg's blue eyes twinkled. "I sort of filled them in on people and events, if you and Hawk catch my meaning."

"I believe we do," Hawk said warmly and slipped an arm around Wynne's shoulder. She turned her smiling face toward him, and his black eyes told her he would have kissed her if they'd been alone.

"They're looking forward to meeting you, Hawk," Peg added. "They've heard a lot about you, of course."

"I'm sure I'll enjoy meeting them," Hawk said, giving Wynne's shoulder a light squeeze.

At least Wynne had no fears over that particular meeting, for both of her parents looked quite Indian. Yes, Hawk would definitely be more at ease with the

Groves but, perhaps, when he saw the easy interaction between them and the Norwoods he would see that such long-standing friendships were not only possible but could be wholly happy.

Hawk visibly tensed when Barry and Steve returned. He has more trouble with the men in my family than the women, Wynne realized. Of course, who could actually blame Hawk with Barry bristling as he was? Peg would definitely need to lecture Barry another time or two.

"Hello, Saddler," Barry said gruffly. "Got a beer, have you? I guess I'll take one, too. You need another?"

"No, sir," Hawk said, his voice chilling rapidly.

But what Barry and Hawk lacked in enthusiasm for each other, Steve more than made up for. "Gosh, Mr. Hawk, it's good to see you again," he said, his blue eyes almost shining out of his head.

"Hawk, ever since Steve met you he's been reading all about Choctaws," Wynne volunteered. She leaned over to hug her son proudly. Steve was such an intelligent kid, as well as being so downright likable and lovable! Couldn't Hawk see that?

Hawk tried. She knew he tried. In fact, he encouraged Steve to chatter away, displaying his knowledge of the Choctaws and other tribes known as "mound Indians." But Hawk's smiles often looked little better than grimaces. He finally stopped Steve when the excited child began talking about bizarre burial customs practiced by long-ago Choctaws.

"See, they put dead bodies up on platforms open to the sun—that was so animals couldn't get to 'em—and after the bodies had dried out a few of the Choctaws who had long, long fingernails—"

"Whoa!" said Hawk abruptly, cutting through Steve's flow of words. "I don't think the folks want to hear about that ancient practice, especially just before supper."

Barry looked entirely interested, but Peg's face had twisted in distaste and Wynne was afraid her own had too. But surely Hawk remembered that kids, *all* kids, relished downright ghoulish things.

Steve gave a disappointed sigh. Then a thought apparently occurred to him and he looked up triumphantly. "Anyhow, only bones got buried under the mounds."

"How come?" Nona piped up.

Hawk shot Wynne a look of near-desperate appeal, and she stood up before Steve could try to devise a more tasteful explanation. "That's enough on the entire subject," she said firmly. "Now I want both of you to go wash your hands before we eat dinner."

The meal was served a short time later in the rarely used formal dining room. The children were subdued, as they always were, in the presence of china and crystal, cloth table covering and napkins—all absolute minefields for kids who tended to be clumsy. Wynne was proud of Steve and Nona when she saw their careful attempts to avoid dropping, breaking or spilling.

Hawk was equally subdued, and Barry was simply not talkative either. He did rouse himself to demand of his wife, "Why are we drinking wine for dinner? You never serve that except on holidays."

"Well, dear, I thought it would add a festive touch," Peg said defensively. "It's really just a light rosé. Let me serve you and Hawk a bit more." Peg, like Wynne, had obviously decided that events might unfold more smoothly if the men were somewhat oiled.

The food was delicious, for Peg was a superb cook. Everyone ate hungrily of meat, potatoes and green vegetables served with Peg's homemade rolls and the strawberry jam she'd made a few months before. Hawk and Wynne both took seconds, their only other meal that day, the fast-food breakfast, having disappeared long ago.

Dessert was lemon pie with high, perfectly browned meringue and a mouth-melting crust. The quality of the food finally loosened Hawk's tongue. "That was a magnificent dinner, Mrs. Norwood," he praised. "I don't know when I've ever had a meal that was quite so good."

"She's a mighty fine cook," Barry agreed gruffly and, for the first time, he looked at Hawk with something like appreciation.

As soon as dinner ended and the table had been cleared, Hawk made his excuses to leave. Relief that the ordeal was over caused everyone to be exceptionally cordial to each other.

Wynne walked out with Hawk to his car. The night was dark, and as he reached the driver's side, he turned suddenly and swept her into his arms. Their lips crushed together, then clung, growing more heated by the moment. Wynne's hands gripped his dark head tightly. When the kiss broke, she whispered, "When will I see you again? You're flying out in the morning, aren't you?" During the weekend they had talked of almost everything except when they would have to leave each other again.

"I have to." Hawk leaned down and his mouth took hers again. "Relocating Navajos—" he stopped and each pause was then punctuated with a kiss "—in Arizona and it's beginning to look like Wounded Knee all over again..."

"Why? What's happening there?" Wynne asked when his hungry lips and tongue withdrew again.

"Government has ordered certain Navajos to relocate—they're living on Hopi Land—but it's sacred to the Navajos too." His mouth caught hers again and couldn't seem to quit kissing her until Wynne drew back a little. "Hell of a thing to have happened between two Indian tribes," Hawk finished.

"I know. When will I see you again?" she repeated, her body curving alluringly against the taut length of his.

"Two—three weeks. I'll write—phone."

"You'd better!" Wynne threatened and tugged Hawk's head back down until their lips touched again.

"God, I want you!" he breathed and she felt the growing hardness of his body against hers. "See what you do to me! I expect you always will."

Wynne felt her body angling even more closely to his in hungry yearning. In a minute even her breathing would be erratic, she knew. "The wine's lowered our resistance."

"What resistance?" Hawk said ruefully, his breath warm as he buried his face against Wynne's. "I never have any when it comes to you! But—yeah, I'm pretty far gone. I don't usually drink both beer and wine."

"I know." She pulled away and smiled. "Don't leave yet. I'll be right back."

"Wh-what?" he stammered.

"I'm going back to the motel with you for an hour or two," Wynne said determinedly. "If you think I'm going to let you leave me for two or three weeks and fly off in your condition—"

Hawk gave a relieved, grateful, rueful laugh. "Please do come!"

Wynne slipped back inside for a whispered word in the kitchen with Peg. "Hawk isn't used to drinking all that we kept pouring down him. I want to drive him back to the motel, then I'll take a cab home."

"Sure," Peg said with a nod.

Wynne paused long enough to inform the children that it was time for baths and bed. They would find their gifts on the top of her overnight bag, she added. She dropped swift kisses on two jam-sticky faces and then she was flying back to Hawk.

"I can't believe I'm actually letting you drive," he teased and his arms reached for Wynne as she slid beneath the wheel.

She gasped as his hands cupped her breasts warmly and boldly. "Stop that, Hawk, or we'll never get to the motel!"

"Okay." He dropped back on his side of the car, but the sexual tension zinging between them was like an eager, vital, throbbing current. Wynne shivered just thinking of that strong tawny body claiming hers again. How is it possible for two people to feel such absolute and simultaneous desire for each other? she marveled.

"Either your driving has improved or I'm drunker than I knew," Hawk said when Wynne wheeled easily into a parking space in front of his motel room.

"I can handle a little car like this," she said.

"I can't wait to see you drive my Blazer. Oh, Wynne!"

"Hawk!"

Somehow they were inside the motel room and coming together with a rush. The bed seemed impossibly far away, and they barely reached it. No further preliminaries were necessary. All Hawk ever has to do is touch me, kiss me and hold me and I'm ready for him, Wynne thought, feeling herself melting, soft and dewy.

In their urgency they removed just the necessary clothes. Wynne's arms opened and Hawk fell into them, his hard aroused body atop her, one aggressive knee parting the softness of her thighs. "I love you!" he breathed and surged into her, making her cry out with joy.

He was wild and hungry, his skin practically burning her mouth and hands, and he drove deeper, harder, seeking to explore more of her than he'd ever possessed before. Wynne gasped, feeling Hawk stretch and fill her. Eagerly she arched up, wanting to absorb each of his driving thrusts, desperately needing everything he had to give.

"I love you, Hawk . . . always . . . always!" she cried.

His lips burned on hers. His body triumphantly owned hers, delighting her, until Wynne went a little crazy, too. Their passion swelled and deepened, building to a tumultuous climax, then they were soaring away into a private Eden where only the two of them belonged.

Chapter Eight

Oklahoma looked like a bright patchwork quilt when seen from the air. Green checkerboard squares bumped sides with brown ones as cultivated land met uncultivated. There were even a few yellow squares as well where occasional fields of wheat ripened. Once in a while a blue ribbon of water glittered far below.

Suddenly a bright yellow-green field of corn appeared. It was unusually large and grew even bigger still when Hawk glided directly over it. A white farmhouse, far below, lay like a pearl in the midst of an emerald sea. Not far from the house was a windmill which, from the air, looked like a child's spinning top.

Hawk drew a hand over his face, still feeling a bit sleepy despite a good night's rest and a couple of cups of strong breakfast coffee. The plane was set on automatic now and flying due west. Soon there would be less green everything on the earth below him and more shades of oyster, tan and rust as he headed across the great southwestern desert.

Hawk loved to fly and had been hooked on it ever since he'd paid ten dollars at a long-ago air show for a quick trip up and around the sky. Now flying lifted him high above all of the earth's problems and helped him to put them into proper perspective. Also, to soar so high that he was often above the clouds satisfied a mystic sense within him. It linked past to present, possibly even bound a life lived long ago to another life to come. Of course, Hawk wasn't really sure about any other lives but flying did give him a sense of the continuity of time. He felt, too, his kinship with fellow creatures since flying made him one with the majestic eagle, as well as with his brother and namesake, the hawk.

Flying was important to him in an absolutely elemental way. He needed it just as surely as he needed food, water, air... and Wynne.

Wynne— Hawk's senses were full of her today. His mouth still held the taste of hers, his nostrils retained her delicate and unique scent. Along with soap, shampoo and fragrance she always smelled deliciously of a young woman's warm and healthy skin. Especially today Hawk's body remembered Wynne's. Her nipples had grown so hard beneath his avid touch last night, but the vale between her thighs was soft and heated. Fire and fury, she'd been just as ravenous as he, and the pulsing, convulsive ripple of her inner depths had finally drained all tension from him. For the moment, at least, he had been whole and replete.

Last night, in little more than two hours, he and Wynne had experienced a dizzying and dazzling spectacle of lovemaking. Between bouts they had rested in each other's arms, then turned back together again, aroused and on fire anew. He could still hear her voice urging him on, then begging for release. She'd uttered exciting little cries of ecstasy until, sated, they each lay gasping and filled with awe.

Now Hawk's body gave a throb of remembrance and he tore his thoughts away from the act of lovemaking, however sublime it had been. Right now he had a plane to fly, and it would do him no earthly good to get heated up all over again, hungering for Wynne. But after last night how could be possibly live through two or three weeks without her? God, it was going to be hard!

And yet, even as Hawk had kissed her good-night for the final time he'd whispered a pledge to her, a pledge that he knew he would keep. "I'll be aching like hell for you before we're together again. But there won't be anyone else, Wynne. There will never again be anyone else!"

"Nor for me, either," she'd said, her radiant eyes shining in her flushed face and her long straight hair, which he'd earlier torn from its prim moorings atop her head and watched fall like midnight about her shoulders. Wynne's mouth had been swollen from all of his lavish kisses and, beneath her knit shirt, her breasts had jutted out more than they usually did, still erotically engorged from the passionate play of his mouth and hands. Standing in the moonlight and looking the picture of an Indian love goddess, she was the most beautiful creature Hawk had ever seen. He knew he would hold that picture of her in his mind and heart and that it would be his talisman, no matter how agonizingly slowly the days passed.

Hawk frankly admitted that he'd been a hell-raiser in his day, but now the time for that sort of thing had passed. He could never risk hurting Wynne or bringing back to her some unwelcome malady from an ugly, promiscuous world.

She was such a lady—when *he* wasn't blissfully tumbling her off her pedestal and all over a mattress! She was a woman he could be proud to have stand by his side and introduce to his relatives and friends: "Wynne Saddler, my wife." The words were alive and real to Hawk for he felt that they were already married to each other in the very best sense of the word. Why, in some strange fashion they had *always* been married, even before he'd asked Wynne and had been accepted, even before Charlie Birdsong's chant over their bowed heads.

Now Hawk wished they could be legally united before September which was three long months away. He wanted Wynne by his side during the day and lying in his bed and in his arms every night. Ultimately, he wanted that flat little tummy of hers to grow large with his child, their child. Already Hawk imagined pressing his face on her pregnant stomach, talking to that child they'd create from their love, and feeling its kicks of response.

If only there weren't those other two blasted kids!

The sudden fierce anger in Hawk's thoughts took him aback. It left him with a mouth gone dry, a heart pounding too rapidly in his chest and hands that sweated more than a pilot's should on a calm, pretty day.

God Almighty, what was wrong with *him* that he resented those two little kids so much? Oh, he'd always had a kind of ho-hum attitude toward various nieces and nephews. He wasn't an indiscriminate lover of all children, the way some adults were.

Hawk could still remember the very different sensations of waiting for his very own child. He'd always remembered that tiny little black-headed boy who had died without ever having lived outside of his teenage mother. As young as Hawk had been, he had certainly loved his child and that was why he so yearned now to create one with Wynne.

So what in hell was wrong with him that he couldn't accept Wynne's other children? Slowly and gradually, Hawk realized that he couldn't make the crucial necessary connection because those kids seemed so *unconnected* to Wynne, at least in his mind. Oh sure, he had seen her kiss them, touch their faces or hair, or flash a warning glance in their direction. Still, none of that seemed quite real. Wynne might have been the babysitter for those fair Anglo kids.

Hawk had even searched their small faces anxiously and hopefully, but only when Nona smiled did he see even a glimmer of Wynne.

At least Nona was growing on him a little, Hawk admitted. She would probably get to him ultimately just because she was cute and cunning, a careless little scamp of a girl. Hawk had grown up with two younger sisters, so the wide-eyed innocence in Nona's green eyes didn't fool him. He could easily imagine himself confronting her when she was sixteen. While he would have ordered Nona home from a date by midnight, he would hear her come creeping in at two. Yes, Nona would need gentle but firm discipline. She was already winding Wynne and her doting grandparents around her clever little fingers.

But it was really the boy—that pale, cool, smart-alecky boy—who kept Hawk's insides knotted up. That boy who, for God knew what reason, wanted to be an Indian and kept shooting off his mouth like he was a Choctaw historian or something. When he was growing up in Mississippi, Hawk had a number of unfortunate encounters with young rednecks who looked an awful lot like Master Steve Norwood. Cold and calculating, they would shortchange any Indian and think only that it was shrewd business. And if you ever found yourself in a back alley with one or more of them, watch out. They fought dirty with a thumb headed toward a guy's eye and a knee aimed at his groin.

No, Hawk did not like Wynne's boy at all, and in his most honest moments alone up here in the sky, he had to acknowledge the bitter resentment that brimmed in his heart.

Yet it was obviously a package deal—Wynne and the kids. She'd certainly made that plain enough to him as they drove back from Tahlequah.

Perversely too, Hawk would not have had her any other way. If she'd been the kind of woman who could leave the kids from her first marriage with their grandparents and go off with any man she fancied, Hawk Saddler would have had little use for her. Grown people had to be *responsible*! You never knew what sort of quirks and twists fate was going to throw at you, so you had to be a mature person who was capable of meeting them. Now, for him Wynne's kids were a couple of those quirks and twists.

"It *will* work out," Hawk heard himself murmuring aloud the same words he'd said earlier to Wynne. "*I'll* work it out!" He had to. Otherwise he would lose her, and Hawk knew he would never get over the deep hurt of that.

But whenever he thought of Steve and Nona, he hurt for a different reason. Deep inside, beyond his resentment and old pain, there lay a tribal knowledge that insisted Hawk behave toward Wynne's children in a willing and generous way. He was supposed to adopt them wholly, and his failure to do so was like a slow hemorrhage, weakening him and gradually wearing him down.

At that moment, alone in the sky, Hawk Saddler knew and faced the worst of himself. The renowned activist was a rotten Choctaw, at least where this one issue was concerned.

Even more galling and unpleasant was that the scholarly, well-behaved Steve Norwood, so relentlessly learning Indian ways and customs, probably knew this too.

Back in Arrow, Wynne was not exactly having an easy time of things, either. Like Hawk, she clung to the memories of their physical union. This helped her to face the reactions of various people when they heard the often startling news of her engagement.

Wynne's parents, who were presently in a trailer park in Brownsville, Texas were obviously happy at the news, but they were one of the exceptions. Another exception came in a rare call Wynne got from one of her brothers. "Hey, Sis, way to go!" Jack applauded. "I'll sure be looking forward to meeting the one and only Hawk Saddler!"

But Wynne's father-in-law, Barry, was anything but happy over the way events had unfolded. "Dammit, Wynne, you don't even know the guy!" Barry blustered.

"I know all I need to know, Dad," Wynne replied quietly. "I love him."

"Yeah? Well, love comes and love goes. Listen to me. You have no way of knowing what kind of husband Saddler would make. And what about the kids? Peg tells me you'll want to haul them off to the wilds of Arizona where that guy lives. Wynne, if you try to do something like that, Peg and I might be forced to take steps."

"What kind of steps would you take, Dad?" Wynne asked quietly. "I'm not an unfit mother, and I've always supported the children."

"That's another thing!" Barry shot back. "I can just see Saddler trying to get his hands on your settlement money."

"My what?" Wynne said, mystified.

"That money you got from the out-of-court settlement with the ski lodge where Tom was killed. That money is for Tom's kids' education and what all!"

"I'm well aware of that," Wynne said coolly. "As you know, I've never touched it."

"In fact, that money may be the reason Hawk Saddler is so all fired up to marry you!" Barry cried.

Wynne looked down at her hands and counseled herself to be patient with Barry. His troubled face told her of the genuineness of his concern. "Dad, Hawk doesn't even know I have that money. We've never discussed finances at all."

"See!" Barry said triumphantly. "You and that guy haven't known each other long enough to get down to the real nitty-gritty. You know what most married couples fight about? *Money!* Just ask Peg how we used to yell and holler at each other when we were young and never had quite enough scratch."

"Dad, I don't anticipate money being a problem. Hawk receives quite large lecture fees and—"

"How large?" her father-in-law interrupted bluntly.

"He usually receives four thousand dollars for a single appearance, although the college got him here for three days at seven thousand. Hawk does lower his lecture fees if he's personally interested in a cause," Wynne said evenly.

Barry's face went rigid with shock. "You know how long I've gotta work to make seven grand? And that guy does it with a snap of his fingers! It doesn't seem right somehow, Wynne."

"You're not Hawk Saddler, either!" Pride left Wynne unable to resist that shot although she regretted it immediately. "Oh, Dad," she cried into Barry's hostile face. "Hawk is a very good man. He'll be kind to the kids and me, I know he will."

"No way you can know ahead of time," Barry said with a heavy sigh.

"Speaking of time, Dad, we're not getting married until September. That will give us *all* a chance to know each other better." Wynne drew a deep breath, marshaling the rest of her arguments. "As far as our living in Arizona goes, Hawk says if I don't like it—or if I find it too far away from good schools—he'll sell his place, and we can move somewhere else."

"Sounds like he's got an answer to everything," Barry said resentfully and sighed again. "Oh, Wynne, Tom's getting killed was such a lousy break for all of us!"

Startled at the deep grief that still echoed in the depths of Barry's voice, Wynne looked up sharply. She knew, of course, that Barry had taken Tom's death quite hard. How could he not? Tom was his and Peg's only child, and he'd been a constant source of pride and satisfaction to them. Now Tom's children were all that Peg and Barry had left and— Abruptly Wynne's thoughts flew off onto another tangent. Oh, of course! *That's* what was really bothering Barry most.

"Dad, you and Peg will always be the kids' cherished grandparents," she said softly. "You'll always be welcome in my home, just as welcome as you've made me in yours. And—and I'll bet you and Peg wouldn't mind keeping the children part of the time—summers or holidays, I mean—so Hawk and I could take a few trips or just—just be by ourselves."

Despite the way Wynne groped for words, it was amazing to watch the relief that washed over Barry's face in a single wave. "Oh—uh, sure, Wynne. We'll always be glad to keep the kids for you."

Wynne's own heart lightened, and she got up from her chair in Barry's den to walk to the desk where he sat. She leaned over and kissed him on the cheek.

Barry frowned ferociously, as he always did when he was actually touched. Awkwardly, he cleared his throat. "I still don't like this business of your marrying Saddler, Wynne," he said gruffly.

But he was no longer threatening to take the kids away from her, Wynne noticed. Not that Peg and Barry could have succeeded, even if they'd found the heart to try.

Her mood thoughtful, Wynne went back to her bedroom. Atop her bureau was a framed picture of Tom as he'd looked when he'd finished college: earnest, sober, likable and young—oh, so very young! By now Wynne had quite left that young man behind for she was nearly thirty. Tom, by contrast, would never grow older than twenty-six in everyone's loving recollections.

In the wake of Tom's death, Barry had been like an almost fatally wounded man while Peg had crept around like a small silent ghost. For months, Wynne and the children had been their only source of comfort even as they had sought to comfort Tom's distraught young widow. It was for mutual consolation more than any other reason that Wynne had agreed to move into her in-laws' large house, the house Tom's parents had built for Tom and the other children they had once hoped to have but which never arrived.

"Wynne, you may regret moving in with Peg and Barry," Wynne's own mother had pointed out to her. "As much as I love them, I have to tell you that."

But she had never regretted it. What Wynne had lost in privacy, the support and love of Tom's parents had more than made up for and each in their way had proved a great asset. Peg was always there when the kids came home from kindergarten or school to feed them a snack and listen to their chatter. Barry was there to set an example for Steve of both masculine strength and gentleness. He had taken the kids to football games and the rodeo, and he let Nona practice her burgeoning feminine wiles on him, often assuring her that she was the cutest and prettiest little girl in the world.

Wynne's relationship with her in-laws had always been warm, affectionate and filled with mutual respect. More than anything else she wanted that relationship to stay just as it was. As Wynne began making plans to remarry, it was very important to her that no one be hurt.

Wynne made no mention of her engagement at work. But because she lived in a small town and worked at a small college, word of it spread quickly.

Dr. Roxie congratulated Wynne warmly. She seemed especially pleased by the small role she had played in reuniting the lovers and hinted that she'd like to come to Wynne's wedding. Wynne assured Dr. Roxie that all of her co-workers would indeed be invited.

The following afternoon, Rick Thompson stepped quietly inside Wynne's office. It was almost 5:00 p.m., and he asked her if he might close her office door.

"Of course, Rick," Wynne said with a smile although her heart sank. She had the feeling that she knew what was coming.

Rick took a chair across from Wynne and made a steeple of his fingers, which he proceeded to regard intently. "Look, Wynne, I—uh, I heard the news yesterday about you and Hawk. It's true, I guess? Somebody said it was even printed in the Tulsa newspaper."

"Yes, Rick, it's true," Wynne said and tried to make a little joke. "See what happens when you get to drive celebrities around."

"Yeah, maybe I'll have a chance with Brooke Shields yet," he said with an awkward little laugh. "Look, Wynne, do you really care about Hawk or is it just *who* he is? You know celebrities don't always make the greatest husbands and fathers."

"Yes, I know, Rick," Wynne agreed, keeping her voice low, soft and hopefully at its most soothing. She could tell that Rick was agitated, and although she knew she really had no reason to reproach herself, she still felt slightly responsible nonetheless. "But I do truly love Hawk. It isn't who he is."

Rick gave a grim-faced nod, and Wynne hoped he would now make an exit line and depart. But Rick was determined not to be easily discouraged. "Wynne, would it make any difference if I told you that I really cared for you?" he asked.

"Oh, Rick! It just makes a difference in my feelings for *you*," Wynne said impulsively. "I'd thought of us as merely casual friends. Now I will always think of you as my very dear and good friend."

Wynne hoped that her reply might make Rick feel a little better. Hopefully he wouldn't think her condescending for she really did like him quite a bit.

"Okay, Wynne." Rick stood up. "Would you answer just one more question for me?"

"If I can," she said, feeling quite helpless when faced with his obvious sadness and disappointment.

"If Hawk Saddler hadn't flown in and swept you off your feet, do you think you could have learned to love me?"

Wynne flinched inwardly. How could she answer such a question to which there was only one blunt reply? But apparently Rick did want the truth. He had asked for it. Maybe he needed it to set him free.

Wordlessly, Wynne shook her head. Rick did not speak again. He simply turned to the door and let himself out.

Wynne told the children separately, guessing correctly that they would have two entirely different reactions to the matter. "Isn't getting married where you have a wedding?" asked Nona.

"Yes, it is," Wynne affirmed and Nona raised shining green eyes.

"Oh, good! I like weddings."

She'd attended just one in her life, that of Becky Grove, a young cousin of Wynne's who had married at Christmas. Since Nona was notorious for coming out with startling statements at wholly inappropriate moments, Wynne would never have taken the child of her own volition. It was Becky who'd insisted otherwise, reminding Wynne that it would just be a family wedding.

Nona had been well coached before the event and, mercifully, behaved herself. Wynne certainly intended to coach Nona further before her own wedding.

"I liked Becky's long white dress and what she wore on her head!" Nona exclaimed excitedly. "Mama, what was that word for the stuff on her head?"

"A veil," Wynne corrected absently. "Look, Nona, my wedding won't be like that."

"Why not?" demanded her daughter indignantly.

"Because it's my second time to get married. I'll just have a nice dress, which won't be white and a bouq—"

"Will your dress be long, Mama? Will you wear a veil? You won't? Why not? Why don't you get a yeller dress? I like yeller, and I'll bet Mr. Hawk does too. Mama, can I throw pedals?"

"Throw *what*, Nona? Oh, you mean rose petals. No, dear, this is going to be a much simpler wedding than that."

"Can I have a new dress? Can it be long?"

Yes, the discussion with Nona definitely took a different tack.

Steve heard Wynne out in silence and only a slight tightening of the child's face gave any indication of his emotions. He asked a great many questions when he was given the opportunity to do so. Wynne answered as best she could Steve's concerns about a new school, new friends and a new home in a different state.

"Steve, we'll all be going to Arizona in another month or six weeks to see Hawk's ranch. I hope you'll like it—I hope we *all* will—but if you don't, I want you to tell me."

"Oh, I'll bet Arizona will be neat." Steven raised an eager face to Wynne. "I've always wanted to go there.

They have lotsa Indians too, y'know. Apaches and Comanches, Navajos..."

His voice trailed off and Wynne saw that tightening of Steve's face again. "What's worrying you, Steve?"

"Well, it's—" He paused, then added confidentially, "Mama, it's Hawk."

"You don't like him?" Wynne said, startled.

"Oh, no! I like him lots. I know he's an important man to the Indians and—and it's great he wants to marry you. But, Mama, I don't think he likes *me*!"

"Oh, Steve!" Wynne found herself pulling Rick's trick; she stared down at a fold of bedspread she held between her fingers rather than look at the child. Anxiously she pleated the material with a nervous hand. "Honey, what makes you say that about Hawk?" Her own question forced her to look up.

"I don't know." Steve gazed back at her with a tenyear-old's honest, candid expression. "I know he acts nice and says nice things. I just don't think he means 'em!"

Wynne could not look into her child's open face and tell an outright lie. A scoffed, "Oh, you don't know what you're talking about!" would not reassure Steve and might even start him doubting his own accurate perceptions—and he would need just such perceptions to move satisfactorily through life.

Wynne selected careful words as she framed her reply. "Steve, I know Hawk isn't used to children and he's not very comfortable around them. That's his problem, sweetheart, not yours. Hawk has promised to try harder to understand you and be your friend. We've talked together about it. But if you feel that Hawk still isn't friendly, or if he ever says or does anything to make you unhappy, you must tell me about this too."

What a way to sabotage a stepfather! Wynne thought, then her common sense asserted itself. To make such a remark to Nona would invite disaster since that little rascal, with her overactive imagination, would dream up God knows what! But Steve was a sensible, levelheaded boy who already liked Hawk tremendously and yearned only to be liked by him in return.

Already Steve's blue eyes were glowing again. He had eyes so much like his father and grandfather, Wynne thought. "Mama, I'll betcha Hawk does okay with Nona and me 'cause he's Choctaw."

"What's that got to do with anything?" asked the mystified Wynne.

Steve was eager to enlighten her. "Well, Choctaws only fought when they had to—and then they only killed *men*. They took white women and children captive. And they adopted the white kids and raised them up to be Choctaws. Then, when the adopted kids got old enough, they became full members of the tribe too."

"How interesting," said Wynne. "What happened to the white women?"

"Oh, they got married off to braves. I wonder how they liked that!" Steve laughed.

"I expect it was something of a culture shock," Wynne said, laughing too. She leaned down and gave Steve a warm hug. "Well, your news about Choctaw customs is reassuring. I'll bet Hawk does okay with you and Nona. Let's give him a chance."

"You bet!" Steve said enthusiastically.

This time Hawk stayed in touch just as he'd promised. He never wrote Wynne more than could fit on a postcard, but he sent those regularly and phoned her every second or third evening. Those chats, while circumspect, still held a quiet and intimate familiarity, almost like that of long-married couples, Wynne thought. Their minds and hearts were so linked to each other.

Also, during his phone calls, Hawk traced the history of the Navajo-Hopi conflict and brought Wynne up to date on the resettlement as it progressed. This was an especially difficult one since it involved sacred traditions of both tribes and each group felt strongly about their position.

Hawk sounded tired a lot of the time, and Wynne wished she could be with him to be sure he ate properly and got enough rest. "What did you have for dinner?" she often asked and grew concerned when Hawk replied too often, "Oh, I just sent out for a sandwich.

"You need proper meals and sufficient sleep to function at your best," Wynne reminded Hawk lovingly.

"You can reform me as soon as we're married, you nag," he responded with a laugh. "Women always do, anyway—"

"We do not!" Wynne interrupted hotly.

"And I'll cooperate quite willingly," Hawk continued with another laugh. "I can't wait to have this solitary life-style of mine altered! Say, should I buy you a diamond engagement ring or something?"

"How about 'something,'" Wynne suggested. She had received a traditional engagement ring from Tom, and that had been fine since she was marrying into his family and traditions. But now she knew Hawk would undoubtedly prefer a different symbol.

"A something it is," he said. "Matter of fact, I've already got an idea. Want me to tell you? Or do you want to be surprised?"

"Surprise me!" Wynne urged as excited as a little kid on the eve of a birthday.

"All right. I'll bring it and give it to you six long, long days from now."

"Oh, Hawk, the time will fly," Wynne said reassuringly.

"It hasn't so far," he grumbled. "It seems like a year or longer since we went to Tahlequah."

So, the days dragged for Hawk while for Wynne, they flew since she was busy with so many new and exciting matters connected with her engagement. But both knew that only when they were together once more would life be really right and good once again.

Eventually the six days passed, and Wynne was excitedly packing a bag to accompany Hawk to Mississippi where she would meet his family.

Chapter Nine

Wynne had flown many times before but never in a small private plane like Hawk's silver Cessna. She sat in the passenger's seat beside him, watching in fascination while this man she loved talked over his radio with what passed for a control tower in Arrow, Oklahoma.

Today Hawk wore a black flight suit with lots of zippered pockets and matching black leather boots. His eyes were keen and alert, his hair as glossy as patent leather, and Wynne watched him eagerly, thinking he was undoubtedly the smartest and best-looking man she'd ever seen in her life.

He was also a well-rested one today, Wynne knew, although Hawk was something less than grateful for this since he and Wynne had spent the night apart. She'd shared his frustration, but when Hawk had first arrived at the Norwoods' house last night, it was already in a state closely resembling pandemonium. Wynne's parents had just returned from Texas an hour before when Hawk was introduced into the assembly, turning it into a riot of greetings, toasts and celebrations.

Hawk had presented Wynne with her engagement present, and she had found breathtaking the ornate silver necklace with its graceful design of corn, a symbol sacred to the Choctaws, Steve had told her excitedly. Wynne's necklace exactly matched the silver ring Hawk wore on his little finger, and he'd allowed Wynne a peek at the simple wedding ring, which matched her necklace. He would place the band on her finger the day they were married.

Overall, it had been a jubilant and happy occasion. Somehow, in the midst of the excitement, Wynne and her mother-in-law had managed to get dinner on the table.

Hawk had obviously liked Wynne's parents, and they had just as obviously liked and approved of him. But Hawk had looked very weary and even admitted to Wynne that he was tired. Shortly after ten o'clock he had bidden everyone good-night.

"Hawk..." Rather anxiously Wynne had followed him out through the carport and to his rental car. There Hawk had turned and swept her up for the kisses he couldn't bestow in front of the others. Then, after a long, breathless, desire-filled yet frustrating time, he had released her gently.

"I know you and your parents have a lot of news to catch up on so I don't expect you to come with me," he had said generously. "I'm bushed, anyway. I doubt if I could do anything for you tonight."

Wynne knew otherwise since she was pressed up so closely against Hawk, but she also knew too, that he had flown that day and would again tomorrow. She didn't like the look of those black circles under his eyes and wanted him to get the rest he so obviously needed.

Now those circles were gone. Hawk had slept for ten hours and phoned Wynne in abject apology because they would be so late leaving for Mississippi. "I understand," Wynne had assured him. "Believe me, I'd rather have a rested pilot than a tired one."

Barry and Wynne had been the only ones in the kitchen at the time of Hawk's call. Peg and the kids were outside, enjoying a sunny Saturday. "Humph!" said Barry, turning away from the coffee pot with a brimming mug. "I wouldn't have that guy as *my* pilot, period."

Wynne bit her lip but said nothing. Apparently Barry was going to have to come around by slow degrees. She made lemonade for the thirsty children as they came clamoring into the kitchen and again answered Nona's questions about why she and Steve couldn't come along on the trip together. "Famblies are s'pposed to be together," insisted the wily Nona.

"I told you, dear. There isn't room for you and Steve at Hawk's parents' home," Wynne had replied to her daughter.

Now, as she and Hawk sat awaiting clearance for takeoff, Wynne wondered if her excuse had been even partially true. The only reason that Steve and Nona were not along, insofar as Wynne knew, was simply that they had not been asked to come.

Wynne could and did make up a half dozen reasons to excuse Hawk. He had been so excessively tired and busy, he just hadn't thought of it. Or he really needed time alone with Wynne to relax and recharge his batteries. Or he felt that he and Wynne required privacy to discuss any number of important matters. Or he thought that Wynne and his family would get better acquainted if— "Et cetera ad infinitum," Wynne sighed to herself.

Her children had been disappointed, and she was disappointed for them. They had never seen the Old South and would have found Mississippi with its meandering bayous and trees draped in Spanish moss quite unlike their own state. The antebellum homes and perfumed magnolias would have been a novelty to the kids. And Steve would have loved seeing a large Indian reservation!

Had Hawk been *ashamed* to bring such white-skinned kids home to his parents? Was he reluctant to introduce Steve and Nona as his future stepchildren?

Wynne looked out the window at the small airfield from which they would depart momentarily and prayed that these were not the reasons Hawk had failed to include the children. But from a wellspring of truth deep inside herself, she wondered and pondered.

The radio crackled. "Cessna, you are cleared for takeoff."

"Roger," Hawk responded, then grinned at Wynne. "Hang on, honey, here we go!"

Wynne nodded and smiled back at Hawk as she watched him push forward on the throttle. The airplane lunged ahead, its engines building rapidly to a loud full roar. They raced down the long, white concrete strip and then, suddenly and more smoothly than Wynne could have imagined, they were airborne and gliding above the end of the runway. She turned to look out her side window and saw the ground falling away and mint-colored fields ahead. Then they were spiraling high into a perfect blue sky and just a faint touch of uneasiness suddenly clamped around Wynne's throat and squeezed.

She wasn't afraid for one minute of Hawk's flying, nor did she question the safety of the plane. No, what suddenly frightened Wynne was the realization that she would soon be meeting her future in-laws. What if they didn't like her? What if they dared say as much to Hawk?

All at once it was quite easy for Wynne to sympathize with exactly what Hawk must have been going through every time he walked up to the door of her house!

"And, Wynne, this is my sister, Lona. Just call her Lonnie. And this is her husband, Buck Tubbe. Well, this can't be everybody! Where's Zia? Where's Heleema?"

Hawk's parents smiled broadly but did not reply. Already Wynne noticed they were leaving the explanations to Lonnie, their chic older daughter.

Wynne covertly studied the two people who had given Hawk life and thought that she could have recognized his father anywhere. Despite being worn and stooped from years of tending cattle and trying to grow crops in red clay soil that was notoriously poor for farming, Hawk's father looked almost exactly like him. Mr. Saddler's face was a pleasing preview of what Hawk's might be one day, still handsome and stamped with kindliness and character.

Hawk's mother was stout and several inches shorter than her husband. Frankly plain, she lacked the physical attractiveness of her husband and children, but the goodness and integrity of her soul clearly shone through her dark eyes. Wynne knew that Hawk considered his mother one of the major influences in his life, so she was pleased and touched to have Mrs. Saddler practically beaming on her. *She'll be another mother-in-law I'll love,* Wynne thought with relief.

Hawk's parents had dressed in their Choctaw finest to meet their future daughter-in-law, and Wynne found their unusual and distinctive attire fascinating. Hawk's mother's blue dress, beautifully handmade, had long sleeves and a full skirt that reached to her ankles. Over the shirt she wore a long white apron. Both dress and apron were decorated with bright designs and multicolored ribbons, and she also wore an elaborate beaded necklace.

Hawk's father's clothes were just as unusual to Wynne. He wore a colorful white shirt trimmed in ribbon and an extravagant ribboned belt atop white slacks. On his head, Mr. Saddler wore a black felt hat with a colorful band. Wynne couldn't help exclaiming over their clothes, and Hawk's parents' smiles grew even broader.

By contrast Lonnie and Buck Tubbe were typical of a younger Indian generation. Lonnie wore smart black slacks, black low-heeled pumps and a hot-pink blouse. Her hair was beauty-shop fresh, short and permed. Buck wore suit slacks and a casual short-sleeved shirt.

"Zia's gone to get Heleema from the clinic in Jackson," Lonnie answered her brother's questions about the others and she and Hawk exchanged a significant glance.

Zia was Hawk's younger sister, Wynne knew. She was divorced and the mother of three small children, a situation with which Wynne could readily identify. Lonnie also had three children although hers were somewhat older. Since all six kids were present here at

the airport, staring at Wynne with undisguised curiosity, she couldn't help but think about the fun Steve and
Nona would have had. Since Wynne's children had
more of Tom's outgoing nature than her own reserve,
they had never been shy about making new friends.

Maybe one day before long we'll all be here, Wynne
consoled herself, then she began to think of what Hawk
had told her about Heleema.

Heleema Wiggins was Hawk's first cousin and had
apparently been quite a favorite of his when they were
kids although she was two or three years older than
Hawk. Almost twenty years ago, when Heleema was a
young married woman, she'd had a nervous break-
down and her husband had promptly abandoned her.
When her own family had proved unable to care for her
adequately, Hawk's parents had taken her in.

"Heleema has never recovered," Hawk had told
Wynne. "Most of the time she's like a ghost, tranquil-
ized out of her skull. But, periodically, she grows re-
sistant to a certain tranquilizer and gets quite agitated.
Then she'll walk the floor talking nonsense for hours
until the folks can get her stabilized on another medi-
cation and calmed down again."

"How tragic," Wynne had said sadly.

"Yeah, Heleema's had a rough life," Hawk agreed.
But he hadn't amplified his statement and, because
Wynne was happy and so much in love, she had been
content not to delve too deeply into the unhappy subject. Now, though, she wondered just exactly what had
happened to Heleema. At some point during the next
couple of days Wynne felt sure she'd have a chance to
ask Hawk or Lonnie about the poor woman.

They left the airport in three cars. The first, driven by
Lonnie, was the one to which Hawk had led Wynne.

Buck and four of the kids were in the lead car while Hawk's parents and the remaining two grandchildren brought up the rear.

Hawk gave Wynne's hand an affectionate squeeze. "Honey, will you understand if Lonnie and I talk a little business?"

"Sure," Wynne said and looked out of her window at the countryside of lush green and rolling hills. She watched a herd of cattle move slowly up one hill and decided that Mississippi looked about like she'd expected. But the summer heat was so humid and intense that Wynne found breathing difficult.

She couldn't help overhearing Hawk and Lonnie's "business," which seemed to be a general rundown on various family members. Pop's blood pressure was staying under control, Lonnie assured Hawk, but Momma just couldn't seem to stick to her diabetic diet. Heleema was neither better nor worse than usual and had just spent a couple of days at the mental health clinic for a follow-up evaluation. Zia was dating a perfectly wonderful guy who worked at the industrial park for Chahta Development. As for Uncle HoPo. . . .

When the conversation turned to more distant family members Wynne ceased to listen and did more looking instead. Lonnie zoomed them down a rippling highway at the maximum legal speed. From a few road signs, Wynne saw that they had apparently bypassed Philadelphia and were headed directly toward the reservation.

"Wynne, we're going to Momma's house first," Lonnie said, interrupting her discourse with Hawk on various cousins. "Momma wouldn't have it any other way. But you and Hawk will spend the nights with Buck and me since we have a guest room."

"Fine," Wynne said agreeably.

Signs soon marked the start of the Choctaw reservation. The green hills and dales, which continued to roll on toward the horizon, were heavily forested, and Wynne identified pine trees, oaks and willows. The car sailed over bridges built to span bayous and Wynne recalled her son Steve's announcement that "bayou" was a Choctaw word. She had been surprised, thinking the word was French.

Now Hawk gripped Wynne's hand again. "Tell me, how does it feel to be near the center of the world?"

He spoke teasingly and Wynne blinked. "Oh, what makes you think we're near the center of the world?" she asked.

"Because Choctaw legend says so. The ancient ones believed that the center of the world was at our sacred mound, Nanih Waiya."

"You mentioned that mound on the first day we met," Wynne said, yielding to an irresistible impulse to reach up and stroke Hawk's cheek. Beneath her palm his skin felt pleasantly warm and smooth.

Hawk turned his head to kiss her fingers. "So I did. But I wasn't sure if you'd remember."

"Oh, I remember everything you've ever told me." Wynne smiled, and Lonnie gave a sigh.

"Ah, true love. Are you two really sure you want to mess it up by getting married?" she demanded.

"*I'm* sure," Wynne and Hawk said simultaneously, their eyes meeting and holding. Then they laughed from the sheer, pure joy of it all. "When will I get to see Nanih Waiya?" Wynne asked Hawk.

"Soon," he said with a significant arch of his eyebrows. "It's an historical site and state park now. Since no one should miss seeing 'the center of the world,' I'll take you there. Incidentally, look around and you'll see a rejuvenated and thriving Indian reservation."

"Oh." Wynne swiveled her head as Lonnie turned off the highway onto another road and large attractive buildings came into view. They sprawled over a hilltop beneath thick pines. Hawk and Lonnie pointed various sites out to Wynne: tribal offices, museum, high school and gymnasium, new hospital and pleasant homes of recent vintage.

"But it's beautiful!" Wynne turned to stare incredulously at Hawk, remembering the dire picture of the reservation that he'd painted for her once.

"Yeah, a lot can happen in almost twenty years," he commented mildly.

It was Lonnie who enthusiastically related to Wynne the Choctaws' economic success story. Over eighty percent of the adult population were now gainfully employed since plants that made automotive parts had sprung into existence. Numerous other businesses had been born and were flourishing as well.

"We've had a very enlightened tribal chief for many years," Lonnie said excitedly. "Not to mention many others in the tribe, like my husband and especially my brother, who caught the vision and fought for progress, education and economic opportunities for our people."

"How wonderful," Wynne said, impressed, then she turned back to Hawk. She watched his proud profile as he stared out at the reservation, obviously noting small but significant changes since his last visit here.

"It used to be commonly thought that Indians were lazy and worthless. Give 'em a whiskey bottle and a government welfare check, and they were satisfied," he said tautly. "*We* knew better!"

Wynne slipped her arm through Hawk's and hugged it tight against her body to say, wordlessly, that she understood.

A moment later, a different question occurred to her. "How did your family escape being driven to Oklahoma over the Trail of Tears?" Wynne's own study of Indian histories had taught her that the Choctaws and Chickasaws were among the first tribes to be moved west.

"According to family tradition, our ancestors knew 'The white man spoke with forked tongue,'" Lonnie quoted.

"Thousands of Choctaws simply melted into the woods. They reappeared later, after the army troops had gone," Hawk added thoughtfully. "Apparently the Saddlers have always been a suspicious lot. Later, as white settlers moved in to claim what had been Choctaw lands, there weren't enough Indians left here to scare them so the two cultures have co-existed ever since. Eventually, of course, there was a third culture as well since many settlers brought black slaves."

"Oh," said Wynne. She glanced through the windshield, her attention attracted by a novel sight. Then she burst into surprised laughter.

"What?" said Hawk.

"The road sign!" she choked.

It was a standard-size Mississippi road sign with a bright green background, but on this one, the road numbers were superimposed over a large white arrowhead.

"Oh yeah, those arrowheads are used all over the reservation," Hawk said, squeezing Wynne's hand again. "Just another mile and we'll be at Momma and Pop's place."

He looked and sounded as excited as the kid he'd once been, she thought, and a great rush of love washed over Wynne as she watched him.

Lonnie, who had slowed the car to a crawl, now began to accelerate again. Up and down they went over a winding road that snaked around the rolling hills.

"There," Hawk exclaimed a few minutes later. "See the house?"

It was a nice-looking brick dwelling set in a grove of tall pines. "That isn't where we grew up by any means," said Lonnie, almost as if she could read Wynne's mind. "We grew up in a tiny tarpaper shack without lights or running water."

"When did your parents buy this house?" Wynne asked.

"Oh, just a few years ago, when my generous brother gave them the money and insisted they get a better place," Lonnie informed Wynne.

"How good of you, Hawk," Wynne exclaimed, swinging back to him.

He looked uncomfortable under the weight of both Wynne and Lonnie's praise. "Pop was looking around for another place, anyway. Actually, I'm not sure Momma's ever been very comfortable in what she calls 'this big grand house.' She's downright *scared* of the dishwasher and still washes dishes by hand. And she thinks air conditioning and central heat are probably immoral."

"Why?" Wynne cast a puzzled look at him, anxious to fathom more of the attitudes and ways of his parents.

"Because summer is supposed to be hot and winter cold," Hawk explained.

"Oh," said Wynne understandingly. Then, as they drew closer to the house, she saw the vast number of cars and trucks parked in front as well as lined up bumper to bumper in the driveway. "It looks like we'll have a lot of company."

"Looks like a whole damned army," Hawk said, his lips tightening in resignation. "My God, Lonnie, just how many folks did Momma invite to drop over?"

"Only the family. A few close friends. A small group of community bigwigs. You know Momma."

"Yeah, that's practically the whole tribe right there." Hawk leaned down and pressed a soft kiss on Wynne's cheek. "Good luck, honey. Try not to get lost in the throng, and if you need me, just yell real loud!"

"Oh, you'll enjoy it, Wynne," Lonnie smiled as she stopped behind a dusty pickup truck.

Lonnie proved correct for Wynne did enjoy meeting all of Hawk's cousins, his lifelong friends and especially his vivacious younger sister, Zia, and her pleasant-faced boyfriend. Everyone was friendly and welcoming to Wynne, and absolutely everybody had brought 'some little something' for a huge lunch, which was held outside at picnic tables set beneath the trees. Wynne thought she'd never seen so much food or so many Choctaws in her life.

Only one encounter proved disturbing to Wynne and that was when she met the unfortunate Heleema Wiggins. Heleema was a tall woman in her late thirties. Although she was amply built, she bore herself with a queen's regal carriage, and it was obvious that she'd been beautiful once. Vestiges of her former beauty still remained, but her huge black eyes held a world of pain and confusion. As Hawk had said, Heleema moved through the crowd like a ghost; she appeared to be searching, always searching, for someone or was it something? When sunlight struck Heleema's long thick braids, Wynne saw that the woman's hair had a substantial amount of gray. Ordinarily, Indian women did not turn gray so young and Wynne's curiosity about the poor, dazed woman increased even more.

Since she didn't know what to do for Heleema, she was relieved to see Hawk reach up and snare his cousin, slipping a gentle hand around her waist. "Come sit beside me, Heleema," he offered.

"Hawk?" Heleema said skeptically. "Is that really you, Hawk?"

"Yes, it's me."

Heleema sat down beside Hawk on the steps of the front porch and peered at him closely. Then, apparently satisfied that he was genuine, she reached out a timid hand to stroke his arm.

Someone else had witnessed the affectionate little scene. "Oh good," breathed Lonnie. "Now Heleema will stay put for a while. Hawk has always had a soothing effect on her."

"Lonnie, whatever happened to Heleema?" Wynne asked in a low voice.

"Didn't Hawk tell you?" Lonnie said, obviously startled by the omission. Then she sighed. "No, I guess he wouldn't. He can scarcely bring himself to discuss what happened to Heleema or to Tishti either. But I know they're the reasons why Hawk lives in Arizona now. Let's see if we can find a place to sit down and talk."

"Good," said Wynne agreeably, then she glanced around in growing dismay. Clusters of people, standing and sitting, seemed to be everywhere. "Gad, *where*?"

"The kitchen," Lonnie said swiftly. "Nobody wants to be stuck in there now that the dishes are done."

Quietly, the two women slipped inside the cool still house and took refuge at the large round table in the deserted kitchen. Wynne declined Lonnie's offer of tea or coffee, and with a nod Hawk's sister plunged immediately into her story.

"Hawk and Heleema were close friends when they were kids, Wynne, as well as being cousins. If you want to know what I really think, I believe Heleema was Hawk's first secret love. Of course, he was only about thirteen or fourteen then and Heleema was three years older. But she was so lovely in those days that a lot of Indian boys had crushes on her." Lonnie paused to draw a deep breath. "They weren't the only ones either."

"Oh?" said Wynne, alert to Lonnie's significant pause. "Who else found Heleema attractive?"

"His name was Todd Wiggins. He was a blond, blue-eyed young man who also happened to be wild and immature. Todd worked on one of the road crews who were resurfacing roads all over the reservation. Apparently, he met Heleema one day when she was walking over to her grandmother's house. It's important to remember that Heleema had been raised like an Indian princess. She really thought she was something special, and there were always men around her who had agreed. Anyway, Heleema and Todd ran off together, and it nearly killed her folks because they knew enough about human nature to know that both those kids were young and weak. It also wrenched the hearts of several young Choctaw men."

A faraway look crept into Lonnie's dark eyes. "Todd did marry Heleema. She'd insisted on it before she'd go to bed with him. But that was about the last decent thing he ever did. He drank too much, and anytime he really got crocked he treated Heleema like a common blanket squaw. Naturally she was outraged, but when she objected Todd beat her into submission. She should have left him, of course, and gone back home the first time he beat her up. But she was too proud. Too young and stubborn to admit she'd been wrong. So she stayed."

"And things just went from bad to worse," Wynne surmised. She felt a sinking feeling deep in the pit of her stomach and wasn't really sure she wanted to hear the end of this story. But she'd asked Lonnie for it, so she had to steel herself inwardly and keep listening.

"One night Todd invited a bunch of his drinking buddies to come over," Lonnie continued. "He and Heleema were living in a mobile home in Philadelphia. Well, the guys played cards at first. Gradually they got drunker and rowdier. At last the guests decided that what they needed were some women." Lonnie paused again, as though searching for words. "Todd proved an overly generous host."

"Oh, no!" Wynne exclaimed, her hands flying up involuntarily to cover her mouth.

"I heard it took four men to hold Heleema down for—for the first man. After that, she didn't fight any more and then men passed her around all weekend. She cried and cried, but they were beyond mercy. When they finally got through using her, someone noticed that she hadn't had a thing to say for hours. By then Heleema was completely mute and catatonic from shock. She didn't speak again for several months."

"Were those beasts arrested and tried for rape?" Wynne asked tightly. Already, though, she sensed the answer.

"No, they got scared when they realized the shape Heleema was in—as well they should! I guess they knew the men in Heleema's family would come after them. So they packed and scattered. Todd, too. He left Heleema sitting there naked in that wreck of a trailer. If her brother hadn't happened by a day or two later, she probably would have died from starvation and thirst. It took months of psychiatric treatment before Heleema could reveal exactly what had happened. She's never come to grips with it, and she's never been the same person since. Oh, so many, many people were hurt by what happened to Heleema!"

"And Hawk was among them," Wynne suggested softly.

"Yes, it hurt him badly. Hawk knew what Heleema was and what she should have become. Instead—" Lonnie broke off with an eloquent shrug of her shoulders.

"God, how awful," Wynne said in a whisper while an involuntary shudder ran through her whole body. The story, sad and depressing as it was, nevertheless helped her to understand Hawk better. At last she could appreciate what had goaded him to lash out at her, as he'd done once. Now she knew why he'd said, "What would you have done if your husband had gotten drunk and beaten you?"

That question, she recalled, had roused both her ire and indignation. But she simply hadn't understood.

Now Lonnie spoke up, revealing an obvious curiosity. "You were married to a white man, weren't you, Wynne?"

"Yes. But my husband was one hundred eighty degrees removed from that creep Heleema married," Wynne said heatedly.

"Do you have a picture of him? And your kids? I'd like to see all of them since we're going to be in the same family soon."

Lonnie's interest was genuine, Wynne saw. "I have pictures in my billfold," she replied. "Now, where on earth did we stash our purses?"

"Momma's bedroom. I'll get them," Lonnie volunteered.

She returned a couple of mintues later, trailed by Hawk's beaming and bright-eyed mother. "Momma wants to see your kids too, if you don't mind."

"Of course I don't mind." Wynne opened her wallet, withdrew the plastic folder that held her photographs and passed it to Lonnie. "That's a recent shot of Steve and Nona. The picture of Tom was taken five years ago."

The women bent appreciatively over the folder of photographs. "Look at that red hair!" Hawk's mother exclaimed in delight and Wynne knew Nona was claiming attention as usual. "Are her eyes really so *green*?"

"Green as grass," Wynne confirmed. "Steve's are blue."

"Oh, let me see!"

The kitchen door swung open. "So here you all are," Hawk said. "I've been looking for you, especially my girl." He draped a possessive arm over Wynne's shoulder, and she smiled up at him. "What are you ladies doing?"

"Wynne's showing us pictures of her late husband and her kids," Lonnie said.

"Oh." Hawk's voice dropped as though chilled by a wintry blast. Wynne felt the arm around her shoulder change from warm vibrant flesh into stone. A moment later, Hawk drew it away.

He had been reminded again, Wynne knew, and he'd reacted as he always did. And, damn it, *why*? Indians traditionally loved and appreciated children. Why, the women had responded to Steve and Nona with exclamations of delight.

Lonnie chose that exact moment to speak. "Wynne, your kids are cute as pie! I can't wait to see them."

"You should have brought pretty children with you," Hawk's mother said to Wynne, and there was just a tiny touch of reproof in her voice.

Wynne could hardly indict Hawk in front of his own mother and announce that it was his fault that the kids weren't along. "Oh, I'm sure you'll meet Steve and Nona before long," she said, even-voiced.

"Your husband was a good man?" Mrs. Saddler questioned, handing back the folder of pictures to Wynne.

"Yes, a very good man," Wynne confirmed.

Hawk's mother nodded with satisfaction. "He has a good face."

Yes, Tom did, Wynne thought defiantly. Hawk's mother could even read it from a photograph. Why didn't Hawk ask to see it and look for himself?

But he didn't. He had turned away, his back to them, and stood at the sink. Slowly and deliberately he filled a glass with water and began to drink it.

All right, so Hawk had a few good reasons to feel as he did. His wife, entrusted to the white doctor's care, had died, and Heleema had been raped and brutalized. But a person couldn't condemn an entire race for the actions of a *few*! There were always the oddballs, the misfits and deviates in any group of people.

If Hawk can't adjust to the fact that I've been married before and have two very attractive and intelligent kids from that marriage, Wynne thought hotly, then he—

Lonnie's voice interrupted Wynne's angry train of thought. "Hawk says you two are getting married in September. What's the date, Wynne? As busy as Buck and I are with the kids, I want to get it circled on our calendar right now."

Hawk's mother beamed again and nodded her agreement. Wynne was uncomfortably aware that Hawk had turned from the sink to stare at her.

He had already asked her twice to set an official wedding date and Wynne had stalled and evaded. Now she knew exactly why she had instinctively stalled. No matter how much she loved Hawk, she wasn't going to give her kids a stepfather who couldn't accept them. More and more, Wynne feared that Hawk would never fully love and accept them.

"I'm sorry, Lonnie, but I'll just have to let you know the date later. My mother has been away, and I've been waiting to discuss it with her," Wynne said smoothly.

She had gone from stalling and evading to downright lying, Wynne knew. Isn't it interesting to see what love can do to a basically honest person, she thought, amazed at her own nefarious talents.

Lonnie looked slightly taken aback. "Do let me know as soon as you can," she urged.

"I promise." Wynne reached over and covered Lonnie's slim tawny hand with her own. "Why, I wouldn't think of getting married without having all of Hawk's family with us."

More prevarication, Wynne knew. Because with increasing frequency, she was beginning to think of not getting married at all! Of course, she couldn't think of completely giving Hawk up either. Maybe they should simply wind up having a very long affair.

Long enough to last until her children had grown up? Nona was only five. Were Wynne and Hawk to wait twelve or thirteen *years* until they could marry and live in peace? Wynne felt skeptical that this could work. And would Hawk even settle for an affair? she wondered with a chilling sense of premonition. She feared that he would not. Hawk wanted a normal married life *now*. He wanted children of his own.

Wynne raised her eyes and found him still standing by the sink, watching her tensely. What had been reflected on her face? she wondered. Hawk looked so somber that a pang shot through her. How she hated for him to be hurt when life had hurt him so badly already! Impulsively she got up and walked over to link her arm through his.

Instantly she felt his warm hand clasp her own tightly. *Oh God!* He really loved her deeply and Wynne knew it. That's what made this whole dilemma so wretched. Wynne smiled up at him, to wipe that tense, tragic look off his face, letting all the love in her own heart shine through. After a moment, his lips gave that little upward quirk.

"What do you say we get out of here?" he asked her tenderly. "We've been polite long enough, and I really do want to show you Nanih Waiya."

"And I want to see it with you," she replied, her fingers tightening over his.

* * *

Later, much, much later, and after a lot of unexpected things had happened, Wynne would still remember that ride in Hawk's father's pickup truck through the green and rolling countryside to quiet Nanih Waiya. Because it lay off the beaten track, it was not a terribly well-visited site. Except for a park employee staying inside a hut with his air conditioner, they had the place to themselves.

Wynne would always remember standing in silence, her hand in Hawk's, as daylight waned and the great sacred mound of the Choctaws—the very center of the earth itself, as they had once believed—lay before them. Then she and Hawk slowly climbed the wooden steps that led up one side of its grassy slopes and surveyed the world from the mound's flat top.

Wynne would also remember how, later that evening at Lonnie's modern home, she and Hawk had slipped back to the guest bedroom. They were each aware of the long weeks that had passed since they'd last been alone together. Across Lonnie's supper table, their eyes met and telegraphed the message of mutual longing and desire.

In the clean and airy bedroom they shed their clothes, then went into an adjoining bathroom and showered together. Hawk claimed the privilege of drying off Wynne, his hands lingering and clinging to her curves. She pressed her own hands on his water-beaded shoulders and felt the heated skin below them.

"Momma's kind of ticked off at me," Hawk admitted as he knelt before Wynne and lifted one of her feet to dry. "She wanted us to stay at her house."

Wynne gazed down into Hawk's thick wet hair and slowly threaded her fingers through its warm blackness. Already she was trembling from just his preliminary touches, and as he pressed a kiss on the sole of her foot her desire for him grew immense. "So why didn't we stay there?" she asked him huskily.

"Because Momma would never have understood that you and I need to be together. You would have been bunking with Heleema while I slept on the sofa!"

It didn't sound like a very pleasant prospect when the alternative was to sleep held fast in his arms. Still, Wynne hated to think of Hawk's mother's feelings being hurt. "Surely we could have put up with it for a night or two?" she said tentatively.

"No." Hawk's voice was decisive. Slowly, ever so slowly, he began to kiss a path up Wynne's leg. From foot to shin, knee to thigh, his mouth blazed flaming arrows. He kissed across the softness of her stomach and then higher still, until Wynne's arms seized him tightly. "I couldn't stand it, Wynne, not when I want you so badly and need you so much!"

His lips caressed the creamy softness of her shoulders and burned up her throat. Mindlessly, Wynne clutched him even closer, finding places on his own cheek and neck to kiss.

Hawk drew back momentarily, and they looked deep into each other's eyes. Then he led Wynne over to the old-fashioned double bed and stretched her out there. His mouth circled the yielding mound of one high-pointed breast, then fastened on the other, sucking hungrily.

Wynne's hands slid down from his waist to his slim hard buttocks where the skin had remained almost baby soft. She was shaking, on fire with the need he could always arouse so easily within her. "Oh, Hawk, I couldn't stand it, either!'' she cried and then, with exclamations of excitement and bliss, they came together again.

Chapter Ten

Talk about one snake-bit trip!

Hawk stood by gate six at the Tucson airport, waiting for word on Wynne's plane which was running late. Just how late, the young airline agent behind the counter didn't know as yet.

Hawk was seething with anger, his insides wrenched by anxiety, but he certainly wasn't surprised. Considering the trouble he'd had trying to get Wynne and her kids out here to Arizona, he wouldn't even have been surprised by a skyjacking.

Not, of course, that he was putting *that* out into the mental ethers, Hawk thought hastily. He was just superstitious enough to know that dwelling on something very often led to its almost eerie occurrence. So, for a few minutes, he simply imagined holding Wynne close in his arms again.

The only trouble with that pretty picture was that Nona immediately stuck her little red head into the act while Steve's pale blue eyes appeared to watch his mother and Hawk with consternation. God, what he wouldn't give to have Wynne arriving here minus children!

But that wasn't going to happen. Instead, Hawk knew he was being given another chance, his very last chance. If, during the next ten days, he couldn't learn to better interact with Wynne's kids then it was going to be all over between him and the only woman he had loved in years.

Scowling, Hawk paced the airport terminal, his fists jammed down in the pockets of his jeans, his boot heels ringing on the tiles. He was grateful that he had been given another chance with Wynne, damned grateful. And yet, perversely, at the very same time, he resented being on this kind of probation. Sure, he had begged Wynne for the chance. And now he felt positively desperate because things just *had* to work out well. But, underneath it all, he was angry too, because Hawk Saddler just wasn't a man to beg and crawl.

God, how had falling in love turned a once sensible man into such a blithering idiot? In Hawk's mind he had become quite a pitiful spectacle indeed.

Once he could have shrugged and walked away from any woman, even a woman he'd known well and had slept with often. But that was before Wynne.

The last six weeks had demonstrated clearly to Hawk that his once incisive mind was simply inadequate to handle this particular matter as he wished. Actually, there had never been a woman he'd *wanted* to walk away from more than Wynne with her pampered, lily-skinned kids yet his heart and his physical senses just wouldn't let him do it.

Six weeks! That's how long it had been since he and Wynne had spent any appreciable amount of time together. It had been six lousy weeks since they'd returned from their long weekend in Mississippi.

Even during those golden days at his hometown they had rarely been alone, except for the hours behind the locked door of Lonnie's guest room. But just remembering some of the sizzling scenes they'd enacted there could cause Hawk's temperature to rise. His lovely, ladylike Wynne became so wanton and wonderful when they were alone together. And that same wonderful woman could be so damn hard and implacable when it came to those fairhaired kiddies of hers!

What did Wynne expect of him where Steve and Nona were concerned—for God's sake, what? Hawk knew perfectly well that he'd busted his butt to be nice to the kids. He'd smiled at them and talked to them, but any time he would glance up at Wynne she would be wearing *that look* on her face. *That look* always told Hawk that he wasn't doing nearly as well as she'd wished.

No sooner had they rolled back down the runway in Arrow, Oklahoma, than he and Wynne had been into it all over again. Of course, in fairness, Hawk had to admit that he'd pressed her hard to set a wedding date. Finally, Wynne had gazed bleakly up at him like a small cornered animal and admitted that she really wanted to wait a while longer to marry.

Hawk had absolutely exploded from rage and frustration. *Great going, Saddler, you not only showed her what one hopping-mad Indian looks and sounds like, you scared her half to death!*

Even now Hawk winced, not letting himself remember that scene in detail. He'd been sorry for his vehement outburst from the moment he first saw the wounded expression in Wynne's ebony eyes.

"Hawk, I have not been 'jerking you around like a ring-tailed monkey'!" she had protested, quoting back to him the very words he'd just flung so angrily at her. Then she began to laugh and cry all at the same time.

Hawk had felt like laughing and crying, too. How could life be simultaneously so terrible and so wonderful? How could love hurt as badly as it did and then heal over so quickly, its agonizing pain soothed to oblivion by kisses and lovemaking? Somehow he and Wynne always managed to scale the whole gamut of emotions. But such heated confrontations left them both wrung out and as exhausted as if they'd fought an actual physical battle.

At least Wynne had not canceled their plans to marry "soon," and Hawk had even agreed to quit pressuring her for a specific date, especially since she had candidly admitted that she wanted to see what sort of home they'd have in Arizona. He knew she needed to gauge just how well the kids could adjust to it, so this long-delayed trip had been planned.

Then everything, but everything, had hung it up. Hawk's own meetings again, with the Navajos and Hopis, had interfered with the first date set for the trip. Next, Nona came down with a stomach upset on the very eve of their departure. Wynne had reached Hawk over long distance barely one hour before he'd been set to fly over to get them.

A week later Nona had recovered completely. But then it wasn't convenient for Wynne's office for her to be away since others in her department were already on vacation. Then, what had happened next? Hawk scowled more deeply and paced another few feet, trying to remember.

Oh, yeah. At that point he'd had an overnighter in Albuquerque and been scheduled to go straight back home after it was over. But when he'd neared the airport, Hawk knew he couldn't wait any longer to see Wynne. So he'd filed a new flight plan and had headed his Cessna east, not west.

He and Wynne had spent a wild and glorious couple of nights at their favorite motel in Arrow. But when Hawk had returned her to the Norwoods' house, old Barry had been out in the front yard watering the grass, and the look he'd trained on Hawk could have paralyzed a panther.

Hawk had slunk out of Wynne's driveway feeling like some foul despoiler of once virtuous women, and never mind that he was actually a respectable man with wholly decent intentions.

Right after that, Becky somebody-or-other who was newly pregnant had begun to have complications and had been hospitalized. Since she and Wynne were first cousins, Wynne had felt she had to hang around until the girl was better.

Snake-bit. Yeah, that sure fit the whole last month.

After Barry's venomous glower at him, Hawk had really not been surprised by the next development. All along, of course, he and Wynne had figured that if they could ever get the Arizona trip settled, Hawk would fly over and pick up Wynne and the kids.

No siree, not according to Big Daddy Norwood! Apparently Barry had raised such Cain over his only grandchildren being in an airplane piloted by that

Choctaw reprobate that Wynne had phoned Hawk hastily to explain the change of plans.

"Steve is just crushed," she had added softly. "He was really looking forward to flying with you."

"Sure." Hawk gave a bitter sigh, but the close-to-tears note in Wynne's voice had stopped him from saying anything more. If Wynne was actually coming at long last, what did it matter if she and the kids flew commercial? Hawk just hoped Big Daddy was the one springing for the tickets.

Now—wouldn't you know it?—the damned plane was late.

His scowl still in place, Hawk stormed back to gate six to glare again at the hapless young woman who worked there. At the sight of him, she gave a small relieved smile.

"Sir, the plane has just landed!"

"Here? It landed here?" asked Hawk suspiciously.

"Yes sir. It's taxiing in right now and will be at the gate in just a mintue," she assured him.

Actually it took a good five minutes—five more minutes for Hawk to fidget, fume and pace. Then passengers alighted, and as they came up the ramp and into the waiting area, he stared at each and every unfamiliar face. Finally the passengers quit coming.

My God, Wynne and the kids must have missed the plane! To Hawk the thought was like being drenched with a pail of icy water. Cold sweat broke out all over him and his heart pounded crazily. By now it certainly looked like all the passengers had deplaned.

Then he saw her. Wynne looked her very smartest in a cool cotton knit sweater, an ankle-length skirt and sandals. Her hair was all twisted up in a sophisticated style and pinned atop her head. She wore a resigned little smile and was shaking her head ruefully as she looked down at Nona.

The boy surged ahead, and his face split in a wide grin as he caught sight of Hawk. "Hi, Mister Hawk!" he called enthusiastically and bounded over. "You'll never guess what that dumb Nona did. She locked herself in the bathroom on the plane and we couldn't get her out for the longest!"

"Oh," Hawk said as sweet relief rushed over him, rich and intoxicating. Unconsciously his hand dropped to the boy's narrow shoulder.

Wynne had seen him now. In fact, her face lit up and she gave him a glowing smile. Nona ran toward Hawk too and began chattering excitedly about something.

"Uh-huh," he said automatically to Nona.

Hawk couldn't wrench his gaze from Wynne's face as she came toward him steadily and serenely, not rushing as the kids had, but her eyes simply spoke volumes. So much love was written there that Hawk felt emotion tighten his throat.

He stepped forward to meet her and forgot completely that he didn't approve of public displays of affection. Nothing could have stopped him from bending down to kiss Wynne, and for a long thrilling moment their lips clung hotly. Slowly, very slowly, they drew apart.

Then, in a sudden rush of sheer exuberance, Hawk bent down and scooped up Nona. She gave a squeal as he settled her on one of his shoulders and Hawk grinned down at Steve. After a moment, the boy gave a hesitant smile in return.

Then, with Wynne in step beside him and Steve walking along next to her, Hawk and Nona led the way into the baggage claim area.

Elation surged through Hawk. He felt good—no, better than good! At last Wynne and the kids were safely here and they were finally on *his* stomping grounds, the one particular part of earth that was his very own territory. No longer were there any outsiders to object, criticize or interfere.

Everything was going to be all right now. Wynne felt certain of it. As she walked around Hawk's ranch she loved every single sight that met her eyes, and how much of everything there was to see!

She could well understand why Hawk had wanted to live up here high in the mountains almost twenty miles north of Tucson. There were majestic mesas, buttes and stark blue-gray peaks that stretched up into the sky. The golden-white sand of the desert was studded with tough bushy mesquite and cactus, more types and varieties of cactus than Wynne had ever imagined existing. She referred often to a small illustrated guidebook on cactus that Hawk had hunted up for her.

There were round funny-looking barrel cactus, clumps of ocotillo and scattered cholla, as well as the mighty green saguaros with their funny arms that usually pointed toward the sky. Since saguaros grew very slowly, the big ones that Wynne admired had stood as silent witnesses to Indian wars, the wagon trains of settlers and the gradual taming and changing of the West.

Now Wynne shaded her eyes and lifted her face. The desert sky was an incredible blue bowl, unmarred by a single cloud, and here on the top of a gradual incline Hawk's house had been built.

Wynne was already in love with the house, even though she had yet to explore it fully. But if she had been asked to envision her dream home, she knew it would undoubtedly mimic the layout here.

The adobe house with a roof of bright red tiles had been erected in the shape of a horseshoe. It curved, Mexican-style, around a courtyard shaded with citrus trees. Here much of the ground was covered with pebble mosaics that led at one end to a merrily splashing fountain and to a cactus and rock garden at the other.

Out came Wynne's guidebook again. Decorative purple cactus, prickly-pear and tall spikeless Burbank grew between pebbles and brightly colored rocks. Why, a small pincushion cactus even wore a delicate ring of pink-purple flowers, Wynne noticed excitedly.

The South-of-the-Border flavor continued inside the house with cool white rooms that had rounded doorways, wood beam ceilings and thick, ornately carved doors. Much of the furniture was also Spanish, heavy and dark, but set within the light-filled rooms it didn't appear oppressive.

I'm going to look all around while Hawk and the kids are away, Wynne decided, for Hawk had certainly encouraged her to do so.

He and the children had left a half hour ago as the result of a minor mishap that had developed almost immediately. Steve and Nona had been horrified to discover that there were no animals on Hawk's "ranch" and Wynne, not realizing that they'd been expecting horses and cattle, lambs and pigs, dogs and cats, had not thought to prepare them.

"Golly, why don't you have *somethin'*?" Steve had cried disappointedly to Hawk. "You've got stalls and corrals in the back. Why, you've even got a dog house!"

"You should have a kitty cat at least," sniffed Nona.

"Hey, kids, I live alone—remember?" Hawk had protested. "I'm away from home fully half the time, flying around the friendly skies in my plane."

Steve and Nona could not quite appreciate the logic of this. Hawk, seeing their crestfallen faces, had provided a quick solution. "Well, even though I don't have all the pets or livestock you'd like, guess who does?"

"Who?" Steve had said dubiously.

"The neighbor whose mailbox we passed on the way up here. Thorn Hightower is his name. He's a good friend, and he's already picked out a couple of ponies for the two of you to ride!"

Wynne's skeptical, "Oh, really?" had been drowned out by her kids' excited whoops.

"Yeah, really," Hawk had shot back to her. "Fortunately I got to talking to Thorn last week about the kids coming and he anticipated this particular problem."

Nothing would do but that each child should see "my pony" right away. Hawk had looked questioningly at Wynne. "Go ahead and take them for a ride," she had urged. Then she added anxiously for Hawk's ears alone, "It's safe?"

"Absolutely." He leaned over and whispered that the "ponies" were two old, slow, broken-down mares.

Wynne knew her relief had undoubtedly been obvious, and she had tugged Hawk's dark head toward her to bestow a grateful kiss. Again their lips clung. But despite her eagerness to be alone with him, she knew there was really little chance for the intimacy they both craved until the kids were sound asleep. Meanwhile, to be alone for an hour or two would give her a welcome break from Steve and Nona, Wynne thought. It would also provide the opportunity to canvas the house at leisure and check on groceries and other supplies. She could also begin learning the names of various exotic-looking cactus.

Wynne finished her stroll across the courtyard and turned back into the house. The living room was absolutely massive with great picture windows on either side. From one Wynne could look up at the towering mountains while from the other she could gaze out across the desert where every changing light produced a shifting panorama of colors to enchant the eye.

The master bedroom, with Hawk's office beyond, lay in a wing leading off from the living room. The bedroom was typically Spanish with a vast double bed, its carved headboard high and wide, and Wynne couldn't repress a little shiver of excitement as she thought of curling up there with Hawk later tonight.

There were two matching night stands and a huge chest of drawers. At the foot of the bed sat a Spanish chest, intricately carved and scrolled. Wynne's gaze touched every item of furniture lovingly for her heart knew already that she was home.

The office presented quite a contrast to the rest of the house since it was pure, late-model-American-everything. Yet despite the impressive array of equipment, the office was obviously the domain of either a wholly disorganized human being or an entirely overwhelmed one. Files stood open and overflowing. Hundreds of books were jammed, crammed and stacked into built-in bookcases. On Hawk's large, plain desk letters had piled up in stacks and his giant-size bulletin board held about three layers of thumb-tacked messages. A book lay open and upside down on the carpet; a manuscript grown to a towering expanse of yellow pages sat on the computer stand next to Hawk's personal computer. Then, for the first time, Wynne noticed a small reproducing machine that kept repetitively flashing a plea to "Please Add Toner."

She laughed aloud, wondering how Hawk or anyone else could possibly get any work done in such clutter, especially when she discovered a telephone lying beneath a magazine. The phone was tipped over on its side and probably the receiver was off the hook as well, Wynne thought as she righted it. She lifted the receiver to check the connection and was reassured to hear a familiar dial tone.

As Wynne looked all around, her fingers itched to tackle all the disorder, for she'd had plenty of experience at organizing and maintaining a functioning office. Also, she had but to remember Hawk's deft automatic movements as he hung up clothes and towels to seriously doubt that he was your basic slob, especially since the rest of the house, including his bedroom and bath, was quite neat. Of course, Wynne knew that Hawk employed a cleaning woman but she had obviously been warned to leave his office alone.

He's literally overwhelmed by paperwork, Wynne diagnosed and was grateful that Hawk had not let all those stacks of paper deter him from the really important things he wanted and needed to do.

I could really be a help to him, Wynne thought with a sense of rising excitement. He certainly needs an administrative assistant to keep his schedule current, answer his routine correspondence and get this place straight. Also, she admitted frankly to herself, she'd been *itching* to get her hands on a computer, and Hawk would surely not be using his all of the time.

Why, I could stay right here at home and have plenty of interesting work to keep me busy and challenged!

Wynne thought in increasing delight. She knew by now that Hawk hated anything to do with financial matters, but she had always loved knowing where money came from and exactly where and how it was spent.

Until the idea of staying home to work suddenly presented itself, Wynne hadn't known just how much she wanted to do that. But she had always worked on an outside job and often her very soul seemed to cry out for more leisure time to do things for her children and, yes, to spend on herself too.

Wynne knew that Hawk would support her in doing any work she wished, and now she knew just exactly what that was. I'll redo Hawk's press releases and bring them up to date, she thought excitedly, and I'll get our finances computerized and—and I'll have a baby, too!

It all sounded like heaven.

She found a bottle of toner and stopped the reproducing machine from incessantly flashing its alarm. Then, with a last slow look all around, Wynne forced herself to leave. Hawk and the children could be back at any time, and she wanted to inspect the rest of the house thoroughly before the three people she loved best were all standing around, competing for her attention.

She walked back through the cavernous living room where a huge circular fireplace of white stone and red tile set a dramatic tone. It also painted inviting pictures in Wynne's mind of chill winter evenings when she and Hawk, Steve and Nona would gather, sitting on the comfortable sofas and chairs to watch a show on the console TV.

A beautiful Spanish guitar sat in one corner of the room, and Wynne's eyebrows rose quizzically as she regarded it. She wondered if that was the guitar Hawk had told her about, the one left him by his friend, Mike.

She passed on into the other wing of the house on the opposite side of the living room. There Wynne found herself in a large Mexican kitchen with a big round table and plenty of shelves and counters. Copper pots and straw baskets hung from the ceiling beams along with strings of dried peppers, garlic and ears of corn. But Hawk had few of the handy electrical appliances so dear to a busy woman's heart, Wynne noticed immediately. An electric can opener and a coffeemaker were all that she saw. We'll need a huge freezer and a microwave first, she itemized.

A quick survey of Hawk's cupboards and refrigerator indicated that he survived mostly on frozen TV dinners, canned soups, crackers and cheese since these were items already opened. But for company he had obviously stocked the larders with everything he'd imagined that Wynne and the kids could possibly eat. Unopened jars, packages, boxes and an overflowing vegetable bin told her he'd practically bought out a supermarket, and Wynne was touched by this evidence of his thoughtfulness.

She left the kitchen and went down a narrow hall where four smaller rooms and two baths completed this larger wing. What a lot of room there was! Wynne marveled, closing the door on two small bedrooms which were presently empty and unused.

The other two bedrooms had obviously been furnished as guest rooms. One held a king-size bed; the other twin beds. Nona's small bag and Steve's suitcase each staked a claim to the two furnished rooms.

Oh, my goodness! Suddenly Wynne realized that Hawk must have put her own luggage in his huge bedroom since it wasn't here in the room she planned to share with Nona. But that would never do! With the

children present, she and Hawk would have to be quite
circumspect—at least until Steve and Nona had fallen
asleep each evening.

Wynne went flying back through the house and, sure
enough, her two bags had been left in the small dress-
ing room between Hawk's bedroom and bath. The gesture was eloquent testimony to his eagerness to hold her
and make love to her, and Wynne gave a shiver of sheer
delight before regretfully hoisting her bags and moving
them into the children's wing. What magic it was when
two people loved and needed each other the way she and
Hawk did!

As though thinking about him had caused him to
materialize, Wynne heard Hawk's Blazer, which had a
distinctive roar, pull back into the driveway. Doors
slammed, then came the ominous sound of Nona's un-
mistakable sobs.

Oh Lord, what had happened to her? She was positively *howling*! Seized by fear, Wynne threw open the
kitchen door and dashed outside.

"Nona! What's happened, baby?" she cried in a
shaking voice.

The sobbing Nona hurled herself at Wynne, screaming even louder.

"There, there," Wynne crooned, cradling the child
in her arms. "What is it, sweetheart? What's happened?"

Nona said something in a tear-strangled voice but
Wynne couldn't make out the child's words. Anxiously
she turned to look at Hawk and Steve who were alight-
ing more slowly.

"It's not serious, Wynne," Hawk said placatingly. "I
know it hurts Nona right now—"

"What happened?" Wynne fairly screamed, feeling Nona's sturdy little body twisted by her tears.

"That dumb Nona decided to *pet* a cactus," Steve informed his mother in the lofty tones of pure disgust. "Before that, she was scared to ride her pony. She started screaming just like *that* when Mr. Hawk tried to put her into the saddle. So we rode instead, and she was supposed to be watching us while Mr. Thorn watched her. Instead she grabbed for a baby cactus 'fore he could stop her. I swear Nona's the dumbest sister anybody ever—"

"That's enough, Steve," Wynne said, cutting through her son's disparaging words. "Nona is just a little girl and you can't expect her to know about everything that you do. Let Mama see your hand, sweetheart."

Nona responded immediately to the opportunity to display her injury. Still crying loudly she backed out of Wynne's arms, her face red and swollen, and held up her right palm in which Wynne could see quite a number of cactus spines embedded. Although they were not deep they would be quite prickly and painful, she felt certain.

"Wynne, Nona wouldn't let either Thorn or me touch her hand—even look at it," Hawk said. Now Wynne saw the grim look in his eyes and heard the harrassed note in his voice.

"Yeah—and she sure messed up our ride, too," Steve said hotly.

"There will be other times for you to ride, Steve," Wynne said briskly, relieved that Nona's injury was actually so trivial. To Hawk, Wynne asked, "Just how *do* we get this cactus out?"

"With a magnifying glass and a pair of tweezers," he responded. "I have both in my bathroom. I'll get them as well as some alcohol."

Nona, who had begun quieting under Wynne's ministrations, began to howl anew. "Not alcohol! It *burns*! Mama, don't let him use alcohol, please! Please!"

"It's okay," Wynne assured both Nona and Hawk since his face was beginning to look almost desperate. "I brought some spray antiseptic with me that doesn't burn. It's in my small shoulder bag, Hawk, if you could get it at the same time."

Wynne had Nona sit at the big kitchen table where the light was good, and when Hawk returned with the necessary implements, she began the tedious procedure of extracting the tiny needles from the small tender hand. Steve watched the process with interest, but Wynne could tell that something was really bothering Hawk. He paced back and forth, his face taut and his eyes fiery.

What now? thought Wynne and wished she could sigh aloud. Between juggling a demanding man and catering to two kids, she certainly had her hands full.

"Mama, I'm hungry," Steve said suddenly. "When are we going to eat?"

"I'm hungry, too," Nona echoed.

Wynne stopped her work to glance at her watch, which was set now on Tucson time. Back home in Oklahoma, it was supper time, and the children's tummies knew it.

"Nona, I can't cook your supper and get the cactus out of your hand too," Wynne pointed out logically to her daughter.

Nona considered the dilemma. Since she had discovered that pulling out the cactus spines really didn't hurt very much she decided to let Mr. Hawk have the honor. "Okay, kid, I'll be right with you," Hawk agreed, following Wynne across the room as she moved toward the stove and refrigerator.

Wynne glanced up inquiringly into his stony face.

"Why did you move your luggage out of my room?" Hawk whispered to Wynne, and she could tell that he was quietly furious.

"Because if I stay with you, the kids will ask questions. They might even carry back tales to their grandparents," Wynne whispered in return.

"Do you mean—?" Hawk looked on the verge of exploding.

"I mean I'll be in to visit you right after Steve and Nona fall asleep," Wynne explained.

"Oh." Hawk looked relieved, yet not completely mollified by her explanation. "I don't want a visitor," he grumbled still in that low voice that the children couldn't overhear. "I want a *wife*!"

With that he stomped back to the kitchen table and began the tedious and time-consuming task of extracting the remaining cactus from Nona's palm.

Once again Wynne wished she could sigh aloud. Instead she turned her thoughts to what she might cook for dinner that all of them would like.

She settled on tacos, and they were a big hit. After they had finished eating, Hawk and the children cleared the table and stacked dishes in the dishwasher while Wynne relaxed over a cup of coffee.

Wynne was glad to see that Hawk's mood had improved again, and Nona's hand, now free of spines, no longer bothered her. With the dishwasher loaded and roaring, both kids looked up expectantly at Hawk.

"Do you two want to watch TV?" Wynne asked, trying to rescue Hawk from the unspoken demand made by her children.

But he had a better idea. "Tell you what, while there's still plenty of light let's walk down to the arroyo. Sometimes, especially after it's rained, you can find arrowheads there and bits of old Indian pottery."

"Oh, boy!" Steve exclaimed. "Let's go."

"What's a roy-yo?" asked Nona plaintively.

"It's a dry creek bed. But it can certainly fill up with water fast enough during the rainy season," Hawk explained.

"When is the rainy season?" Wynne asked curiously since despite the appealing beauty of the desert, it was certainly bone-dry.

"Late summer. The rains should begin in two or three weeks," Hawk answered, holding the kitchen door while the three Norwoods trooped out.

Since Wynne's open-toed sandals scuffed up sand and rocks, she was forced to walk more slowly than the others. Hawk led the way and the children ran eagerly behind him.

They walked for perhaps a half mile, then stopped. When Wynne caught up with the others she saw that they were standing atop a high flat slope. A narrow path led down the slope to the ground, wending its way around rocks and cactus. "The arroyo is right down there," Hawk said, gesturing. "You can see its channel quite plainly from here."

"Yes, I see it," Steve said excitedly. "It looks like a road."

Wynne was struck more by another natural wonder. "Look at that cliff on the other side of the arroyo!" she exclaimed. Unlike this slope with its gentle formation and meandering trail, the immense mountain that lay directly across from them looked completely unscalable. The fading sun had turned the brick-red rock even redder until it seemed to be lit by a savage grandeur.

Hawk led the way down the path, which proved rather slippery, Wynne thought. Also, ordinary steps caused numerous pebbles to dislodge and roll. These in turn frightened a black-tailed jackrabbit that had been hiding beneath a cactus, and it took off running at a zig-zag path to the children's great delight.

"Oh, wow!" Steve said when they had reached the arroyo. He walked its width, kicking up puffs of sandy gold dust at the same time. "Can I dig down here, Hawk?"

"Sure, on another day," Hawk replied with a shrug. "Remind me tomorrow and I'll get you a spade. Also, Steve, if you want to spend much time down here you've got to remember to be careful. Watch out for rattlers mostly, and stay the hell away from 'em! And any time you're directly under a mountain, keep an eye out for falling rocks.

"Okay," Steve said equably. He turned and regarded the huge red mountain with interest. "Hey, Mama, look at those little holes going up the mountain."

Wynne turned, shaded her eyes and saw what Steve had referred to. The red mountain definitely looked pock-marked when one stood up this close to it.

"The holes seem to lead to that ledge that's halfway up. See, Mama?" Steve asked.

Hawk joined them, dropping a casual arm around Wynne's waist. "You're talking about the 'young braves climb,'" he informed Steve.

"What?" Wynne, Steve and Nona all asked in unison.

"It's a Papago Indian legend that Thorn Hightower told to me," Hawk continued. "The mountain was supposedly created by the ancient gods as a test of skill for young Indian boys. At twelve or thirteen, something like that, a boy had to prove his bravery by scaling the mountain and reaching the ledge. Supposedly the small craters that pit the mountain were put there for that purpose alone. That's why they're so small. Most boys succeeded but some obviously didn't and fell to their deaths."

Wynne gave a small shiver. "That was a morbid practice, if you ask me."

"Oh, it was all so long ago nobody knows if it's really true or not," Hawk assured her, then glanced at the children. "Are you kids ready to go?"

Wynne's gaze followed Hawk's. To her horror she saw that Steve's eyes were fixed avidly on the ledge halfway up the red mountain. "Gosh, I wonder if *I* could climb up there," he remarked.

"Me too," echoed Nona.

Hawk reacted before Wynne could. "You two are absolutely *not* to ever try that climb!" he emphasized, raising his voice to the children for the first time.

A shudder she couldn't control rippled through Wynne. "Absolutely not!" she agreed, backing Hawk to the hilt, for just thinking of her children trying to attempt that perilous climb made her feel faintly nauseous.

"Yes sir," they replied in small voices.

For once Wynne had not minded Hawk's sternness and implacability.

They returned to the house at a more leisurely pace. The children were in the lead and Hawk now walked in step with Wynne. One of his arms slipped up to encircle her shoulders, and he hugged her close for a brief hard kiss.

His mouth was warm and tasted of passion. He sighed aloud when he reluctantly let her go. "Don't worry," Wynne whispered encouragingly to him. "The kids should collapse in another hour. They were up awfully early today."

But all the excitement had left them keyed up instead. Steve definitely had the "wide awakes." Long after Nona had fallen asleep in the room opposite his, snuggled up close to Wynne, Steve still sat propped up in one twin bed, reading a book he'd brought from Oklahoma.

Wynne finally took the book away from Steve, and he fell asleep soon after that. She waited an extra five minutes to be sure, then tiptoed down the narrow hallway and glided into Hawk's wing of the house.

He was waiting for her, propped up in bed and scribbling something on a yellow legal tablet. Wynne smiled at Hawk's expression of fierce concentration. The look was almost identical to the one on Steve's face ten short minutes ago.

At the sight of Wynne in her long white nightgown, Hawk dropped his tablet and pen and slid to one side of the bed as Wynne knelt on the other.

"Got room for me?" she asked suggestively and reached out to twine her arms around Hawk's neck.

In a single fluid movement Hawk seized her and rolled her across the bed. He wound up on top of Wynne and then, for the first time, she felt his hard impetuous desire and realized that he was completely naked.

In just another moment so was she.

Chapter Eleven

If Wynne's kids weren't happy as clams by day seven of their visit, Hawk knew that it certainly wasn't *his* fault. He had run their little tails all over Tucson—hell, all over Pima County and clear to the border for that matter!

Hawk had personally escorted Wynne and her kids to the Desert Museum and Old Tucson; to visit the studio of the late, great artist, DeGrazia, who had specialized in painting Indian children; to Saguaro National Monument and the Papago Indian reservation. He had driven them to Nogales so the kids could brag about their having been in Mexico, and Hawk had stopped to haul them through historic old mission churches along the way.

He had driven and spent and paid. He had stage-managed events and scoured his brain to remember good restaurants and fun-filled events. He had neglected his work and put off answering some really important letters, telling himself that winning over Wynne and the kids came first. But all he had to show for it now was a flattened wallet, a case of exhaustion and the depressing certainty that nothing he'd done had really made the least bit of difference.

Oh, Wynne and the kids had been exquisitely polite and uttered all the right expressions of appreciation. But Wynne still hadn't mentioned visiting any schools, and she hadn't set a wedding date. As for the kids, they seemed to be happiest when they were just left alone to dig up the arroyo. They were acquiring quite a collection of arrowheads, some brightly colored rocks and shards of pottery, too. At least this was free entertainment for them and quite readily available.

Hawk had frankly been surprised by the kids' ability to entertain themselves. On other occasions, he could drive them down to Thorn's and leave them for a couple of hours. Now that Nona had conquered her fear of the big gentle horses, she and Steve would ride around and around in the pasture with Thorn keeping an eye out for them. So Hawk had actually found himself with a lot of time alone with Wynne and that was the last thing he'd expected.

They had walked, talked and made love. They had cooked meals together, cleaning up afterward, and Hawk had never known before that stacking the dishwasher or peeling potatoes could be fun. More than ever their being together seemed right. But Wynne still evaded Hawk's efforts to get serious. Although she and the kids planned to be around for another three or four days, Hawk didn't see any signs that she'd change her mind.

Did Wynne fear marriage in general? He had occasionally wondered. Or was it, as he really believed, that she simply feared marriage to *him*? The desolate thought that what he was and what he could provide just weren't enough—that he didn't quite suffice and couldn't really measure up to what she'd known with her WASP husband—was still a constant source of torment to Hawk. Each time Wynne came to his bed late at night or slipped from it so early in the morning, all of Hawk's old feelings of inadequacy returned to plague him again.

He had vowed over and over that he wouldn't mention marriage to her again. Yet like the man plagued from a sore tooth who couldn't stop his tongue from constantly exploring the source of his suffering, Hawk had been unable to quit asking Wynne to marry him. He wanted things settled! He needed to know, and not remain suspended in this hellish limbo.

The kids! In Hawk's mind, it always came back to the kids. If he could just win them over completely and get them to fully like and accept him, then he knew he'd have Wynne. But kids had the honest, irritating way of holding at least part of themselves aloof until they felt they were loved and wanted. And Hawk knew full well that he neither wanted nor loved them.

But, paradoxically, he had actually started to *like* them much better. Nona could be a real pain in the butt, howling like a banshee when she didn't get her way or had suffered some trivial injury, but you really couldn't expect great maturity from a five-year-old. Most of the time the kid really was cute and funny. But then Hawk had always half liked Nona if for no other reason than the fact that she had Wynne's smile.

No, to Hawk the real surprise was Steve. Except for bitching occasionally about Nona—and what big brother didn't feel himself put upon, especially if cursed with *girl* siblings?—Steve was actually a pretty good kid. When he set himself a project such as digging up and down the arroyo, he really stuck to it. Also, the boy had a way of meeting and conquering fear that Hawk liked. At first, Steve had been just as scared of his horse as Nona, his face so chalk-white that Hawk could see the bluish veins showing through. But Steve had still pulled himself into the saddle and ridden off, scared or not.

"He's a nice kid. They both are," Thorn Hightower had surprised Hawk by saying just the day before. Coming from Thorn, who was half Papago and half Pima Indian, any praise for a kid who looked like Steve was bound to be sincere.

The boy just might make a geologist or an archaeologist. He certainly had brains enough for either, Hawk mused. Then as he remembered how Steve had proudly spread out his growing collection of Indian artifacts and thought of all the Indian-related questions the boy could ask, Hawk felt it more likely that Steve would become an anthropologist.

Hawk just wondered if he would be around when Steve achieved his almost predictable success. No, I won't be, he thought, if Wynne doesn't quit pushing me so dangerously close to the edge. Hawk felt himself dangled like a puppet by her refusal—or inability—to decide on their marriage.

That night the loving with Wynne was fierce and sweet. It felt almost like an exchange of souls to Hawk, and he wondered if, in these dark lush nights, he and Wynne were creating a new soul as well. The modern

American part of Hawk momentarily scoffed at his superstitious Indian nature. Wynne had once delicately implied that she was taking care of matters related to contraception. Naturally, such an up-to-date woman as Wynne would be availing herself of the very latest medical knowledge. The only problem with all of that was that no method Hawk had ever heard of was completely one hundred percent foolproof.

Now, as he felt Wynne gliding toward sleep in his arms, Hawk heard himself whispering the very words he'd vowed never to say again. "Marry me, Wynne. Please marry me!"

"Hawk, don't," Wynne said in a spent, sleepy voice.

He let his arms slide away from her. Now he felt entirely different words—those other words that he couldn't, *mustn't* say—trembling on his lips. It would be easy, so very easy, for him to say, "Damn it, Wynne, I want you for all time, not just for a late-night roll in the hay! Now either you set a date for our wedding or you can haul your little butt back to your own bed, and back to your own house in Oklahoma, and you'll never hear from an Indian named Saddler again!"

The ultimatum kept banging on the door of Hawk's mind and as the hot words tumbled so very close to utterance, he could feel them actually trembling on his lips. He was tired of being treated like a second-class citizen! Tired of feeling like the tentative and reluctant choice of second husband—unless or until someone better came along.

Bet my ultimatum would wake her up as fast as a speeding bullet! Hawk thought angrily, aware now of Wynne's deep regular breathing.

Inside him he felt something already tested, now strained to the limit. He wanted to seize Wynne's shoulders and shake her awake. Wanted, in fact, to shake her until her head bobbled and her hair tumbled all around her face.

No, she's tired. She needs her sleep. And you're thinking like a savage!

By a superhuman effort that found Hawk clenching his fists on the sheets, he stopped himself from waking her, shaking her, railing at her.

Glumly he stared up into the dark night. For once Hawk's magic technique that had always enabled him to fall quickly asleep had failed him. An hour passed slowly; he watched the minutes change on the automatic clock on his bedstand. Its numerals glowed a luminescent green.

Outside a coyote howled at the moon again and again, baleful and forlorn. Hawk knew just how the frustrated, lonesome sucker felt. Finally he slipped out of bed, determined to utilize the time if he couldn't sleep. By the time Wynne woke up next morning he had written replies to thirty-seven letters.

Wynne knew that something was wrong with Hawk, she just didn't know what. She awakened at dawn to find him in his office, the printer connected to his word processor spitting out a veritable chain of letters.

"Hawk." She said his name softly, then bent over him from behind, encircling his shoulders and pressing a soft kiss on his cheek. "Have you been awake long?"

"I never went to sleep." His voice was an exhausted monotone and sounded somehow remote from her. Beneath her hands Wynne could feel the tenseness of his shoulders.

"Oh," said Wynne, puzzled both by Hawk's insomnia and the remoteness she heard in his voice. Since he said nothing else, instinct warned her to leave him alone. Maybe he was in an especially creative mood or something. She backed out of the room and returned to Nona's bedroom.

An hour later, when Wynne called Hawk to join them for breakfast, he appeared willingly but ate very little. His eyes were deeply circled and his replies to the children's chatter were monosyllables. Immediately upon completion of the meal he asked the children to clear the table of dishes. Then, without any further comments to them or to Wynne, Hawk went back into his own wing of the house.

Wynne debated following him. But she sensed that Hawk was fighting some lonely inner battle, so perhaps it would be wiser just to leave him alone until he had fully resolved it. Also, by then the children were clamoring to go to the arroyo and dig for more arrowheads. Was she actually to have an hour or two for herself? Wynne wondered. What should she do with such luxury? Try a new hairstyle? Take a nap? Read a book?

She tried to tell herself that whatever was going on with Hawk had nothing whatsoever to do with her, but she didn't believe it.

"Mr. Hawk!" Nona's voice was a shriek of panic. "Oh, Mr. Hawk, please come quick!"

Hawk leaped up from his desk, trying to decipher Nona's next cry. It seemed to garble "Steve" and "snake."

Oh, my God! Hawk dashed out of his rarely used back door, which led outside, and moved instinctively in the direction of Nona's cries. They sounded like they had come from the garage or adjacent storeroom where he kept gardening equipment such as shovels and rakes, hoses and shears. His heart pounded like a runaway engine. God, had the dumb kid gotten himself snake bitten? Hawk wondered with a sense of dread. If Steve had been bitten, Hawk felt drearily certain that Wynne and the Norwoods alike would find some way to blame it on *him*.

Nona continued to yell, not even trying to use words any longer. Hawk raced around the edge of the garage, then skidded to a stop. Steve, wearing the grin of a triumphant gladiator, held a bloody shovel in his hands while a large but very dead rattlesnake lay at his feet.

The minute Steve glimpsed Hawk, he turned to Nona who danced up and down and continued to squeal. "Shut up, dummy," Steve growled and Nona at last fell quiet.

"What's happened here?" Hawk asked, a dangerous edge in his voice.

"I guess Nona an' me stirred up this old snake when we went in the storeroom," the boy explained. "'Cause when I came back out with the spade, the snake was right in our path. See?" With his thumb Steve gestured to where the snake lay stretched out.

"Why didn't you step off the path, walk carefully around the rattler and come get me?" Hawk demanded.

Steve looked taken aback. He had obviously expected praise for his noble deed and was meeting with condemnation instead. "Well, Hawk, there's so much cactus off the path—" he said, gesturing futilely.

"There's cactus everywhere! You're supposed to pick your way around that too!" Hawk's voice rose to a roar for his head ached relentlessly from weariness. In his exhausted, irate state it was a relief simply to yell at someone. "Didn't I tell you just a few days ago to stay the hell away from snakes?"

"Yes sir but it started rattling—"

"There aren't any 'buts'!" Hawk felt something poised for an explosion snap in two within him. In an instant he had lost control of himself completely, seizing the boy's slender shoulders and giving them such a shake that Steve's head wobbled. "No, instead of getting out of the snake's way you had to bait it. Scare it, provoke it into striking! Do you have any idea what could have happened to *you* if you were bitten on the wrong place? On your face, say, close to the brain? You might *die* before I could get you to a hospital! The nearest one is almost twenty miles from here!"

Automatically Hawk punctuated his furious words with more shakes of Steve's shoulders, jerking the boy's head to and fro just as he'd imagined shaking Wynne's last night. Even Nona's aghast wail did not deter him.

"You were showing off, weren't you?" Hawk raged. "Trying to impress little sister. Well, say something! Admit it!"

Light rapid steps rounded the side of the building. "What's going on here?"

Wynne's angry and frightened voice, speaking from behind Hawk, broke the evil spell. Hawk's hands fell away from Steve's shoulders and he looked down tiredly at the boy.

Steve's enormous blue eyes in his paper-white face made Hawk feel like a child abuser. Although Hawk knew he hadn't really hurt Steve physically, he had still lost control of his temper and jumped on the boy. In his relief that the stupid kid hadn't been bitten and his leftover rage at Wynne, he had said and done far too much.

He was messing everything up, losing his very last chance with Wynne, and the funny thing was that Hawk Saddler had never been a natural screw up before.

"Hawk, why were you shaking Steve? What *happened*? Steve? Nona? Somebody tell me something!" Wynne said indignantly.

Hawk turned away wearily. "I'll discuss it with you in the house," he informed Wynne.

As he walked away he could hear the children finding their tongues. "Steve killed the snake, Mama, but it made Mr. Hawk real mad and he yelled at Steve and shook—"

"Mama, I just killed the snake 'cause I was afraid it would bite Nona," Steve said piously. His voice trembled.

By the time Wynne came back into the house, Hawk had fixed himself a cup of instant coffee and stood waiting for her in the kitchen.

"I've sent the children down to the arroyo to play," she said tightly.

A moment of silence passed while Hawk stirred his coffee and awaited the consequences. When Wynne spoke next her voice was cool instead of heated with anger, as he'd expected. But cool could be deadly too. "Hawk, do you know what you've done?" she asked.

"Yes," he said truthfully and stirred the coffee some more.

"You could have had the children's love and respect, especially Steve's." Now Wynne's own voice was beginning to shake. "Steve's had a case of hero worship on you from the beginning, just in case you haven't noticed. Now, when all he was trying to do was *protect* his little sister—"

In a pig's eye, thought Hawk, withdrawing into an aloof place deep within himself. I was a big brother myself. I know how they show off. Steve risked getting rattlesnake bitten to impress the hell out of Nona. But I'll bet he thinks twice before he ever does something like that again.

"You shouted and shook him," Wynne was saying. "He's not used to that sort of treatment. Now you've completely alienated him, probably permanently and irrevocably!"

That's a pretty good line, Hawk thought from his mental distance. I need to remember that one. Wynne's good with words.

"Hawk, do you know what you've *done*?" she said again, still in that cool yet shaky voice.

"Yes." He set down the cup of coffee that he had yet to taste.

"I know you've tried, Hawk. I've watched you trying. But this will simply *never* work! Unconsciously you're so hostile toward the kids that it wouldn't take long before they picked it up, if they haven't already after your temper tantrum today."

"I said I knew what I'd done, Wynne." Hawk spoke in an even voice and turned around to face her squarely. "I've done what you couldn't seem to do. I've ended it."

Her black eyes grew enormous while the color washed out of her face. Momentarily Wynne looked stricken and very, very young. A small involuntary sound of pain escaped her, and suddenly it felt like a dagger being plunged into Hawk's heart.

"Yes, I've ended it," he went on quietly, explaining so that Wynne would understand. "Because I've reached the very same conclusion you have, that it just won't work. And it hurts like hell, Wynne, and I know the pain is only just beginning. But I feel a sense of relief too. I can't spend the rest of my life tiptoeing around your kids.''

She nodded but didn't speak. She looked actually incapable of speech.

"I guess there are a lot of things we overlooked when we fell in love,'' Hawk went on softly. "I don't think old man Norwood would ever accept me. And as far as my friends go, most of them are activist too. Maybe 'purists,' some people would say. I've already wondered how I could explain two white stepchildren to them.''

"I—I never even thought of that,'' Wynne stammered.

"I did,'' Hawk said frankly.

"So we're *never* going to get married?'' Wynne asked, and her voice was shaking again.

"Never is a long time.'' At first Hawk hedged because of the pain these words were causing him. He was even finding it hard to breathe, but hedging wasn't fair either. "As much as I've begged for marriage, Wynne, right now I have to admit that *not* getting married sure seems like a swell idea.''

She looked down, but not before he had seen the tear sheen gathering in her eyes. "You're right. But it hurts, Hawk,'' Wynne said in a small whisper. "Dear God, it hurts so bad!'' Then her own control cracked. She buried her face in her hands and began to cry.

He had never been able to bear the sound of her unhappy sobs and nothing that had happened between them could change his feelings about that. Swiftly Hawk crossed to Wynne and suddenly they were locked in each other's arms, clinging and kissing in a desperate farewell.

His tongue scooped the tears off her face, then traced the outline of those lips he'd so loved kissing. They parted for him and his tongue plunged inside. Wynne's arms were shaking but still held him in a fierce grasp.

Their kiss was searing and so were the several others that followed it. They clung together both as lovers and as lost souls, who could not really conceive of life apart from each other but knew their future together was being dangerously threatened.

At last, when Hawk began to reluctantly draw back, Wynne was the one who objected. "No!" she said in a hoarse whisper. "Oh, Hawk, I need you—now!"

He stared down at her, shaken himself almost to the point of tears by the frankness of Wynne's wanting him. Shaken too by his own desperate need for her now that his anger had blown itself out like a swift summer storm.

"The kids?" he asked.

"They'll stay at the arroyo for an hour or two. You know how they enjoy it down there," she added.

Hawk gave a numb nod. Yes, the kids had loved playing there in the shadow of the great red mountain, and they had been tanning considerably in the process of their digging and scooping for Indian artifacts. Even Steve's light skin had taken on a slightly darker hue although his nose was peeling a little.

What strange thoughts to have when he was about to make love to Wynne for the very last time! Hawk's mind surprised him with its painful convolutions or—or were they just painful evasions? *God, how could he live without her?* he wondered as his arm slipped strongly beneath Wynne's knees. He lifted her into his arms, and their lips met again.

This time, when the kiss ended, he carried her to the bedroom they had shared through most of the nights. Swiftly they stripped off their clothes, then fell across the bed straining together, their pain transmuted briefly into passion.

This lovemaking was different—poignant and heart-stoppingly tender. Generously they offered themselves to each other while clinging together. The pain also made the culmination more intense than ever before. Wynne's ecstatic cry sounded like a wound being inflicted, and Hawk's deep shudder of release brought him to the top of a summit then seemed to drop him off the jagged edge. At the bottom of that peak was an exhaustion so deep that it went far beyond the merely physical. Slowly their bodies separated. They were apart again, and each was left alone with his loss and despair.

Wynne reached out and gently stroked Hawk's cheek, feeling the smooth beardless face beneath her fingers. "I used to wonder why I felt so empty inside," she told him tremulously. "And all the time it was because I was missing you, needing to meet you, wanting to love you and have you love me. I wonder now if I'll have that awful empty ache back inside of me again. I'm afraid I will for the rest of my life."

Hawk turned his head until his warm lips met her stroking fingers and then her soft palm. "I just don't understand, Wynne," he said very softly, as though to speak louder of these matters would absolutely break his heart. "Charlie Birdsong—you remember him?—said all that we needed to do was cherish each other.

And we have. We always have! But it wasn't enough after all."

Wynne heard the utter desolation that ached and throbbed in Hawk's voice, and she heard the exhaustion too. Briefly she hugged his dark head to her bosom, her gesture almost maternal. Then slowly she relinquished him and slid from the bed.

"Try to rest, Hawk," she urged him. "You sound so tired! And—and I don't want you to hear me, see me, doing what I have to do."

"All right." Obediently his eyes shut, and Wynne tiptoed from one window to another, darkening the room by closing the heavy drapes. Then she pulled on her jeans and shirt.

Just as she started to leave the room, he spoke again. "I'll never be able to quit loving you, Wynne. Oh God, I just don't understand...."

But she understood. She understood far more than Hawk even knew he was telling her now. He needed someone badly. He wanted to marry and have children. He was thirty-eight years old. He wouldn't—couldn't—wait around for Wynne Norwood's two kids to be grown and on their own. And she didn't really want those years of lonely waiting for him.

Alone in the hallway, Wynne fought and won the battle of emotional control. Then she dashed away the last of her tears and forced her mind to think on practical matters. Call the airline. Pack the kids' clothes and then her own. Finish cleaning up the kitchen which had been left in disarray. Then phone Peg and Barry to tell them that she and the kids were coming home sooner than planned. That, she knew, would be the very last thing she did, she dreaded it so.

The airline had three spaces available on an early-evening flight so Wynne booked them, then began packing. Every movement she made seemed painful, as though it hurt her heart. She had loved it here in Arizona so much! So had the kids.

She had loved Hawk so very much! Momentarily her rigid self-control wavered, and Wynne felt her lips quivering, her eyes stinging. Would Hawk take any better care of himself in the future than he'd done in the past? Or would he keep right on working too long and hard, trying to do too much, eating the wrong food, living alone and lonely.... Maybe the woman who became his wife, whoever she might be, could help him to slow down.

I'll never be able to quit loving him, either! Wynne thought fiercely.

She finished packing her things and Nona's, finding her daughter's belongings strewn all about—a doll under the bed, a sock on the bathroom floor, a bedroom slipper behind the drapes.

Steve's things were tidy, as always. Wynne packed for him in record time.

Now what? she wondered bleakly and her mind, frantic for activity, suggested she start lunch. So Wynne headed back to the kitchen. She decided to make a large green salad, full of crunchy health-giving vegetables. If only I could have stayed here and married Hawk, I could have had a garden, Wynne thought and paused briefly to wipe her eyes.

I could have had a baby too...our baby, she thought, and scrubbed at her eyes more vigorously. Then she chopped, peeled, sliced and tossed. So intent was she, both on her task and her feelings, that it took several minutes before the now-rare sound began to impinge.

That sounds like rain, Wynne finally thought in surprise. She set down her knife and went to the nearest window to look. Rain was indeed falling, a thick gray curtain beyond the kitchen window. Quite fitting, Wynne thought, considering her own bleak mood.

I'd better start sandwiches since the kids will come tearing in here any minute, Wynne decided. Not that her two hardy kids feared a few raindrops but neither did they like being drenched. Although drenched, they would probably be considering the distance to the arroyo, even presuming they hurried back.

Wynne had finished a platter of sandwiches, even trimming off the crusts on one for Nona, who preferred hers that way, when the first twinges of uneasiness struck her. It was really raining quite hard now but still the children had not come in although they were undoubtedly soaked by now.

Suddenly words that Hawk had said several days ago slammed into Wynne's pain-numbed mind. "An arroyo is a dry creek bed. But it can certainly fill up with water fast enough during the rainy season . . . The rains should begin in a week or two."

The knife Wynne was holding fell clattering into the sink as she stood stock-still, rooted momentarily in place. She knew very little of ecology but one thing she had heard of was that dangerous flash floods could happen in the desert because water did not soak into the sandy soil but ran off it much as it ran down a pane of glass.

Wynne doubted if her children knew even that feeble little bit of information. For all of Steve's brightness he had still only lived ten years. Great gaps existed in his education that the next decade would have gradually filled.

With a frightened shake of her head Wynne threw off the creeping paralysis of fear. She dashed back toward Hawk's wing of the house, screaming his name in terror. "Rain! It's raining, Hawk! It's pouring, and the children are still outside!"

Wynne's cries awakened Hawk but he came back slowly, as if reluctant to face reality, when she burst through the door. He propped up in bed as she automatically hit the light switch, but his dark eyes looked dazed as he blinked at her.

"What, honey?" he stammered.

Terrified, Wynne stood in the center of his room and repeated her words. It was raining. It had been raining for some time, quite hard rain. And the children had not come back from the arroyo.

"Rain!" For a moment Hawk tilted his head, listening. Then, as Wynne watched, his face seemed to freeze, stamped by fear. He leaped out of bed, grabbing for his jeans and shoes.

"How long?" he snapped, managing to yank up his jeans and snap them all in one motion.

"The rain? Oh, maybe fifteen minutes," Wynne stammered. "Oh, Hawk, tell me my children are *all right*!"

He did not respond to Wynne's entreaty except to stamp first one foot and then another into his worn jogging shoes. "Raining this hard the whole time?" Hawk demanded instead.

"Yes—this hard or even harder. Oh, Hawk!" Wynne began to tremble but before the attack of nerves had gripped her fully Hawk was standing beside her. He seized her elbow, rushing her out of the room with him, and Wynne heard the jangle of his key ring already poised and waiting in his hand.

Heedless of rain or the fact that he was only half dressed, Hawk ran through the downpour to his Blazer, pulling Wynne along with him.

She sank gasping into the passenger's seat. Rapidly Hawk started the engine and it came alive with a powerful roar, then the Blazer sped out. Wynne felt fear now digging like iron claws into the sides of her mouth; it almost squeezed her throat closed.

"Hawk—Hawk, tell me my kids are okay?" Wynne said in a frantic whisper.

The look he threw her was desperate. "They are if— if they knew to take shelter on the high hills when the rain first started. Would Steve know that?"

"No." Wynne wasn't sure if the word even made it past her lips so she shook her head instead.

"My fault!" Hawk said in a choked voice. "I never dreamed the rain would start this early in the year. Or that I'd be asleep—*asleep*, for God's sake!—if it did."

Hawk's hands were clenched tightly into fists on the steering wheel, his mouth a hard, straight, uncompromising line. At that moment Hawk hated himself, Wynne knew.

"It wasn't your fault," she cried, trying to console him, but by now there was only room for terror for them both.

The Blazer lurched up and down, jolting her body almost unbearably, and Wynne stared out through the windshield at a desert totally and ominously transformed.

The rain was slackening off now and no longer falling in torrents. On the desert floor innumerable little rivulets had formed, winding in and out among the rocks and cactus. The rivulets met and joined everywhere. Muddy cascades of water rolled across the slopes while miniature lakes were forming in the flatter areas.

The Blazer careened and rumbled like an old buckboard as Wynne cowered, trembling in her seat. She could feel even her lips quivering as her mind relived every important and significant moment in the life of each child. She saw them again as fat babies, held in the arms of their father or snuggled up against Peg. She remembered tottery steps, adorable toothless grins, big eyes opened in awe at Christmas trees and magic Disney creatures. She saw birthday cakes and counted candles—so few candles!

Hawk stopped the Blazer so suddenly that Wynne almost fell against the windshield. At the last possible moment his hand shot out, steadying her. "I'm afraid to drive any closer," Hawk muttered, then he was jumping out of his door and letting it slam shut behind him as he plunged ahead in the driving rain.

Wynne tried to follow Hawk, but her knees would barely support her. Like a very old or thoroughly terrified woman she tottered after Hawk, understanding why he must not wait for her and praying, simply praying, that he would arrive in time.

She forced herself up the gradual slope, which she knew would overlook the arroyo. She saw Hawk stopped at the top, his brown bare back as rigid as stone. What was he seeing below? Wynne wondered desperately and tried to make herself believe that he was simply standing there, scanning the area and finding the children safe.

But, deep in her soul, she knew better. A rush of adrenaline gave her the extra energy she needed to push onward and upward, even wading through a shallow half-grown river that lapped at her ankles and tried to impede her path.

Gasping again, she managed the final ascent and topped the crest. Then she looked down and reeled, aghast. Far below she saw the gushing flood of water. White-capped, turbulent and muddy, it stampeded down the arroyo with a distant but still thunderous roar, sweeping everything before it.

A flash flood at its height, it carried tons of sand, gravel and even large stones in its wake. The water driving relentlessly down the arroyo uprooted trees and tore away bushes along the banks. Even as Wynne watched, the torrent swelled and the burden of debris increased.

"My babies!" she cried and suddenly a terror unlike any she had ever felt gave her an almost manic strength. She started to dash down the slope, completely indifferent to her own life and safety, but immediately felt Hawk's steely strength attempt to restrain her.

For a moment she almost escaped him, so wild was she to be free. "Let me go!" she sobbed. Then she began beating at his arms where the muscles were bulged and knotted. "Let me go! I've got to find Steve and Nona!"

"Wynne...oh God, Wynne. They're gone! They must be gone!"

As the man's voice brought home to her the worst realization on earth and as the cascading waters thundering down the arroyo really registered, Wynne looked up in total despair and mental confusion. "Tom. Oh Tom, our babies are gone. Steve and Nona are gone!"

Chapter Twelve

Hawk's own worst moment also came with his realization that the children had undoubtedly been swept away to their deaths, and it was his fault, all his fault. He had arrogantly assumed that *he* could certainly take care of the little brood, and he had failed colossally. Failed unforgivably. Wynne's calling him "Tom" did not matter or impact him at all, except as a barometer to the extent of her dazed, shocked horror.

As he stood holding Wynne, Hawk felt himself breathing as heavily as though he'd just finished running a marathon. His chest ached as if he had absorbed a tremendous blow there, right over the region of his heart.

Steven and Nona were gone! And just a couple of hours ago they had been so utterly alive—running, gesturing, talking to him. Now, obviously, they were dead. Steve and Nona... and Wynne might as well be, too.

She would not recover from this, Hawk saw, staring down into her now horrified face. She had already suffered one grievous blow when she had lost the father of her children; she could not get over losing the children as well.

Until this past week Hawk had not really felt Wynne's inner connection to those two kids. But seeing her solely in charge of them with much more of the mothering side of her nature on display, he had finally felt her relationship to them.

It was certainly their mother who sagged now in his clutch, no longer able even to stand upright. She had carried those children in her body, each for nine long months, and now she had just seen them returned so horribly and prematurely to the darkness from which they had sprung. He felt her spirit absorbing the almost unbearable blow although her mind was still too dazed to grasp it entirely.

The Wynne he had loved so much was dying now with Steve and Nona, Hawk realized with yet another almost devastating rush of guilt, grief and remorse. Why hadn't he realized before that a part of her sheer lovability sprang from her feelings for her children? Now in this woman in his arms, shocked almost beyond comprehension, he saw another Heleema in the making.

And if Wynne was utterly destroyed, Hawk knew he was not far behind. Already he was shaken to the depths of his soul, and yet, at the same time, he felt as though he had awakened from a bad dream that had held him in thrall. He had *never* wished any child injury!

Good God in heaven, what had been wrong with him? How could he, a grown man, have resented those attractive and pleasant little kids? He had been given a great opportunity; he could have been a worthy stepfather to a couple of fatherless tykes, and he had blown it to hell and gone! What had their skin color to do with the inner self of each kid, a self that he had found himself actually beginning to like? In the enormity of the moment, Hawk would have torn the skin from his own body if only it would change anything, give back life to Wynne's children and place them safe and well in his sight once again.

"Please…" he heard himself praying silently and the God he beseeched was neither white nor red.

Wynne kept quaking as though rocked by internal earthquakes, and Hawk caught her even closer, his own hands trembling as he attempted—entirely futilely, he knew—to offer comfort. Blindly he stroked her wet black hair. "Oh, please…" he whispered again, his lips against Wynne's silky hair because neither she nor her children had deserved anything like this.

For a moment Hawk's own eyes closed in utter helplessness. He had never before known what it was like to hurt in quite this way because he had never before felt himself so much to blame. He had been so wrong, indeed almost criminally wicked in his negligence and arrogance.

But even in the wake of this terrible tragedy, he had to keep functioning. There was so much to do—guide Wynne back to the house, phone the sheriff and begin that arduous, heartbreaking task of notifying the Norwoods and the Groves.

Hawk wearily opened his eyes again and found that the rain had now almost stopped, the drops smaller and thinning out. The sky was turning lighter and brighter. Too late. It didn't matter. He discovered his eyes focused on the red mountain across the arroyo and sud-

denly, to his absolute amazement, Hawk saw something
small and bright moving there on the rock face.

He squinted, his heart banging on his ribs. Had he
imagined—

No! There, right there! It moved again, something
alive and in colorful attire. But so tiny. And beside the
first something clung a second, even smaller. Squinting
through the still-lingering rain haze, Hawk looked
across the gushing, pounding floodwaters to see the two
small figures dangling on the red mountain. They were
practically specks against its steep rock wall, but they
were Wynne's children and, incredibly, they were still
alive!

"They're not dead!" Hawk cried in sheer relief. His
heart, which had pounded so sickeningly before, now
gave joyous leaps and bounds inside his chest. He seized
the dazed, uncomprehending Wynne and swung her
around to face the red mountain. "Look! There, on the
left!" Hawk pointed for her benefit, and saw her own
eyes focus. "Less than halfway up, not too far from the
ledge. Your kids, Wynne! They're still alive!"

He felt the jolt that ran through her slender body like
a shot of life-giving electricity. And, indeed, perhaps it
was. But after just that one moment of staring incredulously across the chasm, she swayed again in Hawk's
grip with renewed terror.

"Hawk, how long can they stand to *hang* there?" she
said in a strangled voice.

By now Hawk's initial jubilation had, like Wynne's
realization, given way to somber reality. The children
had obviously retreated up the rock face to escape the
flood, and a smart bit of fast thinking on Steve's part
that had been, Hawk thought, his admiration for the
ten-year-old rising steadily.

But Wynne was right. The children could not cling indefinitely, their feet tucked into one set of small pits on the red cliff, their fingers growing increasingly pinched and painfully twisted as they clung to another. Eventually those little fingers would tire and weaken. Then the children would fall into the flood they had sought to escape, if they weren't killed striking boulders and rocks on the way down.

"Steve, you've got to climb up to the ledge. It's your only chance!" But would the boy dare do the one thing Hawk had told him *never* to do? He must make Steve listen!

So fierce was Hawk's concentration, as his mind honed in on the only realistic solution, that he wasn't aware he had spoken aloud until he felt a shudder radiate through Wynne's body.

"No!" she gasped.

"Honey, it's the only way. He's *got* to go for it and persuade Nona to follow him," Hawk said rapidly to Wynne.

"No!" she wailed again but it was a cry of despair, not actual resistance. "Hawk, that cliff is so sheer, so slick—"

And now it's wet too, which makes it even slicker, Hawk thought to himself. I doubt if even the young braves were required to climb when the rock face was ever this wet.

Still, it was one chance, the only chance, for the children to move up to the ledge and then sit there and wait to be rescued. But could Steve figure all that out? Burdened with the responsibility of Nona, a flash flood at his feet, and clinging like a fly to that cliff, could the poor kid possibly avoid panic long enough to figure it all out? For that matter, faced with such a life-threatening emergency, Hawk wondered if even a grown man could decide what to do.

"C'mon, Steve," Hawk thought, concentrating with all his might. "C'mon—go! Before your hands and feet get too stiff, just go!"

And at almost that exact moment, Hawk realized that the spunky little kid was doing just exactly what he was praying for. The boy had started to move, cautiously, yes—slowly and carefully, true—but he was moving straight up in the direction of the ledge. A moment later Nona began to crawl too, as though in response to Steve's command.

"Attaboy, Steve," Hawk whispered hoarsely. "Go, go! Don't take time to stop again and get scared. Don't look down. Just go!"

Hawk scarcely heard Wynne's moan or felt her frantic clutch as she gripped his neck and buried her face in his shoulder. He was too intent on the desperate life-and-death drama being played out across the swirling, white-flecked flood waters.

Steve moved again, over the sheer rock wall, plunging his small hands and small feet into the shallow pits that reputedly were only child-sized. Behind him Nona scrambled like an agile little monkey.

"Wynne honey, they're moving. They're going the right direction—up. Yeah, kid, c'mon. That's right... go, Steve! Don't look down. Just keep moving slow and easy. Yeah, fella. *That's right*!"

Just as Wynne couldn't bear to watch the new peril to which her children were now exposed, Hawk couldn't tear his own gaze away. Something hot and salty splashed into one of his eyes, making it sting. Distractedly he rubbed away the drops of perspiration on his forehead, not realizing that the clammy sweat of tension was seeping now from practically his every pore.

"Yeah, that's right, Steve. You're halfway now. Just keep... no, not so *fast!* God, don't slip and fall now!"

Time had ceased to exist—or, if it did still exist it had slowed to a crawl as paralyzingly slow as the long painful crawl up that cliff by Wynne's children.

Wow, look at little Nona! She sure had spirit to match her red hair, clambering along so gamely after her brother.

How much time had passed? Ten mintues? Fifteen? It seemed like hours had gone by, but Hawk knew it really couldn't have been very long. He was still drenched in perspiration and Wynne was no longer able even to quiver convulsively in his arms when, at long last, Steve crawled up to relative safety on the narrow shelf of stone. The sun broke through almost at that very moment, and now the rain had virtually stopped. Hawk could see that the child was utterly exhausted by the way he bent over, his hands on his knees. Then, with a last great effort, he dropped to his stomach, leaned over the ledge and used both his arms to drag Nona up beside him.

"Way to go, fella! Now just stay *right there*," Hawk heard himself congratulating the kids as though they could hear him. With a muttered, "They're safe," he shook off Wynne's grasp and ran for the Blazer. There wasn't time now to deal with Wynne too, and anyway she would be okay as soon as he got the kids down. The next order of business was to arrange for the rapid rescue of those children from the ledge. Those kids! How about those two unbelievable kids! Hawk thought exultantly. Never at any time or place during his colorful life had he felt any prouder of two people.

* * *

The next couple of hours passed like a blur in Hawk's mind. His frenzied ride back to the house, his emergency phone calls—to summon help for the kids and send Thorn Hightower after Wynne. He then drove down through the mountains to the helicopter pad. The Tucson Search and Rescue crewmen knew Hawk and had decided to wait until he arrived before taking off although he had advised them not to.

But the decision was wise, as it turned out. Hawk's presence in the chopper and the encouraging gestures he made to the children gave them the courage to move to the edge and crawl, one by one, into the rescue basket while the helicopter hovered precariously over their ledge.

Nona was lifted into the helicopter first. Still wet from rain, scared and squalling, she grabbed at Hawk with the same death grip her mother could employ. But within a few short minutes Nona's natural aplomb asserted itself. By the time the chopper landed, Nona had already charmed its experienced crewmen and her ordeal soon became an adventure.

The boy didn't squall. But his soft blue eyes were enormous from shock, fear and the superhuman effort he'd had to exert. He was wet too, as well as filthy, scraped and scratched. His thin knees shook uncontrollably. Hawk swept the boy, dirty, wet and all, into his arms and hugged Steve hard against his own bare chest. One of his hands instinctively stroked the child's hair, and he recognzied its familiar silky touch.

"I didn't know what to do, Hawk," Steve related, his voice high and thin. "I know you told us not to climb the mountain, but when I heard the roar of the water coming—"

"You did exactly right, Steve. You used your own best judgment as you always must, and it was right on target."

"—so I did. I pulled Nona up the red mountain, but we both got so tired of holding on. Then I thought . . . I know this sounds crazy . . . I really thought I heard *you* tell me to climb to the ledge."

Hawk's eyes squeezed shut, and he hugged the boy even tighter. "You heard me, Steve," he finally said, his voice husky. "I guess you and I must communicate pretty well."

"Yes sir . . . Hawk."

According to an old Indian legend, a child always arrived at the right teepee. Certainly this one had. After another moment, Hawk felt the boy's silent sobs begin, releasing the tension Steve had been under for so long. But that was okay, right now Hawk wasn't seeing very well himself.

Mama was at her bossiest, Steve thought wearily. Oh, he hadn't really minded all the hugging and kissing she did on him and Nona because he knew she'd been worried and scared. But she kept asking a million questions, and he felt too tired to answer them.

"Why are you carrying him, Hawk? Steve, are you hurt?"

"He's not hurt, Wynne, I promise. The kid's just worn out."

"But his legs! Hawk, just look at the way his legs are shaking."

"I know they're shaking, honey. He was scared to death like any sensible person would be, that's all. Now the reaction is catching up with him—"

"Are you *sure*? Why isn't he talking? Steve, are you—?"

"I'm all right, Mama," he managed to say, then leaned back against Hawk's shoulder again. It sure felt good and strong.

"Don't you think he needs to see a doctor, Hawk?"

Feeling vaguely ashamed, Steve looked down at his uncontrollably shaking legs. "Look, Wynne, he'll be all right. Trust me. The same thing's happened to me a couple of times in my life."

That made Steve feel a lot better. It sure helped that Hawk knew what was happening and that he understood as well.

"But Nona isn't—"

"Nona is still too young to really know what almost happened," Hawk said firmly.

"Am not!" Nona's chin jerked up like it always did when she got mad. "I know we near 'bout croaked!"

There was a moment's silence, then Mr. Thorn Hightower and Hawk burst out laughing at the same time, and after a minute, Mama did too.

Then she hugged and kissed Steve and Nona some more.

Wynne had asked for one miracle; she had never expected to be blessed by two. And yet that was apparently just what had happened, she thought wonderingly, as she watched her two children and Hawk talking, laughing and eating ravenously.

At first Steve's case of the shakes had frightened her. So as soon as she'd finished scrubbing Nona from head to toe, Wynne had invaded Hawk's wing to check on Steve. Her son had been so wobbly that Hawk was helping him to clean up.

Wynne had forgotten about a young boy's touchy modesty until Steve fairly *screeched* at her. "Will ya get out of here and let us guys take a shower?" he'd demanded so Wynne had beaten a quick retreat, assured that her son was recovering quite nicely.

Now her eyes rested lovingly on the three bright heads gathered around the table. They were all so different, and yet somehow all akin as they voraciously attacked the second plate of sandwiches she had fixed.

How quickly life returned to the ordinary, Wynne marveled. It became baths and clean clothes, antiseptic and Band-Aids, plus a lunch so long delayed that it was served practically at supper time. Yet, in the midst of the absolutely ordinary, the positively miraculous had also occurred. How grateful she was!

The adventure remained foremost in Nona's mind. "Mama, did you see us ride off in the helicopter?" she inquired as Wynne sat back down beside her.

"I sure did," Wynne said feelingly. "I was watching with Thorn Hightower, and my heart was in my throat every single minute!"

"Have *you* ever been in a helicopter?" Nona asked.

"No, I never have." Wynne yielded to the urge to caress Nona's smooth cheek. "Goodness, sweetheart, but you must have been so scared through the whole thing!"

"Mostly I wasn't," Nona informed her mother. "I was scaredest of all when we climbed to the ledge. But Steve kept yellin' at me that Injun kids did it, and since we were part Injuns, we could too."

"Kinda proud of having Indian blood, aren't you, son?" Hawk asked, ruffling Steve's hair.

"Yes sir," agreed Steve. "Aren't you?"

Hawk paused a moment, then he grinned again at Steve. "Yeah, sure. But, you know, Indians aren't really superior to other folks any more than they're inferior. Actually, we're all just the way we're supposed to be. I have your mama to thank for that lesson."

Touched, Wynne looked down at her plate. She was afraid if her eyes met Hawk's, she would cry again, and she didn't want to shed more tears in front of the children.

"I think I'll go out and watch the sun set," Hawk said, rising and excusing himself from the table.

"I'll join you soon," Wynne promised.

"Say, Hawk—" Steve suddenly spoke up.

"Yeah, Steve?"

"This morning, with the snake, you were right. I was showin' off. I'm sorry."

Again Hawk's hand went to caress Steve's head. "I'm sorry I lost my temper and shook you. It was very wrong of me."

"Aw, that's okay, Hawk."

They exchanged another grin, then Hawk strode outside and Wynne turned back to the children. For once they admitted to being pooped. They were quite happy to take bowls of ice cream into the living room and sprawl on the carpet to watch TV.

Wynne went into Hawk's office to assure herself of privacy, then placed several brief long-distance calls. She hung up smiling and went outside to join Hawk.

He wasn't on either the porch or the patio. But after a moment's reflection, Wynne knew just exactly where he would be.

Already the hot Arizona sun had baked the desert almost dry again. There were still leftover pools of water that would evaporate more slowly.

As Wynne had expected, Hawk was atop the slope overlooking the arroyo where they had stood crucified in agony several hours earlier. Only a scant few inches of water trickled down the arroyo now. High above, the dying sun was painting the sky in radiant and spectacular colors.

"Hawk," Wynne called softly.

He turned and then instinctively their arms went around each other's waists. How good Hawk looked and felt, Wynne thought, her grip tightening. Oh, he had to be the single most desirable man in the whole wide world!

His lips brushed her forehead and even that light grazing brought her senses awake to eager, clamoring life. "Hey, did I hear right?" Hawk demanded. "Were you *canceling* your plane reservations before supper?"

"I sure was," Wynne said, snuggling up closer to his warmth and strength.

"You mean despite rattlesnakes, flash floods and crazy Indians, you're still going to take a chance on Arizona?" He spoke in surprise.

"No," Wynne replied very, very calmly. "I'm taking a chance on you."

Hawk stared down at her for a minute, his face almost blank in its total amazement. "Hey, you're really not kidding, are you?"

"Not a bit! I know it's a trifle soon but I thought the twentieth of August would make a wonderful wedding date. It's okay with Lonnie and your folks." She took a deep breath. "Still want me, you rare and wonderful man?"

"You've got to *ask*?" Hawk shouted and now Wynne saw the absolute jubilation that fired his black eyes.

Their hands tightened even more, and they moved closer still, staring at each other and smiling in mutual joy and elation.

"You won't be sorry, Wynne. It'll be okay with me and the kids," Hawk vowed.

"I know. I can tell. I think this afternoon definitely made a daddy out of you!" she laughed.

"As well as aging me twenty years!" Hawk agreed.

"But what about your Indian friends?" Wynne said carefully. "You said some of them wouldn't understand your having white stepchildren."

"Anybody who doesn't accept my kids is no friend of mine!" Hawk said fiercely.

That was the answer Wynne had hoped to hear, but now she herself added a qualifying phrase. "Oh, just tell them that they'll like the looks of our next one."

Hawk's delighted laughter rang out and echoed across the chasm. Then, abruptly, his face sobered. "Steve's done me a big favor. He's proud of his heritage." Hawk drew a deep breath. "I didn't realize it until today, but I *haven't* always been proud of mine, for all the speeches I've made and all the writing I've done."

Wynne moved even closer, standing so near she could feel the rhythmic rise and fall of Hawk's chest as he breathed, but she dared say nothing. It was important that Hawk verbalize this.

"I guess I absorbed part of the 'Indians are inferior' message when I was a kid," Hawk went on after a moment. "I think I got another dose of it when Heleema ran off with that white guy. She had a half-dozen fellas on the reservation who were in love with her but, clearly, she thought white skin was better. I guess I thought the same was true of you, Wynne. I kept being afraid I couldn't measure up to Tom, that's how inadequate I felt and how insecure I was. And that's the real reason I couldn't like Tom's kids.''

"Hawk Saddler, you'll always measure up to anybody!" Wynne whispered emphatically. "It's the rest of the world that has trouble measuring up to you."

With that, Hawk gathered her so close that their bodies touched in dozens of places, her softness cradling the hard male limbs and taut muscles. They, in turn, supported her.

His lips against Wynne's ear, Hawk whispered, "It's okay. After Steve and I showered, I asked if he had a picture of his dad. He showed me the one in his wallet. I guess it's the same one you carry."

Wynne nodded, the suspense almost overwhelming her as she awaited Hawk's reaction.

"Faces usually don't lie," Hawk said slowly. "And Tom's—well, he looks a whole lot like my friend, Mike McCormick."

It was a moment before Wynne could trust herself to speak. "I'll have to replace Tom's picture with one of you. He would understand, Hawk—understand that I love you so! Oh, I know I've said it before, a hundred times or more, but there's never been *anyone* who means as much to me as you do! You're my partner, my other half, the piece of myself I was always and forever missing."

"I think I can finally accept that." Hawk leaned down and kissed her then, his lips so warm and tender that Wynne wanted them covering hers again and again and again. He would never be able to kiss her quite enough, even if he devoted himself zealously to that project!

"All my life I've needed to know that someone felt the way you do about me," Hawk admitted when their lips parted at last. "I know I was always looking too... looking for the one woman on earth who *would* care, the one I could love back the very same way."

Wynne felt the western sun touch them as they stood clinging together rapturously. Like a ball of flame gliding down toward the horizon, the sun now streaked the sky with lavish, extravagant colors of orange and umber, red and yellow. Like a golden firestorm it encircled and enveloped the two of them.

So the old Indian prophet they'd met on the road to Tahlequah had been right after all. Cherishing each other really was all that had ever been needed.

Silhouette Special Edition

COMING NEXT MONTH

FIRE AT DAWN—Linda Shaw
As New Orlean's finest tried to put ghetto doctor Brittany Schellenegger behind bars, rugged police detective Hammer Curry intervened to save her...and soon two hearts were captive in a dangerous enthrallment.

THE SHOWGIRL AND THE PROFESSOR—Phyllis Halldorson
Carefree Reno showgirl Sunshine Smith wanted tutoring in math, and intellectual professor Chad Fitzhugh III was happy to give her *very* private lessons. But theirs was a case of opposites attracting in a nearly disastrous collision.

HONORABLE INTENTIONS—Kate Meriwether
Though anti-nuke lobbyist Libbie Greer and Army lieutenant Cole Matthews fiercely clashed on political issues, even more explosive was their sudden, unbidden, impossible passion.

DANGER IN HIS ARMS—Patti Beckman
For globetrotter Dusty Landers and ex-CIA agent Mack O'Shea, life was a series of exciting escapades. Still, constant adventure left little time for leisure...and less for loving.

THEIR SONG UNENDING—Anna James
When plane failure stranded conservative investment counselor Logan Addison and flamboyant entertainer Justine Hart on a romantic island paradise, calamity rapidly led to desire. All too soon, though, grim reality threatened to shatter their unlikely new love.

RETURN TO EDEN—Jeanne Stephens
When she learned that her childhood idol had wed her on the rebound, Mia had had the sense to flee the sham marriage. Now David was pursuing her in earnest, but how could she give her whole heart to the man who'd once broken it in two?

AVAILABLE NOW:

FOR NOW, FOREVER
Nora Roberts

SHADOW ON THE SUN
Maggi Charles

ROSE IN BLOOM
Andrea Edwards

THE EXECUTIVES
Monica Barrie

GOLDEN FIRESTORM
Anne Lacey

OBJECT OF DESIRE
Jennifer West

Silhouette Intimate Moments

MARCH MADNESS!

Get Intimate with
Four Very Special Authors

Silhouette Intimate Moments has chosen March as the month
to launch the careers of three new authors—Marilyn Pappano,
Paula Detmer Riggs and Sibylle Garrett—and to welcome top-
selling historical romance author Nancy Morse to the world of
contemporary romance.

For years Silhouette Intimate Moments has brought you the
biggest names in romance. Join us now and let four exciting new
talents take you from the desert of New Mexico to the backlots
of Hollywood, from an Indian reservation in South Dakota to
the Khyber Pass of Afghanistan.

Coming in March from Silhouette Intimate Moments:

SACRED PLACES: Nancy Morse
WITHIN REACH: Marilyn Pappano
BEAUTIFUL DREAMER: Paula Detmer Riggs
SEPTEMBER RAINBOW: Sibylle Garrett

Silhouette Intimate Moments, this month and every month.
Available wherever paperback books are sold.

IM-MM

ATTRACTIVE, SPACE SAVING BOOK RACK

Display your most prized novels on this handsome and sturdy book rack. The hand-rubbed walnut finish will blend into your library decor with quiet elegance, providing a practical organizer for your favorite hard-or soft-covered books.

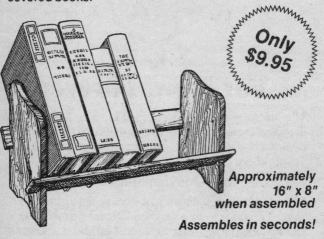

Only $9.95

Approximately 16" x 8" when assembled

Assembles in seconds!

To order, rush your name, address and zip code, along with a check or money order for $10.70* ($9.95 plus 75¢ postage and handling) payable to *Silhouette Books.*

Silhouette Books
Book Rack Offer
901 Fuhrmann Blvd.
P.O. Box 1325
Buffalo, NY 14269-1325

Offer not available in Canada.

BKR-2R

*New York residents add appropriate sales tax.